IN THE SHADOW OF AN OLD MASTER

IN THE SHADOW
OF AN OLD MASTER

P. J. Blake

Copyright © 2014 Pierre Viarnaud

The moral right of the author has been asserted.

Apart from any fair dealing for the purposes of research or private study, or criticism or review, as permitted under the Copyright, Designs and Patents Act 1988, this publication may only be reproduced, stored or transmitted, in any form or by any means, with the prior permission in writing of the publishers, or in the case of reprographic reproduction in accordance with the terms of licences issued by the Copyright Licensing Agency. Enquiries concerning reproduction outside those terms should be sent to the publishers.

Matador
Unit 9 Priory Business Park
Kibworth Beauchamp
Leicester LE8 0RX, UK
Tel: (+44) 116 279 2299
Fax: (+44) 116 279 2277
Email: books@troubador.co.uk
Web: www.troubador.co.uk/matador

ISBN 978 1783065 080

British Library Cataloguing in Publication Data.
A catalogue record for this book is available from the British Library.

Typeset by Troubador Publishing Ltd, Leicester, UK
Printed and bound in the UK by TJ International, Padstow, Cornwall

Matador is an imprint of Troubador Publishing Ltd

For Janice, Tania and Marc

Author's Note:

This book takes inspiration from the life and the events surrounding Eric Hebborn, the "Prince of Forgers" and his mysterious death in Rome in 1996.

This book, however, is a work of fiction and does not claim to explain the circumstances surrounding his death, nor to describe with any degree of accuracy, characters or events that touched Eric Hebborn's life.

The names and characters and incidents portrayed are the work of the author's imagination.

Prologue

On the night of the 8th January 1996, shortly before midnight, a distinguished looking Englishman wearing a full beard was seen leaving a bar in Trastevere. It had been raining all evening and the streets were empty and no one saw him walk from the bar to Piazza Trilussa. When he reached the northeastern corner of the square, a sturdy Italian accosted him. An angry exchange ensued between the two and when the Englishman tried to walk away the Italian pulled him back causing him to lose his balance. They continued to argue. The Italian hit the older man, sending him flailing backwards against the marble steps. The Englishman fell, his head hit stone.

The aggressor hesitated, looked around him to make sure no one had noticed the altercation. He saw two drunks and their dogs huddled under the statue of Trilussa, the poet, too far gone to realise what had happened. He bent down, checked that his victim was still breathing and hurriedly searched his pockets. He pulled out a set of keys and walked briskly away from the Piazza.

He knew exactly where to go. He unlocked the heavy green front door of a building a few hundred metres away, entered the long dark corridor, climbed the stone steps that led to the first floor, and let himself into one of the apartments with the stolen keys.

Once inside he proceeded cautiously, making sure there was no one there, until he felt confident enough to switch on the lights. Within minutes he had searched drawers, cabinets and cupboards thoroughly and found what he was looking for. He then made sure that everything was as he found it, switched off the lights and left, locking the door carefully behind him.

At about 1:30 in the morning someone called 118, the medical emergency line, to report that a man was lying on the cobbled stones of Piazza Trilussa in Rome with what appeared to be head wounds. The caller, who did not identify himself, added that the man was semi-conscious and incoherent.

An ambulance was dispatched to Trastevere and the paramedics found the man at the foot of the steps, bleeding, incoherent, and soaked from the rain. When they picked him up, one of the paramedics noticed he smelled of wine and assumed he was drunk. The man was taken to Trastevere's Regina Margherita hospital where he was examined by a nurse on duty. It was a particularly busy night and the nurse, wrongly assuming he was just another drunkard, left him to attend more urgent cases.

A few hours later a doctor came to check on him, and placed him under observation after having noted that he suffered from several contusions, in particular to the head. The attending nurse noticed the papers he carried revealed he was an Englishman by the name of Eric Hargrave. He wore flannel trousers, a woollen jacket and a relatively clean shirt, and was in possession of a wallet with cash in it. The assumption that he was a bum was quickly dispelled.

Hargrave's condition worsened and arrangements were made to transfer him to San Giacomo hospital, where he underwent a brain scan. The scan revealed a serious brain haemorrhage that needed to be operated on immediately. The San Giacomo did not have a neurosurgery department and he was therefore sent on to the San Giovanni hospital, where doctors carried out an emergency surgical intervention before sending him back to San Giacomo, where he remained in a deep coma until he died two days later.

Chapter 1

On the 12th of January, Eric Hargrave's death made the front page of most of the Italian newspapers which wrote about "the mysterious death of the king of art forgers". His photo was dug up from the archives in a hurry and details of his colourful life were given to a wider audience than those who had read his autobiography five years earlier.

Questions were raised about the cause of his death and various theories proposed by journalists who had a lot more imagination than facts. At first, the police did not see the need to investigate, indicating that the medical report was consistent with an accident. They attributed the probable cause of death to a fall caused by his state of advanced inebriation. But the theories developed by the Italian press continued to multiply, foreign journalists started to call the police for statements and the British Embassy eventually sent an official request to the Foreign Ministry to ask for an investigation.

At this juncture, a magistrate asked that a preliminary investigation be carried out and demanded an initial report within forty-eight hours.

The *Commissario* of Trastevere looked incredulously at the single sheet of paper Alberto Conti, one of his most senior inspectors, gave him.

"Conti, what is this?"

"The preliminary report on Hargrave you asked for."

The *Commissario* raised his eyebrows in mock surprise and shook his head. He read the report aloud.

Eric Hargrave, Englishman, 60 years old, living in Rome since 1965. Owner of three properties: Trastevere, the Aniene Valley and the Eolian islands. He paid his taxes, had no criminal record, and was a peaceable man. He had a wide circle of friends, from all walks of life. A professional painter, he earned his living from his art – paintings, drawings, sculptures. In 1991, he published his autobiography in which he explained that he forged and sold a thousand drawings in the style of the Old Masters. His book created quite a stir in the art establishment and needless to say, made him a few enemies.

Eric Hargrave appears to have no family living in Rome. He was homosexual and his last lover lived abroad, and visited him regularly. Hargrave was also a regular and heavy drinker, some might even have said an alcoholic. He was also known to have the occasional dalliance with young male prostitutes. He was picked up in an inebriated state, with his wallet, but no keys.

The medical report of the forensic doctor stated that Hargrave died from complications of a blow to the head, but neither confirmed nor excluded the possibility of a homicide.

The *Commissario* looked up at the inspector with a quizzical expression. "Conti, please tell me that this is the introduction of your report and that the rest is being typed!"

"No, that's it. It is the initial report."

The *Commissario* contained his frustration. Hard as he tried, he had not been able to find a common ground with his senior inspector. Conti showed no political sensitivity, could not care less about football, and had gained the reputation of a loner who disliked authority. But he had a good track record and was invaluable to the department.

"A twelve-line summary after two days work! I can find out as much about Hargrave, if not more, by reading the papers."

Conti looked out the window, seemingly unconcerned.

"Since I have put you in charge, would you do me the favour of entertaining me with some theories or at least explain what you intend to do next?" the *Commissario* asked calmly.

"There is a lot to do. The man had enemies after admitting he was a forger, and it is very plausible someone wanted him out of the way. He allegedly said so to a friend."

"He said someone wanted him killed? And you did not think it was worth mentioning in your report?" The *Commissario* hit his desk with his index finger.

"It needs to be checked. It may, or may not, be relevant. We have no proof it was a homicide. Hargrave could simply have fallen, hit his head, and died."

"You have until the end of this week to come up with a proper report…go, go now," the *Commissario* half shouted, losing his composure and gesturing towards the door.

Conti nodded and turned around, a half-smile on his face.

The death of Eric Hargrave continued to make headlines in the Italian press for several days, and each time a new development was reported in one of the major dailies, furious exchanges took place between the Interior Ministry, the *Commissariato*, the office of the Magistrate who had requested the investigation, and sometimes the Foreign Ministry. Was the information accurate? Who had leaked it to the press? Why couldn't the investigation proceed faster and more discreetly?

The *Carabinieri*, it was suggested in an internal memo, should take over, since contacts with Interpol and art forgeries were at the centre of the investigation. But the central office of the *Carabinieri* did not show any enthusiasm, and the *Commissariato* claimed it was a purely local matter and that no final conclusion had been drawn on whether the death of Eric Hargrave was of an accidental or criminal nature.

The head of the Trastevere police was in a foul mood; he turned his frustration and annoyance on his investigators and Alberto Conti was asked to give the Hargrave case the utmost priority.

After a week of frantic communication, however, no new theory came to light and no discovery made the front page. Romans shifted their interest to the football derby match between Roma and Lazio, and the British Embassy appeared satisfied with the promise that all efforts would be made to explain what had happened to Eric Hargrave.

Contradictory instructions were passed on to the prosecutor and the *Commissario*. Written memoranda requested that the investigation be given priority while informal discussions in the corridor of the Palace of Justice suggested that accidental death was the most logical and acceptable conclusion.

Chapter 2

The drumbeat of the rain against the roof tiles of Anticoli's church accompanied the congregation's silence more effectively than a funeral march.

Father Luciani raised his head slowly and stared at his flock without speaking, for what seemed a long time. His church was full, with people spilling outside, huddled under dark umbrellas, who followed the service despite the miserable weather. The villagers were there of course, as every Saturday evening, but there were many new faces; some had come from Rome, others from abroad.

Judging that his pause had been used to good dramatic effect, the priest started his sermon.

"Eric Hargrave is no longer with us. He was called back a week ago by the Lord our Shepherd and we are gathered here today to bid him farewell and pray for his soul." He paused again, straightened his back, hands on lectern, and did his best to pretend that he had not noticed the video cameras spanning the crowd and zooming in on him.

"Eric was part of our community and was held in high esteem. He counted many friends who will remember him for his generosity, his kindness and of course for the talent that God had bestowed on him. We will remember him in particular, for this wonderful painting he donated to our church a few years ago." The priest glanced to his right at a large unframed canvas that depicted the Last Supper, Christ and his disciples dressed in jeans and casual shirts. Many in the crowd followed the priest's eyes and craned their necks to get a better view of the work by *Il Maestro*.

The village of Anticoli, despite its forbidding appearance, had provided countless beautiful models to the artists' studios of Rome since the time of the Renaissance. Partly because of the reputation of its women, Anticoli continued to attract painters, sculptors and writers. Eric Hargrave's gregarious nature and understated manners won him the goodwill if not the friendship of many in the hilltop village. From a humble background, he had learned to accept success with modesty and react to troubles with equanimity.

The inhabitants of Anticoli were not exactly known for their warmth and sense of hospitality. But Eric had seemed blissfully unaware of stares and gossips. At first they mocked his ability to drink large quantities of red wine. Then someone pointed out, maybe Cesar the owner of the bar, that he only drank the product of Anticoli's vineyards, and soon Eric was seen drinking with the regulars, exchanging views about the last vintage, commenting on the weather or asking for advice on how to prune fruit trees.

When asked what he did for a living, Eric Hargrave replied that he studied. For him, drawing, sculpting, painting were all means to acquire knowledge.

Father Luciani blessed the crowd with a sweeping sign of the cross and stood by while pallbearers struggled to lift the casket onto their shoulders.

Giulia Vasari did not wait for the pallbearers to balance their load. She hastily crossed herself and stepped out of the church. Recognising familiar faces she nodded to acknowledge some, but continued walking until she reached the main piazza a few hundred metres away.

Small groups of people were scattered around the square waiting eagerly for the funeral procession to emerge from the narrow streets, hoping to recognise a well-known face or catch fragments of conversation that could be repeated and become gossip.

Giulia observed the scene and shook her head in disapproval. Why was it that people were attracted to scandals the way moths are drawn by light? She wondered who among these people had really cared for Eric and would genuinely miss him.

The thought of Eric filled her with sadness. She would miss him; she would miss his wonderful sense of humour, the way he told stories, the way he tugged at his beard before admitting he had misbehaved, the way he had been there for her.

Her thoughts were interrupted by the arrival of the procession. A hearse was waiting for the casket to drive it through the wet cobble-stoned streets that wound down to the cemetery. The procession was led by two of Eric's siblings who had flown in from England, slowly walking beside the hearse.

The crowd dispersed and spread across the square. Children broke into a run; a group of older men in black entered the bar to order a grappa and coffee while small groups formed only to break away again a few minutes later.

Beside the fountain that marked the centre of the square a young dark-skinned man, in a black leather jacket raised his voice. The couple he stood with stared at him disapprovingly and the woman said something that made the young man even angrier, and he shouted loud enough to be heard across the square. "No, I cannot accept that. And anyway you have no rights. None! He told me many times, everybody knew it!" In between his shouts he burst into tears, and sobbed he too was hurting.

He turned his back to the couple and marched away. Before Giulia could move, their eyes met, and he recognised her. Willie was probably the last person she wanted to talk to at this moment but there was no way she could avoid him, so she composed herself as best she could and watched him approach.

"Willie, are you all right?"

The young man was still agitated and did not bother to answer. His right eye was twitching nervously and his mouth quavered.

"They have no rights. None! I told them. Why should they get everything? Eric did not even want to see them!"

"Willie, calm down please. People are looking at you. This is neither the time nor the place," she said, taking his arm gently.

"I don't care. They can look all they want!"

"Let's walk," Giulia suggested, pulling him away from the piazza. "Willie, you must be devastated. It must have been a shock to hear about it on the phone. Were you in Canada when you found out?"

He looked at her quizzically as if he was not sure what she was talking about, before answering, "Yes, I was in Canada. They called me in the middle of the night. It was like a nightmare…He loved me, you know."

He broke into tears. It was not clear whether it was a sign of grief or frustration, or a combination of both. Giulia fetched a glass of water from the bar and made him sit down on a wooden bench.

"Next time I take a lover, I will make him sign a will right away. I won't be cheated again," Willie proclaimed.

It was difficult to feel sympathy for someone who betrayed such ignoble thoughts on the day his lover of the last five years was being buried. But Giulia stayed with him patiently, until he spotted someone else in the crowd and darted away to repeat his sorry tale.

The cemetery hung precariously from the steep hill among pines and cypress trees, below a sharp bend of the road. Giulia Vasari strolled through the alleys, between headstones and funerary monuments, until she found her friend's final resting place. She stopped and the reality of his death hit her. By now the hearse had reached the gate of the cemetery and people were pouring in. Giulia stepped aside and made the sign of the cross.

Fog was slowly filling the valley and a persistent drizzle made the marble stones shine faintly.

"*Anche il tempo e triste, non e vero?*"

The man who spoke was looking straight in front of him and Giulia was not sure he had addressed her. Studying him from the corner of her eye, she saw a man in his early forties wearing a light-coloured raincoat and a scarf around his neck. His hands were clasped behind his back and his chin jutted out, making his face look angular. She found the half-consumed Tuscan cigar sticking out of his mouth offensive and out of place although he made no attempt to relight it.

"*Conosceva bene il defunto, Signora?*"

This time he half turned towards her and he was more difficult to ignore.

"Sorry, I am not Italian," she said, although she spoke Italian fluently.

"Ah, you are English then?"

If she was hoping that her answer would deter further questions she was disappointed.

"Did you know Eric Hargrave well?" he continued in English.

"He was a client of mine," she hesitated, "and a friend."

"A client! What work do you do?"

Giulia looked for an opening in the crowd but saw none. She was cornered at a time when she most wanted to be alone.

"Oh, I am sorry. I must present myself. My name is Alberto Conti. I am a police inspector, and you are?"

"Giulia, Giulia Vasari," she answered.

"My pleasure, *Signora*."

It was unlikely that the police inspector was a friend of Eric's, she thought. But she could not be sure, as Eric had a wide circle of friends from all walks of life.

"Are you from Anticoli?" she finally asked.

"No, from Rome."

Before Giulia could utter a word he quickly volunteered, "I am investigating the death of Signor Hargrave, and if you are in Rome, I would like to talk to you."

"To me? What about?"

"About the kind of person he was, your friend."

"I was not even in Italy when the...when he died," she protested. "I don't see how I can help you."

"I am sure it will be helpful for me if we could talk. Maybe you know his friends, I noticed you comforting one of them on the piazza, and maybe you can tell me what he was working on if he was your client, or what his plans were, that kind of thing."

"Well I guess...I could," Giulia conceded, realising she did not have much of a choice.

The policeman handed her a visiting card.

"Call me when you arrive in Rome."

Giulia watched the police inspector disappear behind a marble monument and pocketed the card, although she had no intention of calling him.

The priest gave his final blessing, the grave had been sealed and the crowd melted rapidly. She felt chilly, her shoes were soaked and her toes felt numb. She trudged back to where she had left her rented car, alone.

Her white Fiat Punto was blocked by a Mercedes that had double-parked and she was forced to wait in the rain. As minutes passed her annoyance slowly grew into anger towards the inconsiderate driver, and she made no effort to conceal the irritation her face betrayed.

"Is this your car?" she asked a man walking slowly towards her in an expensive dark cashmere suit.

The man did not reply and made no visible effort to hurry. Giulia crossed her arms and glared at him. She noticed he limped slightly.

"I'm sorry but I walk very slowly. An old knee injury."

He stopped in front of her and extended his arm, placing his umbrella over Giulia's head.

She took an instant dislike to him for this unwanted familiarity although he probably meant well. It had been a long and draining day; she was in no mood for small talk, and would have stepped away except that she had her back to the Mercedes. He stood there a few centimetres from her, and apologised again.

Giulia noticed his expensive tie and long white hair. He smelled of cigarette and after-shave.

"It has been a long day and this rain..."

"My name is Giorgio Monticello," he said offering his hand. "Can I at least offer you a coffee to be forgiven?"

Giulia declined the invitation and did not give him her name. All she wanted to do was drive back to her hotel close to the Piazza del Popolo in Rome, take a long hot shower and go to sleep.

Monticello bowed ceremoniously to signify he accepted her refusal gracefully and stepped aside, but his appraising eyes did not leave the attractive woman's face.

"I'm sorry if I seem to stare but…haven't we met before?" he finally asked.

"No, I don't think so," Giulia answered curtly.

She inched past the front of the Mercedes to her car, but in doing so was forced to look at Monticello.

"Maybe you came to my art gallery," he offered as an explanation, "it's in Trastevere, Via della Scala. I have many engravings by Signor Hargrave."

Giulia looked up briefly but continued to distance herself.

"Perhaps," she said before turning her back on the Italian to insert a key into the lock of the Fiat.

The drive back to Rome took Giulia through the meandering roads of the narrow Aniene valley onto the A24 that linked Castel Madamma, Tivoli and the Italian capital. The highway left behind an imposing monastery that clung to the edge of a gorge and crossed a low mountain range partly covered by olive groves and oak forests. Soon it descended into the Roman plain with its umbrella pines and houses in *tufo*, the characteristic brownish volcanic stone.

Giulia drove carefully because of the rain and had time to reflect on what had dictated her presence in the little village east of Rome. She remembered the phone call she received in London on the evening of the 10th January from one of Eric's friends she barely knew. Eric was in hospital in a serious condition, she was told. He had been found in the early morning of the previous day, lying in the street, apparently unconscious from a blow to his head. And no, the caller was not sure in which hospital he was, because he had been moved several times.

She made frantic telephone calls to find out where he was and in what condition but in vain. On the 11th she managed to find him listed in the intensive unit of the San Giacomo hospital but was told she was too late, he had not survived surgery and had died in the morning.

Giulia had spoken with Eric on the morning of his fatal accident. He had said he was ready to meet in London before the end of the month to discuss his new book, and promised it would be even more scandalous than his autobiography. Giulia recalled how she had smiled and retorted that she hardly thought it possible. Eric's words were now engraved in her memory. "What would you say if I now told the world not only what I did, but how?"

They exchanged a few more bits of news when he finally admitted he was not in the best of form. All the partying since Christmas had taken its toll on his health. He had, however, reluctantly agreed to meet a friend for dinner, but it would be an early night for him as he was being taken to Anticoli the next day to settle the matter of an exorbitant water bill; there had been a leak in the pipe that brought the water down the hills through the woods to his property.

Giulia had told him to take care of himself a little bit better, and try to drink a little bit less. He had thanked her for being such a good and loving friend.

Four days later he was dead.

She rejected the thought that Eric Hargrave could have been killed. Somehow she could not reconcile her memories of a gentle-spirited Eric with the spectre of a violent death. Of course, she knew that he had made a lot of enemies and there was no saying how far some people would go to buy his silence.

Chapter 3

The unpretentious façade of the Locarno Hotel fronted a quiet one-way street between Lungotevere, the avenue that followed the course of the Tiber, and Piazza del Popolo. Although it was described as a four star establishment, the small hotel seemed designed more to make its guests feel comfortable rather than to impress, and its only remarkable feature was its Art Nouveau front door. Hotel guests, for instance, could not be sure whether the old lady they crossed in the creaking lift was the Contessa who had retained the top floor of the building as her private apartment, or a visitor like them. Both were greeted in an equally cheerful way by the ancient doorman in striped livery.

Giulia Vasari was under the shower when the phone rang and she wondered who could be calling her at nine o'clock on a Sunday morning. She hurriedly put on the hanging white bathrobe before reaching for the telephone.

"Am I waking you up?" the voice on the line said.

"No Victor, you're not. But it's early for you, and on a Sunday!"

"Yeah, well, with my being away on Monday, I wanted to catch you before you left Rome."

Victor Edelman headed the London office of Seldom House, a leading American publishing company Giulia was contracted to. He was known for his total dedication to the company and did not distinguish between working days, week-ends or holidays, despite having lived in Europe for twenty years.

"You're leaving for the states next week then?"

"Yeah, and that's why I needed to talk to you."

"What about?"

"New York called yesterday about Hargrave. They want a reprint of his autobiography and they are excited about publishing his new book."

"His new book?"

Giulia knew what Edelman meant but was not quite ready to discuss business so soon after having buried her friend.

"Yes. You know exactly what I'm talking about," Edelman said, sounding impatient.

"You do realise that Eric is dead and that this book you are talking about may not have been completed," she answered firmly.

"But we don't know that. You told me yourself he had promised to bring you what he had written so far."

"I didn't say that. I said he was coming to London to discuss his new book."

Giulia understood that Eric Hargrave's death was generating a tremendous amount of publicity and Seldom House wanted to use this to their best advantage.

"Who's the executor of Hargrave's will? His Chinese boyfriend?"

"I don't know. If Eric died intestate, his family I suppose."

"Good. You know what to do then. Go and meet them and explain that you have to go over his papers because we had a deal going and he had promised to deliver his manuscript this month!"

"Which he had not promised," she corrected him, highlighting the word promised.

"No," and Edelman dragged on the word, "but you know very well he intended to, don't you?"

She bit her lip and knew she had been cornered. To end the conversation she made the vague promise of, "I'll see what I can find out." This appeared to satisfy Edelman but she knew better, and was sure that he would pursue his objective relentlessly. They didn't call him "Pit Bull" for no reason.

Giulia put on a pair of jeans and a black cashmere sweater. She slipped her feet into her suede walking boots, grabbed her jacket and left the hotel. She had no other plans for the day but to wander the streets of Rome and once again feel part of the city she loved. The sky was overcast but the temperature was unusually mild for January and a group of Northern Europeans sitting in their overcoats occupied several tables outside the *Café Rosati* on the Piazza del Popolo.

Giulia could have easily passed for an Italian. It amused her to hear two male backpackers describe her as a typical Italian beauty. She had naturally tanned skin, big dark brown eyes, a strong nose, and a full mouth and wore very little make-up.

Her dark shoulder length hair was tied back in a ponytail. Her leather jacket stopped at the waist, her jeans hugging the curve of a shapely bottom.

She paid for a cappuccino and cornetto and enjoyed her Roman breakfast standing by the counter together with the bar's regular customers. One of the backpackers who had not understood that he had to pay before ordering his coffee stood by, frustrated, trying to communicate in pidgin English. She tapped him on the shoulder and told him what to do.

The backpacker looked puzzled. He was no more than eighteen with striking blue eyes and fair-skinned. "You speak English very well," the boy said.

"Maybe because I'm American," she retorted with a smile. "Well, I'm partly Argentinian and have lived in Rome for a few years."

"That explains it," he replied.

He thanked her and took the two cups of cappuccino and brought them outside to his waiting companion. Giulia left some change for the barman and passed by the two backpackers' table on her way out. This time the young boys waited until she was far enough away to comment on the way her hips swayed from side to side as she walked. Giulia smiled to herself, the innocence of youth, she thought.

She crossed the piazza and entered Via del Corso between the two 17th century churches of *Santa Maria dei Miracoli and Santa Maria di Monte Santo* that faced the arch of Flaminio. It was busy for a Sunday and motorcyclists had to swerve between people who strolled in the centre of the street. By the next square several stands were being erected by sellers of football emblems. Giulia recognised the red and gold colours of the Roma club and remembered that Italian soccer games took place on Sunday afternoons.

She also remembered how Robert had learned to love watching the games during the four years they had lived in Rome. They had been married less than a year before he received his first Foreign Service posting and could not believe their luck when the news came it was to be Italy. They discovered Rome together and in a short period of time were comfortably conversing in Italian with their new-found friends. Giulia remembered how Robert never lost his American accent and how she used to tease him about it.

She headed for Piazza Farnese, down the familiar routes that she and Robert had taken many times in the past, discovering and rediscovering the many treasures of the historical centre. She walked half the length of Via del Corso, recalling in amusement an article she had read, that a pope had it paved during the fifteenth century using funds collected from a tax on prostitution. When she reached the column of Marcus Aurelius she turned towards Piazza Navona, leaving the guards of Palazzo Montecitorio, the lower House of Italy's Parliament, to her right. She continued through the narrow streets, passed the Pantheon until Piazza San Andrea di Valle, reaching Piazza Campo di Fiore still littered with leftovers from the open market and passed under the bridge designed by Michelangelo to connect Palazzo Farnese, one of the most beautiful Renaissance palaces in Rome and its gardens. In Via Giulia, she peeked into antique windows to get a glimpse of old prints, hanging chandeliers, ceramic dishes and porcelain dolls seated on Louis XIV style armchairs. Tired, she sat down to rest on the top of the steps that led to the edge of the waters of the Tiber. The river was brown and uninviting, its level swollen by the recent rains. She had never understood the fascination the Tiber had exerted over Robert. For her it was just one of the features of Rome, and not one of its more attractive. She didn't bother to understand what made it so special to Robert then, but now that he was gone she saw it as a failing on her part and was filled with melancholy.

The clouds had finally lifted and a hazy sun came through. Giulia crossed the Ponte Sisto and made her way in the direction of the Botanical Gardens. Only then did Giulia realise she was standing in front of Eric Hargrave's front door. His name was there, by the doorbell, handwritten in elegant calligraphy. Giulia shivered and crossed her arms. She crossed the street and turned, looking at his windows. Strangely, the shutters were open. Someone pulled the curtain aside and was looking down from Eric's apartment. The apartment was dark; as the building stood in the shade she could not make out the face and she had no wish to find out who it was. She walked away briskly towards the Piazza Trilussa where she entered a bar and sat down at a small table far from the door to calm down.

Giulia saw him before he saw her. He was standing at the entrance of the bar, surveying the room systematically, from one corner to the next. He was wearing the same light-coloured raincoat he had on at the funeral the evening before, but now Giulia was able to make out what he looked like in the light of day. Alberto Conti cut an imposing figure, taller than the average Italian, with wavy brown hair and bushy eyebrows to match. He had strong Italian features and hazelnut coloured eyes that she would later notice changed hue depending on how the light hit them. Before their eyes could meet, Giulia looked down and applied herself to stirring her cup of coffee without letting the spoon touch the sides of the cup.

"Signora Vasari, very nice to see you again."

She looked up and acknowledged the inspector with a forced smile.

"Inspector Conti, what a coincidence! How are you?"

Without waiting to be invited the inspector sat down in front of Giulia and unbuttoned his coat.

"I saw you a few minutes ago, and thought that this would be a good chance to talk."

"You work on Sundays too? Were you in Eric Hargrave's apartment?" she asked.

"To your second question, no, I was watching his apartment like you were. And to your first, yes, the case has been put on top priority and that means we work round the clock."

"What is it you wanted to talk to me about?" she asked curtly.

"Please do not be angry with me. It's my job to investigate the death of Signor Hargrave. You were friends you said, and so you must want to find out what happened, no?"

His conciliatory tone surprised her.

"Yes, he was a friend, a good friend," she finally said, in a softer tone. "In fact, he called me the night of the accident to say he was not feeling well but he was going out to dinner with a friend."

"And did he say with whom?"

"No, only that it would be an early night."

Conti made a mental note to follow this lead. He motioned to a waiter to bring him a cup of coffee.

"You said he was also your client. What do you do exactly?"

"I work for a publishing company in London."

"Did your company publish his autobiography then? It made a big scandal here."

Giulia nodded.

"Why do you think he wrote it?"

Giulia hesitated, not quite knowing what response was expected from her by the police inspector.

"I think he was looking for recognition…and I suppose he wanted to get back at the dealers, the people who see art as a way to make a lot of money."

"But it is a little dangerous to attack so many people so publicly, don't you think?"

"I guess it can be," Giulia conceded.

"So it would be reasonable to say that many dealers wanted Signor Hargrave silenced. Maybe some wanted it enough to kill him or have him killed?"

Conti studied the inside of his empty cup of coffee, giving Giulia the chance to study his face.

"What about his lover? Did he have a reason to want him dead?"

"No, I am sure he did not wish him any harm."

"But he was very angry at the funeral. He was shouting."

"He was angry because Eric had not left a will and the family wanted to keep everything. At least that's what he told me."

"It is true. There was no will found and the family will receive everything. By the way, do you know whether he was close to them?"

"I don't think so. They may have tried to keep in touch with him but his life was so different from theirs, that I think he felt he did not have much in common with them."

"When did you first meet Signor Hargrave?"

"At his one-man show in Tivoli."

"You mean a painting exhibition I suppose."

Giulia wondered whether Inspector Conti had a hidden list with prepared questions, as they followed each other in quick succession.

"Did you know that he was doing…what is the word? Fake drawings?"

"No, I found out much later, when he asked me whether Seldom House would be prepared to publish his autobiography. I was already living in London at the time."

"And how did you feel about him after you read his book?"

Giulia had never really thought about it. She remembered her surprise when she first read Eric Hargrave's manuscript and had thought at the time that her friend had a darker side to him. As there were things about her she had not shared with Eric, she naturally accepted that there would be things about him that she did not know. And Giulia told Conti precisely this.

Alberto Conti smiled and said, "You really liked him, didn't you?" Giulia nodded.

"Out of curiosity inspector, have you read his book?"

Expecting an answer to the contrary, it surprised Giulia when Alberto Conti answered, "Yes".

"And what did you think?" she asked.

"I would have liked to have met the man," he stated simply.

Chapter 4

For someone who had dedicated most of his life to the study of Old Masters and borrowed their styles in what many would later call his infamous activities, Eric Hargrave's choice of Villa d'Este to exhibit his own watercolours was fitting. The palace itself, which was built during the 16th century for a cardinal, was a shadow of its past splendour. Frescoes slowly faded into humidity stains, many windows and shutters, warped or eaten by woodworms, had been nailed shut and the tiled floors were so uneven that visitors often stumbled on their way to the gardens.

In fact it was the garden with its spectacular fountains, water jets, cascades and grottoes, rather than the palace, that attracted visitors nowadays. Carved from the steep hillside, it commanded a spectacular view of the thermal city of Tivoli and the valley below it.

Hargrave, understated and soft-spoken, spent the day sitting in the garden with a glass of red wine in hand, rather than inside in the room where his paintings were hung. This is where Giulia had first met him when she visited Villa d'Este on the invitation of a mutual friend to view the exhibition.

Many of Hargrave's watercolours depicted Tivoli and were sold on the opening night. Hadrian's villa, the hills around Rome, and several views of the village of Anticoli completed the exhibition.

Giulia and her husband had wished to purchase one of the watercolours and were told they could find Eric in the garden. "He is the one with the beard and a glass of wine," they were told. Eric had invited them to sit with him saying, "The views from this terrace are much more spectacular and they are free."

Eduardo, seated next to Eric added with a sweeping gesture, "Behold, the Valle Gaudente, otherwise known in English as 'the Gay Valley'. He was as exuberant as Eric was quiet and Giulia had liked them both. They talked of art, of living in Rome, of London which Eric had turned his back on thirty years earlier, and of course of food and wine, a very Italian habit he had made his own.

When Robert explained they were interested in one of the

paintings and wondered if they could pay for it over two months, Eric had said of course they could, and invited them to pick it up from his villa in the woods below Anticoli once the exhibition had closed its doors. Giulia had complimented Eric for the quality of his works and the prestigious venue, to which he replied, "Italians have a lot of respect for their past. If you visit the small towns around Rome you will find that each one claims to have a hidden treasure worth a visit. Anticoli, where we live, for instance," deferring to Eduardo, "was famous for providing models to the best painters and sculptors in Rome."

"I don't think Anticoli provides models these days, or needs to," Eduardo interjected, and struck the pose of the dying slave of Michelangelo, lifting his shirt with no inhibitions.

To which Eric quipped, "Now we import models into Anticoli, as you can see."

Eduardo was quick to match Eric's wit, and without much ado, gracefully moved from his dying slave impersonation to Michelangelo's rebellious slave pose.

Before saying their good-byes, they exchanged telephone numbers and Eduardo jotted down directions on how to reach their house, inviting them over for lunch two Saturdays hence, when they could also collect their painting. Their first meeting ended on a high note, and was the beginning of a tight and loyal friendship.

Chapter 5

Christopher Donovan's ambition drove him to take chances and live on the edge. When he opened his art gallery, St. George's Fine Art, close to Bond Street, the Irishman only had enough money to pay the deposit and the first three months' rent. But he was able to convince several artists and another art dealer to lend him works on consignment to mount his first exhibition. A good organiser and publicity monger, it turned out to be a great success and with it Donovan felt he was one step closer to becoming a well-established art dealer in London.

When he decided to represent Eric Hargrave in the United Kingdom, less than a year after Eric's book had created havoc in the London art scene and beyond, he knew it was another gamble. But Donovan often acted on instinct and something told him it was a gamble that would pay off.

St. George's Fine Art was on the first floor of a Victorian building on Hanover Square and the brass plate that announced it also said "by appointment only". He normally placed a double-sided board on the pavement, to which he pasted posters advertising his exhibition or a reminder that he dealt in contemporary prints, to catch the eye of passers-by.

Giulia Vasari found Christopher witty and entertaining but was also well aware of his propensity to take risks. During the opening of an exhibition of Eric Hargrave's work, a year earlier, he had cornered her in the kitchen of the gallery and tried to kiss her. When Giulia asked him what he would tell his wife, who was in the next room, if she happened to come in, he replied "I'd say I'm taking care of customer relations," and left the room laughing.

When Donovan called to invite her to the gallery for a chat, the incident was still fresh in Giulia's memory and she reminded herself to be on guard. She rang the bell, and the door buzzed open almost immediately. The lanky frame of Donovan appeared at the top of the stairs welcoming her. He had put on some weight since she had last seen him but it looked good on him, she thought.

"Giulia! How nice to see you again!"

He kissed her on both cheeks and raised both hands, palms up.

"Have no fear. I am a completely reformed character."

"I'm not quite sure I believe you, Christopher."

"I've been trying very hard," Donovan swore, a hand on his heart.

"Good, keep it up," she answered playfully.

"You are a difficult woman to please, Giulia."

He took her coat and draped it over a chair by the desk. She examined the paintings that hung on the walls. From a distance, the vibrant colours and strokes conveyed a sense of place and mood. Closer up the splashes of paint appeared disconnected and meaningless.

Giulia read the artist's name aloud.

"Who is he?" she asked.

"Scottish guy, young but very promising. It's his first show in London."

"He reminds me of someone else…"

"Hodgkin maybe?" Donovan suggested.

"Yes, you're right. Howard Hodgkin."

"Do you like this?"

Giulia said she preferred the works on paper to the oils. There was more power in them, she thought.

The telephone rang and the gallery owner excused himself to take the call. Giulia walked leisurely to the next room where Donovan had a few prints in gold leaf frames, a Picasso, a Modigliani and two Matisses, all signed in pencil. She also noticed there was no work by Eric Hargrave to be seen, and told him so as he joined her.

"That's right. It's not good for business to mix his work with the rest! Anyway, I'm in no rush to sell what stock I have. His prices are bound to go up."

He sounded pretty much like an investment banker, she thought.

"Can I invite you for lunch? There is something I would like to talk to you about, and, well, it is about Hargrave. Do you have time?"

Giulia checked her watch and said she did, doing her best to hide her curiosity. She took her coat and walked down the steps ahead of him.

The small Italian restaurant was run by a family from Naples just like a Neapolitan household. It always sounded as though they were about to throw dishes at each other rather than serve them to their guests. It was badly lit and noisy but the food was good and the prices affordable. Giulia had been there several times before and when Carlo, the owner's son, recognised her he quickly led them to a table by the window which stood away from the rest. They could at least have a normal conversation without having to compete with the din in the room. Carlo and Giulia exchanged pleasantries in flawless Italian after which Carlo took their orders.

"Did you have a chance to speak with the Hargrave family at the funeral last week?" Donovan asked Giulia as he planted his fork into a ball of mozzarella.

"No, I didn't. Why?"

He gave her an appraising look before answering, as if he had to assuage a last minute doubt. He knew he would get a direct answer from Giulia, but he also knew she would read between the lines, questioning his motives.

"I'll be honest with you…Eric was working on a commission for a client of mine and…he never got it to me."

"What was it?"

Carlo, who came with two steaming plates of pasta *matriciana*, al dente, and a carafe of red wine, interrupted them with a broad smile and walked away.

"Well," Giulia prodded.

"I would rather not say."

"Then what's the point of telling me in the first place? Shall we then just enjoy our meal and forget about all this business of commissions?"

Donovan felt trapped. She was right of course.

"You must promise me that you will keep it confidential. My client insists on it," he said leaning over to Giulia in a conspiratorial way.

"You know I can be discreet when you want me to be," she smiled teasingly at him.

In a low voice, and first checking that what he was about to say was out of earshot of the nearest table, Donovan said, "Giulia, I'm serious. An important client of mine wanted a view of Venice in the style of Canaletto from Hargrave. He agreed to paint it, over six months ago, and told me a few days before he died that he only needed to wait for the paint to dry before I could have it."

"Why don't you ask his family for the painting?"

"I have, but they claim they don't have it. They didn't see it in Rome."

"You mean someone could have taken it, or you think they're not telling the truth? But I don't see what I can do. His family is not likely to give me a different answer. Why should they?" Giulia countered.

"You were Eric's friend. They might be more inclined to talk to you," he said.

"But you were Eric's agent, and that gives you certain rights, Christopher."

Giulia had hit on a sore point. Relations between Hargrave and Donovan had not been trouble-free the last couple of months, although Hargrave had promised to fulfil all his obligations to Donovan, including the consigning of the Canaletto. There had been some terse exchange of correspondence, and if Eric's heirs got hold of it, they might give him a difficult time.

"Can't you explain to your client what happened?"

"I can't."

Giulia twirled the spaghetti around her fork and watched an edgy Donovan splash tomato sauce on his shirt and curse. Carlo, who had spotted the accident, came rushing over with some white powder that he guaranteed would remove any stain.

"Look, I really need your help with this. I'm willing to compensate you financially for your trouble. My client is quite wealthy."

"Did your client leave you an advance?"

"Yes, but it's not the money. He…well, insists that an agreement is an agreement and cannot be broken."

"Who are you dealing with, the mob?" she asked half-jokingly.

"Of course not. But, of course, he did pay a substantial amount up front."

Meaning, Giulia thought to herself, that if Donovan did not deliver, he would have to return this "substantial amount" to his client, and knowing how Donovan stretched his finances to the hilt, he probably had no money. So no money, no painting, he was clearly in deep muddy waters.

She thought about it for a moment and said that she would help him, but with no guarantees.

"What exactly am I looking for, Christopher?"

"St. Mark's Square in Venice, seen at an angle, from the Piazzetta by the Grand Canal."
"How big?"
"A metre by a metre and a half."
Giulia looked up surprise. That was big. "Substantial" took on a slightly different meaning and she could understand Donovan's consternation.
"At what stage was the painting when you last saw it?" Giulia asked.
"Nearly done. Eric just wanted to add the finishing touches. So when we last talked on the phone and he said he was just waiting for the paint to dry, I had no doubts the delivery could take place before the end of this month. Eric would be receiving the rest of his share so it was in both our interests to get the deal done. But for now, I've got my back to the wall," he said with a heavy sigh.
Giulia promised she would get in touch with the Hargraves and get back to him. Donovan appeared to relax a bit, and the crease on his forehead faded away. He even asked Giulia, with a mischievous grin, whether she had noticed that it was Carlo who came over and served every single dish to their table despite the many women servers in the restaurant.
Giulia repressed a giggle and told Christopher that Carlo was gay, and his domineering mother, the cook, had outlawed young male servers to keep Carlo "out of trouble". "So, you see Christopher, Carlo was in fact not flirting with me, but had his eyes on you all the time."
They shared a good laugh when Donovan said that after all, sometimes, it was not such a bad idea to have his back to the wall!

Chapter 6

Giulia stopped her car in front of a road sign and rolled down her window. According to the directions Bernard Hargrave had given her, she was to turn left a few miles before Brighton to avoid the centre. She re-read the notes jotted down on the back of a postcard before driving on.

Eric had not talked much about his family, so Giulia knew very little about his siblings except for what she had read in his autobiography. Eric had introduced her to some of them at the launch of his book in London but she had only a brief exchange with them. On the phone Bernard Hargrave had sounded helpful and accommodating. Giulia imagined he was a retired accountant or a civil servant leading an orderly and tedious life. She wondered what difference his brother's notoriety had made to his life. Did he boast about his brother's fame or was he ashamed of it?

Bernard Hargrave's house was exactly as Giulia had imagined. It was one of the many terraced houses along the seafront on the outskirts of Brighton: red brick walls, grey roof, windows with floral curtains, and a narrow patch of garden before the front door.

She parked her car and went to ring the doorbell but hurriedly stepped back as she was greeted by the barking of dogs. She heard a man's voice shout at the dogs before the door was opened. Bernard could not have looked more different from his brother. While Eric had a beard and was strong as an ox, Bernard was a wisp of a man, slightly stooped, clean shaven with thinning white hair.

"Miss Vasari, how nice of you to come!" he said. "Please come inside and meet my sister Alice."

Alice explained in a deep voice that she was Eric's youngest sister and gave Giulia a vigorous handshake.

Bernard and Alice appeared to perform very distinct roles. Alice served tea and cut the fruitcake. She made small talk about the weather, how delightful Brighton was and asked how Giulia enjoyed living in London. She swore when a piece of cake fell off her plate and giggled at her clumsiness. Alice had no airs and was likeable, but her brother kept his distance and said little. He sat to Giulia's right and stared, smiling occasionally. Now and then he would correct his sister or nod in approval. That was until Giulia mentioned Eric's work and his autobiography, at which point Alice quietly withdrew from the conversation and sat back while Bernard moved forward to the edge of his armchair.

He made no attempt to hide his curiosity and asked Giulia what her relationship was to his brother. He had probably forgotten that they had briefly met at the book launch. She told them of her years in Rome, of how she and Robert had met Eric through common friends and of the friendship that had developed, and about her involvement with Seldom House.

"So you knew his, hm…friend Willie?" Bernard asked.

"Of course, we met for dinners in Rome," she replied.

Eric's homosexuality was clearly not a subject his brother wished to dwell on and he changed the subject quickly.

"You said earlier that you had helped him when he published his autobiography. So you knew that he…well, made these drawings?"

"Only when I read his book did I know about the controversy over his drawings in the style of the Old Masters. We bought a watercolour from him many years ago but it was an Eric Hargrave watercolour. He may have used techniques he had learned from his studies but it was nevertheless his own style."

Alice giggled and repeated, "Of course, a genuine Eric Hargrave!"

Bernard glared at her.

"We did not see each other very often," Bernard felt he had to explain. "Eric lived in a different world. His whole life centred around his study of art and nothing else mattered very much. It was he who chose to stay away from us," he continued rather sadly.

The dogs' sudden barks provided a welcome distraction. Both Bernard and Alice rushed to check on them. Giulia noticed the bare walls save for a couple of photographs of dogs and a print of an insipid Mediterranean landscape. The furniture was tired, and there were too many prints and patterns that mingled and clashed, from the retro carpet to the floral upholstery of the sofa with its matching curtains. The only peaceful piece of furniture was the brown leather armchair that Bernard had been sitting in. On an upright piano were several silver-framed pictures of a younger Bernard and someone Giulia assumed must have been his wife.

At this point, Alice returned to the room and said Bernard was very attached to his dogs who had won prizes in numerous dog shows. She pointed to the display of medals beside one of the pictures of Bernard's wife.

Giulia nodded in acknowledgment, and turning to the photo of the woman, asked whether she was Bernard's wife.

"Yes," she answered. "She passed away three years ago, cancer," Alice added, as Bernard walked into the room.

"I am sorry," Giulia murmured.

Bernard nodded discreetly, not saying anything.

"It must be hard," Giulia said almost to herself.

There was a pause, Bernard lost in his thoughts, Giulia remembering her own loss. Then Alice, uncomfortable with the silence announced, "I'll go and make us a fresh pot of tea."

They resumed their conversation about Eric's autobiography.

Alice returned to the room and poured more tea and she took her place beside Giulia on the sofa.

Giulia thought it opportune to mention the purpose of her visit.

"Eric was writing another book and we were to meet in London to go through it together. We spoke about it shortly before his accident," Giulia explained. "Seldom House is interested in publishing it."

"What is the book about?" Bernard asked candidly.

"Eric's theory was that drawing was a language and that one could study the use of lines in artists' drawings to understand them and to recognise the author of a drawing."

The explanation seemed lost on both Bernard and Alice.

"You see, we don't know anything about publishing books. But well, do you sell a book, like you sell a...say, a painting?" Bernard finally phrased the question he had in mind.

"Not exactly. If the publisher is interested in a book he will offer to pay an advance to the author, a down payment. Once the book is published, the author will receive a percentage on the book sales, so called royalties."

"And could we ask how much Eric received for his autobiography?"

"If I remember correctly, he got close to 10,000 pounds sterling as an advance on royalties. What he made in the end, I cannot say for sure, as the book rights have been sold for translation, and our accounts department would be better informed of the figures."

Bernard and Alice exchanged glances. This they could understand.

"And where is the manuscript of Eric's new book?" Bernard asked.

"I was hoping you had it among Eric's personal belongings," she answered.

"It could take some time," Bernard explained. "We have just arranged for the contents of his apartment in Rome to be transported back to England. The lorry should be here in a week; only then can we begin to go through his things."

Giulia offered her help and assured them that she would be glad to drive back to Brighton if they needed her.

Although she had not mentioned the Canaletto painting of Christopher Donovan she now knew that most of Eric's possessions were on their way to Brighton and Donovan would have to contact the family himself.

Giulia remembered what Eric had said to her when she left Rome for London. There would always be good reason for them to remain in touch. She now knew this to be true.

Chapter 7

As Giulia drove back to London, the visit to Bernard and Alice in Brighton triggered memories of her first visit to Eric in Anticoli Corrado, a few years back.

It was a beautiful summer day and the anticipation of a lunch al fresco, in what promised to be good and entertaining company, made even the traffic getting out of Rome acceptable.

There were two ways to reach Eric's house: down from the village of Anticoli or up from the foot of the hill. Both paths required about half an hour's trek through the woods, on a muddy slope, slippery most of the time because of natural springs.

Robert had decided to park the car at the bottom of the hill, figuring that a climb up to start the day was more logical, and would make the trek down after a full lunch a whole lot easier. Giulia could not but agree with his logic.

They had brought along two bottles of Chianti red, a home baked apple pie, and a book by fellow American, Michael Mewshaw entitled "Playing Away". Bushes along the narrow track had been cut back and after a good twenty minute hike they eventually reached a clearing with fruit trees, flowering bushes, and an orchard at one end. Framed by an amphitheater of century old oak trees, the house sprawled the width of the clearing at the other end.

Eduardo, clad in shorts and a t-shirt, and a long flowing scarf tied around his neck, dashed to greet them saying, "Welcome to our home. Don't you think this," tugging at his scarf, "makes me look like Isadora Duncan?" It was lost on Robert, but Giulia said "Yes, but keep away from convertibles!"

Eric was standing in the shade of an apple tree, wine glass in hand, his signature Panama hat on his head, conversing with a group of friends. He went over to greet Robert and Giulia, and Eduardo went about arranging the table and chairs together with other guests. Introductions were made. Gianni, an Australian composer discovering his Italian roots in Roviano, greeted them with a wide smile. Luisa and Marco and another couple from Rome apologised for not being able to prevent their small children from running around the hammock, and Martin, an abstract sculptor from Germany who lived closer down the river, shook hands with them without interrupting his discourse and invited them to join in with a broad sweep of his arm. Martin's interlocutor turned out to be a retired literature professor with a colourful toupee, known only by the nickname of Texas.

Eric took Robert and Giulia inside the house to show them the painting they had purchased two weeks earlier. He explained that the central part of the house had been a square stone refuge for shepherds. It had been extended to accommodate a living room with a large stone fireplace and a guest bedroom and bathroom. The living room, which they had entered from the garden, gave way to a small studio, with a spiral staircase that led to the floor below, a master bedroom with its own bathroom and a kitchen that led on to a terrace paved with flag stones and lined with enormous terracotta jars brought in by car from Greece. Each door and window had been carefully recycled from a crumbling castle in Roviano, the tiles from the roof and the red bricks of the floor taken from old farms that had been abandoned. The different elements of the house blended well with each other and it seemed that it had stood there for as long as the oak trees.

Giulia helped bring out the dishes from the kitchen. Everyone had brought something and there was an assortment of food laid on the long wooden table. The buffet consisted of appetising plates of cold cuts, olives, dried tomatoes, local produce; three kinds of salads and a cold pasta dish; an authentic humus dip made by their Italian Lebanese friend Antonio, whose Filipina wife had prepared deep fried baby spring rolls. A side table had the wines, waters, juices and fizzy drinks. The guests helped themselves to the starters, and some sat themselves on the edge of the veranda, others on garden chairs.

When everyone complimented the fare and said they had all eaten more than they should have, Eduardo appeared with the main course for the day, coq au vin, that both he and Eric had prepared. Lunch was a great success, coffee was served, and everyone agreed that space needed to be made before the various sweets on offer would be ready for consumption. Some guests took to the hammocks for a snooze, while others formed into little groups on the lawn. Others took refuge from the midday sun in the living room kept cool by the thick walls. Among them, Giulia and Robert.

Giulia commented on the many books that lined one of the walls of the living room and Eric, always ready with a story for a willing audience, went over, took one from the shelf and handed it to her.

"Would you like to know where that book came from?"

She nodded, smiling.

"I happened to be in Yorkshire where I stayed at a small inn some years back, and as I had drunk rather too much for lunch and after lunch," he chuckled, "I decided to go for a walk in the countryside. I must have walked for a good hour, got thoroughly lost until I saw a mansion on the other side of a stream. I crossed a wooden bridge and approached the house. On a bench sat a very dignified white-haired gentleman who greeted me politely. I told him I was lost and asked whether he could show me how to get back to the inn. The old gentleman introduced himself and asked whether I wanted to come into his house first."

Eric drank some wine before going on. "I said I would be grateful for a glass of water and followed him inside the house. The house was large. It had a courtyard with a lawn and at its centre a well, and on the right side you could see the stained glass of a chapel. After showing me the ground floor, he asked if I would care to see the library. I said I would be delighted and watched him while he selected a key and opened the door. He said I should take my time and enjoy the books and that he would come back a little bit later. The library was magnificent but it was quite humid and cold and I remember wondering how much damage the humidity was inflicting on the books. When the old man returned, I had in my hands a book by William Blake with some interesting engravings. He said that if I liked it he would be happy to give it to me. I politely declined of course, but as he insisted I was glad to accept it. I remember his exact words. He said, 'Books are the last things I need now.' He then gave me directions to the inn which turned out to be only ten minutes away. Upon reaching the inn I went straight to the bar and ordered a whiskey. I made conversation with the barman and told him I had visited the mansion that stood about ten minutes east of the inn and met the owner who showed me his library. The barman looked at me in disbelief and shook his head. An old man who was sitting at the other end of the bar turned to me and said, 'That house has been closed for over ten years and no one has lived there all this time.' I asked him how he knew this and he answered, 'I am the caretaker of the place. I live beside the house, but these days I only look after the garden.' When I asked about the owner of the house he sighed and said that he had drowned in the river, and that his heirs were still fighting over his inheritance."

Giulia felt goose pimples on her arms.

Eric continued, "Maybe I dreamt it, but then, where did the book in your hands come from?"

To break the eerie silence that had fallen upon the room, the ever practical Robert asked Eric whether the humidity did not create problems for the many paintings that hung on the walls.

"The paintings do not suffer too much, it is more of a problem for the drawings," Eric replied.

"You can always make some new ones," Eduardo had said floating into the room, his scarf no longer around his neck."

Giulia would later remember his comment.

Chapter 8

"I knew the man well and there is no doubt in my mind that he was a skilled draughtsman. The claims he made, however, are preposterous and I am convinced that he could not have fooled experts time and again....

Eric Hargrave's claim to have produced hundreds of Old Master drawings is delusional if not downright dishonest. But what else can you expect from a self-proclaimed forger?
I viewed the drawings he exhibited last year at the St. George's gallery and found them interesting but lacking the fluidity of genuine Old Masters and frankly, easy to dismiss as forgeries."

Tarquin Littlejohn

Giulia read the excerpt from an article in an art magazine a second time before she cast it aside. What infuriated her was not so much the argument as the pompous and condescending tone the columnist had used to dismiss Eric Hargrave. He hadn't even bothered to get his facts straight. It also did not suit his purpose to mention that some works cited in Eric's autobiography did in fact get their attributions changed. But like the art historians who would only accept a change in the attribution to read, for example, "a follower of Mantegna" instead of "by Eric Hargrave", our columnist readily acknowledged that Eric was a skilled draughtsman, but would not admit to Eric being able to produce an Old Master drawing!

Of course, Eric Hargrave's confessions had sparked a controversial debate that made headlines for months. How could he have fooled the art community for so long? Were the art experts from the leading auction houses as inept as he made them appear?

What vast amount of money did the dealers make? What was the real value of a work of art? These were among the questions debated to the consternation of the art establishment and the delight of the general public, who saw the forger as a modern day Robin Hood.

Eric's sudden death had revived the debates, and emboldened experts, who no longer worried about a confrontation with the famous forger, were divided into two groups: those who claimed to have known all along he was a forger, and those who dismissed his claims as gross exaggerations.

Seldom House was hosting another cocktail reception at the Grosvenor Hotel that evening. Giulia found the venue old-fashioned but Victor Edelman stubbornly refused to consider alternative venues. She never looked forward to these business functions, finding them tedious, but today was different. Something compelled her to go.

Guests were led through a thickly carpeted corridor lined with prints of castles and cathedrals in heavy gold frames to a private reception room, where a white-gloved barman awaited them. The lights of the crystal chandelier had been dimmed to enhance the reflections of a wood fire against the bookcase that covered one of the walls. It was easy to understand how guests felt they had been invited into a private home rather than a hotel.

Giulia was talking to one of the guests, a former Ambassador to India who had high literary ambitions and very little talent in this field but excellent connections in the banking community, when someone grasped her arm.

"Sorry to interrupt you, Giulia. Can we speak when you've got a moment?"

She nodded to a tanned young man in tight black jeans and an open white shirt.

Giulia turned her back to the Ambassador, apologising for the distraction.

His attention was diverted by a wobbly matron who held a glass of champagne in each hand, handing him one, and launching into a description of her last trip to Rajasthan.

Giulia took the opportunity to go in search of Sebastian Greenwood to see what it was he wanted to talk about. She waded through the crowded room, catching bits of conversation ranging from the state of the stock market to the latest crisis in Whitehall, or how the service was unacceptable at the newly opened restaurant in Knightsbridge.

Giulia spotted Sebastian Greenwood standing by the door and waving at her. She quickly went over to join him.

"Giulia, I must speak to you about something important. Can you spare a few minutes?"

Giulia nodded. Greenwood produced documentaries for television. Interviews, reportage, on whoever and whatever was of topical interest. They had met when his company had produced the BBC programme on Eric Hargrave that was aired on prime time as Eric's autobiography hit the bookshops.

The producer led her to one of the bars of the Grosvenor Hotel and they sank into facing armchairs.

"Well?"

"I'd like to do another programme on Eric. I need your help."

He couldn't have put it more simply.

"Do you have anything new to say?"

"I've got a few ideas, but I'm not quite sure ..."

"Okay, let's hear what you have in mind," she said encouragingly.

"His death! I thought of starting with a dramatic reconstruction of his death. Late night in the narrow streets of Rome, rain, slippery cobble stones, dark corners where someone could have been waiting, you know what I mean. And then I try to retrace his last days to establish what or who could have caused his death."

Giulia remained expressionless.

"Hmm, you're not buying it. Probably too commercial. And not exactly the style of the BBC. Another idea would be to focus on Hargrave's legacy, have his work and his views discussed by serious personalities from the art world."

This provoked a reaction from Giulia.

"It would be a character assassination exercise, you wouldn't be short of candidates for that one," she replied.

"I'm sure we could find someone sympathetic," he suggested.

"I guess so."

"What I really need is to find a good starting point."

Sebastian studied Giulia's face eagerly. "Something he left behind maybe, a testament of sorts?"

Giulia did not say anything, and Sebastian waited patiently. Finally she shook her head.

"Seb, why talk to me? Did Edelman suggest it to you?"

"No, I mean not exactly. I called him because I was interested in following up a story or something on Eric. The mysterious circumstances surrounding his death provide fodder for a good story, a good film. We enjoyed filming with Eric in Anticoli and in Rome. I've got lots of unused footage, and Giulia, I am a film producer, it's my bread and butter, and I go where I think there's a good chance of making a worthy film."

Giulia half heard what Sebastian was saying, annoyed that Edelman might yet again have prematurely made announcements about a new Hargrave book.

"What exactly did Edelman tell you?"

"He mentioned that Seldom House was going to publish a posthumous book by Hargrave and that it would create another scandal. If I can use this material it will help me sell the idea to the BBC and the exposure would of course help Seldom House sell the book."

"Edelman forgot one tiny detail. There may not be a book to publish!"

A surprised Greenwood looked at Giulia and asked, "What do you mean?"

"I'm sorry, but there is nothing I can do now to help you with this project."

During the week that followed Giulia avoided the office of Seldom House and Victor Edelman under the pretext of carrying out research on Eric Hargrave and Old Master paintings sales of the last decade. She visited the main auction houses in London as well as the National Gallery and the Tate, did some research in the library of the Victoria and Albert, but mostly stayed in her Kensington apartment where she re-read Eric Hargrave's autobiography.

Robert's life insurance had made it possible for Giulia to purchase a tiny two-bedroom apartment in Kensington, not far from the gardens of Hyde Park, easy walking distance to the shops and public transport. She had taken the few pieces of Italian furniture that Robert and she had picked up at antique fairs, and mixed these in with contemporary pieces she had purchased in London to create an eclectic and tasteful look. She had no trouble filling her bookshelves with new buys and was careful not to clutter her small but comfortable apartment with more than she needed. This was home for now.

Giulia took regular walks with her friend Tessa in the park. She was one of the reasons, aside from the job offer at Seldom House, that persuaded Giulia to make the move from Rome. They had known each other as children in New York and had maintained a close friendship ever since. Tessa had married her first love, David, who had brought her back to London with him. Giulia had married Robert, who had taken her to Rome.

She had come back from today's walk feeling lighter. Giulia had told her about her frustration with Edelman, about her trip to Rome, about how she still missed Robert, and about the unrelenting Alberto Conti.

She noticed the red light blinking on her telephone and pressed the play button as she took off her coat and kicked off her boots. First message, Victor Edelman's stentorian voice blared over the phone. He demanded that Giulia call him back and come to the office the next day. Second message, her younger half-brother, calling in to say hello. He was in Jordan and had just been on a camel. That was so like him, to call at the strangest of times, from the strangest of places, having been…Giulia caught herself smiling, doing the strangest of things. Third message: Bernard Hargrave, asking her to call him back.

The phone rang six or seven times before Bernard Hargrave finally picked up.

"Mr. Hargrave, Giulia Vasari here. How are you?"

"Oh, very well, very well, thank you. How nice of you to call me back so quickly, Miss Vasari."

Bernard Hargrave coughed discreetly, a habit he had when he felt uncomfortable.

"Miss Vasari, do you know a person named Tarquin Littlejohn, Professor Tarquin Littlejohn?"

" Littlejohn? The journalist? No, I don't know him personally. Can I ask why?"

"He called me yesterday with a most impertinent request."

"Yes?" Giulia said slowly, remembering Littlejohn to be the columnist whose article had irritated her.

"He asked when it would be convenient for him to go through the papers and personal effects of Eric. He said it was a matter of some urgency and since he was in England, he could come right away to see me."

"Did he give any explanation for his request?"

"He claimed to be the curator of an important museum in America and said he needed to find proof that his theory was correct."

"I wonder if Eric maybe knew him..." Giulia said more to herself than to Bernard.

"I asked him the very same question but he mumbled something incoherent. He only repeated that checking Eric's papers was of great importance to him."

Giulia was as intrigued as Eric's brother.

"I told him I would think about it and he left me his number in Cambridge," Bernard continued. "I was wondering..." Bernard hesitated.

"Yes," Giulia said.

"Well, the boxes from Rome have arrived and, well, I, we, were wondering whether we could ask you to, well, to help us go through Eric's papers. It's all a bit too much for us and, well, you might be able to sift through them more quickly and see whether there is anything important. That is, of course, if you have the time, and you are inclined to do so?"

Giulia could not believe her luck. It was a favour being asked of her that she was most happy to carry out.

She tried to contain her eagerness when she accepted to help.

"So Monday it is. Thank you so very much, Miss Vasari."

Chapter 9

Victor Edelman stuck his head through the office door and saw that Giulia was waiting for him. "Don't go anywhere. I'll be with you in half an hour," he barked before closing the door again. His secretary shrugged resignedly and mumbled something Giulia did not catch. "I'll go through the art magazines you store in the back office," she told her.

Giulia picked up an "Art in America" magazine that dated back several years and leafed through the pages. She continued through the row of magazines for a while when a short article caught her eye. The text mentioned that Professor Littlejohn had joined the Silverstein Museum in Los Angeles in 1993 as curator of the European drawing collection. It mentioned that he was an internationally acclaimed scholar who had held important positions in several British museums and that his appointment was a coup for the California museum. Giulia put the magazine aside, eager to see what else she could find related to Littlejohn and the Silverstein. She quickly went over the editorial contents of the next magazines when she came across one entitled "Sex and Forgery in California, a Court Case". She glanced through the article and spotted the name of Littlejohn. As she was about to take a copy of the articles, Edelman's strained voice distracted her. "Well, go and get her, goddamnit," he ordered his secretary. Giulia pressed the print button and watched the printer spew out several pages of text and pictures. She slipped the copies into her bag and made her way to Edelman's office.

Victor Edelman was not an easy man to work for. He made no attempts to control his bouts of temper and Giulia was glad she did not have to spend much time in the office of Seldom House. As she had expected, the head of the publishing house wanted to know whether she had found Eric Hargrave's manuscript. Giulia briefly told him about her meeting with Bernard and Alice. He leaned back against his chair and grinned in self-satisfaction. "Way to go. Charm them, bully them, promise them anything they want, but get me this manuscript. Our first quarter financial results are not looking good and I need something to give the Board."

Giulia needed to gain time.

"I'm going over to Brighton on Monday. Some of the boxes have arrived," Giulia started cautiously, not wanting to raise Edelman's hopes, "and the Hargraves have asked me to help sort them out."

"That is good news. If you also need to fly to Rome, go ahead. We'll of course pay for your expenses," he suggested generously.

Christopher Donovan looked worried and for once was at a loss for words. Yet the person who sat in front of him looked anything but threatening. Balding and overweight, dressed in a dark blue suit, immaculate white shirt and an eye-catching red tie, he lifted his glass of wine to his lips with a theatrical movement. He displayed a thick gold ring with an embossed crest on his right hand and a gold Rolex watch stuck out from under the sleeve of his shirt.

"Do not force me to have to repeat to you what I said last week. Your problems are of no interest to me. I have given you another three weeks to carry out your part of the agreement and this is final," the man said before putting his glass down.

Donovan knew it was pointless to argue.

"Fine, I understand," was all he replied.

Donovan's interlocutor looked over the gallery owner's shoulder and stared at the attractive woman who had just entered the restaurant. Donovan turned around and saw it was Giulia. He winced, and turned his head, hoping she had not seen him. But his guest was quick to notice his reaction.

"Do you know her, Christopher?" he asked.

Donovan gave a noncommittal nod.

"Why don't you invite her over to our table?"

"I don't know if…" Donovan started to protest.

"Hurry, before she gets away."

Donovan stood up slowly and walked over to Giulia who was being led to a table by the waiter and guided her towards their table.

"Greg Watkins, a pleasure to meet you, "Donovan's guest said extending his right hand.

She smiled and shook it, immediately feeling the tension between the two men.

Watkins stared at her unashamedly. Donovan looked up to the ceiling wondering what to expect next.

"Giulia, may I call you Giulia?" he asked not waiting for her to reply, "Where does the lovely Giulia come from?"

I'm half American, half Argentinian," she replied curtly but with a smile.

"Please call me Greg, as our friend, Christopher here does," he said turning to Donovan who felt like a third wheel.

Giulia noticed the awkward expression on Donovan's face. He had remained silent the whole time, carefully watching her, admiring how she could so effortlessly adapt to any given situation. What he heard next made him sit up straight in his chair.

"Tell me, Giulia, do you like art?"

She could see Donovan was not too happy with the direction the conversation was going.

"Are you in the art world, like Christopher?" Giulia asked with an ingenuous smile.

"You could say that, I have quite a few artworks hanging on my walls," he smiled.

"And what do you collect, Mr. Watkins, I mean Greg?"

"Old Masters mainly."

"Any particular period?" she asked.

Watkins wanted to impress and tell her he could afford any and the best but decided against it.

"Italian and French Renaissance painters," he finally offered.

"And if you could choose a painting to own, which one would you have?"

"La Gioconda, by Leonardo da Vinci."

"And may I ask why?"

"Because it will remind me of the smile on your face," he said with the sweep of a hand as he placed his napkin on the table and stood up to leave.

"Giulia, it was a pleasure meeting you. Here is my card. Please call and I would love to show you my collection one day. I am sure you will enjoy it." He looked towards the standing Donovan and said simply, "Christopher."

As he left Giulia turned to Donovan.

"A friend of yours?" she asked provocatively.

"A client. That's all."

"Is he by any chance the one who commissioned the view of Venice in the style of Canaletto?"

The Irishman looked up sharply.

"Do you have any news for me about the Canaletto?"

"Yes, I have," she said, noting that he had dismissed her question.

"And?"

She looked at him calmly.

"Giulia, please don't play games with me. It's really important."

"I thought you liked to play games," she said.

"Not now. I really need to find this painting."

Donovan sighed and sat back in his chair. He raised his hands above the table in mock surrender, hiding his rising frustration as well as he could.

"What do I have to do to get this information?"

"Eric's things have been shipped over. I'm going down to Brighton on Monday and I'll let you know if your painting is there," was all she volunteered.

"By the way Christopher, did Eric ever mention the name of Professor Tarquin Littlejohn?" Giulia asked as she stood up to go.

Donovan shook his head, "Why do you ask?"

"I'm just curious. I read an article in which Littlejohn claimed he had identified forgeries in a museum in California which he believed were done by the hand of Eric Hargrave."

Donovan shrugged.

Chapter 10

The day Christopher Donovan first visited Eric Hargrave in Rome, the eternal city drowned under a torrent of rain and traffic was brought to a standstill.

Donovan had found Trastevere run down and chaotic, lacking the sophistication of London and wondered what Eric liked about it. But once he entered Eric's home, his impression changed completely.

The apartment was on the "piano nobile" of a fifteenth-century building that used to be a monastery. The internal walls that once divided the room into cells had been removed to create a large room, divided by three arches, with high ceilings and antique wooden beams. The entrance was illuminated by an elegant chandelier that hung over a baroque mirror and on the whitewashed walls hung paintings, drawings and engravings.

On the eighteenth-century English desk that stood in a corner, a marble statue of a youth's head was casually resting against the wall. A four-poster bed faced an oval fresco that had lost some of its colour but none of its beauty.

Eric was working on an exquisite landscape in oil, in the manner of Claude Lorrain for an English client, and without hesitation he explained to Donovan how he had selected the subject, and what material he was using, pointing out with a broad smile that he was painting it on a contemporary canvas, not an 18th century one, "It should make the question of attribution a rather simple one to answer, wouldn't you think?"

Donovan had suggested the principle of a contract between them and Eric agreed readily, waiving the need to consult a lawyer. The gallery owner explained he was prepared to pay Eric a monthly stipend in exchange for the exclusive rights over his artistic production. Eric, who considered money to be a necessary evil, was delighted to be able to free his mind from such mundane concerns, and Donovan was convinced that his investment would at some point be very profitable.

A few months after signing, Eric had agreed to produce a series of drawings in the style of "a broad spectrum of Old Masters" to be exhibited in the London art gallery. The objective, Donovan had explained, was to show the variety of styles he had mastered. The wider the range the better, he had insisted. Eric proposed names and subjects as casually and confidently as if it was only a matter of selecting them from a catalogue.

When they met again in London, Eric handed the dealer a worn out portfolio and said, "Here they are. I hope you will find them suitable." Donovan opened the portfolio with a mixture of anticipation and concern. As he pulled out the first drawing he was left without any doubt that the exhibition would be of the highest quality. He gazed in admiration at each of the twenty drawings in turn.

Eric Hargrave had found inspiration among French, German and Italian Old Masters from the early fifteenth to the early nineteenth century. He had used ink, chalk, gouache and pen to correspond exactly to the medium used by each artist in such different styles that, had he not just consigned the portfolio to Donovan, it would have been impossible to believe that all twenty drawings were made by the same hand.

The first image was of St. George slaying a dragon, drawn with pen and brown ink on vellum paper in the style of Jacopo Bellini. And although Eric had not copied an existing drawing, he had borrowed various elements from known works and combined them into his own composition. The slightly stilted style of Bellini contrasted with the study of a woman's head in black and white chalk, in the style of Bronzino, but which could have passed for a preparatory work by Leonardo da Vinci. The tilted head was typical of sixteenth-century Florentine masters, smooth and mysteriously romantic.

Next were a group of Roman soldiers with horses in the style of Zuccaro, an artist from the sixteenth century, whose works included frescoes in the Palazzo Farnese in Rome and who was known for his expertise on Roman friezes. The composition, with brown wash and white gouache, drawn on blue tinted paper, stood out from its background as a bas relief would have.

The rest of the drawings were as interesting in their own right and the art dealer recognised the styles of Watteau, Fragonard and Boucher, Giambattista Tiepolo, Piranesi, Annibale Caracci as well as Durer. There were others for which Donovan guessed that Eric had borrowed the style of several Dutch artists which he could not identify immediately and some of a lesser known artist from the Florentine school of the sixteenth, or maybe seventeenth century.

"Remarkable, brilliant really," was his comment to Eric Hargrave who smiled benignly. "I will have them framed by one used to working with Old Masters," he announced.

After a long lunch at an expensive Italian restaurant in Mayfair, Donovan returned to the gallery and perused the portfolio of Hargrave's works once again before sitting at his desk to write the outline of the catalogue he intended to produce for the exhibition.

The variety of styles Eric Hargrave was able to "borrow" was truly amazing and it was not surprising that experts had been fooled again and again into attributing works by the hand of Eric to a variety of Old Masters. There was no common feature to be found between a charcoal done in the style of Durer, another in the manner of Watteau and a third by Tiepolo. Eric had succeeded in adopting such different styles and techniques in the same way a talented linguist would master languages.

Donovan remembered that Eric once claimed to have restored the Leonardo cartoons when he was a student at the Royal Academy. According to Eric, a caretaker had carelessly left two large preparatory drawings by Leonardo da Vinci leaning against a heater in the basement of the Academy. The heater was faulty and leaked onto the drawing causing irreparable damage, to the consternation of the curator. Eric, whose talent had not gone unnoticed, was asked to repair the cartoons but in fact redrew them entirely as they had almost disappeared. Eric was of course sworn to secrecy and, not long afterwards, the Royal Academy actually sold the cartoons for a very large sum of money at a public auction.

Studying the drawings in front of him, Donovan had little difficulty believing Eric's claim.

Chapter 11

The rain fell parallel to the windows of the train compartment and each drop that grazed the glass traced a line against it, as if hatched by an invisible hand. It was already dark outside and the reflections of the lighted compartment bounced off the glass.

Three wet-haired teenagers giggled four rows away from Giulia. Across the aisle and one row ahead of her a young man in jacket and tie stared at his laptop, casting annoyed glances in the direction of the teenagers. The compartment was nearly empty and she could hear each passenger although she could not see them all. A nervous woman talked to a young child, an elderly man constantly coughed, and, at the other end of the carriage, someone was speaking loudly in a foreign language. Slowly but inexorably all these individual sounds melted into one and became no more distracting than the raindrops against the window. Giulia closed her eyes, and leaned back against the head-rest of the seat.

Her day with Bernard Hargrave had been a rollercoaster of emotions. Eric's personal belongings had been cast away in removal carton boxes as you would dispose of unwanted things. Books, clothes, silverware, ceramic plates and piles of paper had been mixed without care. Whatever remained of a collection of small terracotta statues lay partly buried in undergarments and shoes and several were broken when Giulia pulled them from a box. Drawings and watercolours had been packed separately and with more care, but each one was damp.

Sifting through the contents of each carton, Giulia felt she was attending her friend's funeral a second time, as if the disposal of his treasured possessions completed the burial of his body. Bernard Hargrave's questions were as predictable as they were unemotional: "What do you think the value of this book, or this statue or that drawing is?" Most of Eric's books now stood in piles in his brother's guest bedroom, many of them damaged, covers bent, pages stained by paint, illustrations foxed by humidity; each one was a reference, a milestone in the study of Old Masters which Eric had pursued relentlessly.

Giulia had recognised one of the watercolours as having been exhibited in Rome at the last show she had visited with her husband before he died. She recalled Robert had liked the upturned hulls on a Sicilian beach and said they should go there sometime. There were also letters from friends she did not know, from the bank, from Eric's boyfriend, and even a hastily scribbled note from her to thank him for a dinner party.

She felt something was missing. Eric was preparing for an exhibition and there should have been many more drawings or watercolours. He had told Giulia he would meet her in London and show her the draft of his new book, yet no manuscript was to be found. Giulia had pointed this out to Bernard as they sat drinking tea, limbs stiff from lifting heavy cartons throughout the afternoon. Eric's brother had frowned and said the instruction had been to pack everything except for the furniture. Giulia felt she had reached a dead end.

The thatched roof of the cottage just outside Cambridge and its garden had the unkempt appearance of a house seldom used and badly maintained. On the ground floor, a disproportionately large fireplace dominated the living room but its roaring fire did not succeed in warming the whole room.

The dining table had been positioned close to the fireplace. On its polished top, reams of paper were lined up in neat piles around a laptop computer.

A tall man entered the room, with a glass of whisky in hand. He sat down at the dining table and drank from the glass before placing it in front of him. While he stared at the papers he played with the gold ring decorated with a coat of arms he wore on a finger of his left hand. Slowly, he picked up the first document and started to read it yet another time. The request for a trial against the Silverstein Museum of Los Angeles had been filed by the law offices of Goldman and Stratton in Santa Monica on behalf of Professor Tarquin Littlejohn, the plaintiff. The complaint file alleged that the museum had committed fraud and broken the contractual relationship with the plaintiff, at the time curator of the Department of Drawings at the Silverstein Museum. The first allegation asserted that Littlejohn was a well-respected art historian and lecturer, who had held key positions in leading British museums and was the author of various scholarly publications such as "Tiepolo's Art," "Roman and Florentine Drawings," and many more. The Englishman read the first allegation a second time with obvious self-satisfaction. He was, after all, respected and a well-known figure in the art world and he would be damned if the Silverstein Museum of Los Angeles was not forced to acknowledge it publicly and admit he was right and they were wrong. He had discovered that several drawings in the Museum's collection were forgeries by Eric Hargrave and pointed this out to the Board of Trustees of the Museum. Of course it was disturbing! Large sums of money had been spent by his predecessor, Professor Spencer, to purchase forgeries. It was not only damaging for Spencer's reputation but reflected badly on the Museum's Trust. The Trust contacted the previous curator, who staunchly denied there was any truth in Littlejohn's assessment. That was when the troubles started.

He put down the document and dialed a number on his phone.

"Goldman and Stratton Law Office. How can I help you?" the voice said.

"Give me Jack Goldman, Professor Tarquin Littlejohn here."

An irritating tune started to play while he was made to wait.

"Jack Goldman. How are you, Professor?"

Littlejohn did not believe niceties and polite remarks were what the law firm was paid for, even though he had actually not paid out anything and would only owe the firm if his court case was successful.

"When did the Trustees contact Professor Spencer, and which one of the trustees contacted him? Have you been able to find this out?"

"Hmm, not just yet. But we are working on it."

"It is critical, as you know, because my so-called communication problems must have started right after the Trustees talked to him…."

"I know that Professor, I understand the importance of this element. As I said, we are working on it."

"Another thing, Mr. Goldman. Why did we not ask for a specific sum of money as reparation? I am still not convinced that 'punitive damages in an amount sufficient to make an example of, and punish, defendants' is the best approach."

"We have discussed this before. We know that the sums spent to acquire these forgeries amounts to well in excess of two million US dollars, but we felt that punitive damage 'based upon the wealth of the defendants' would allow us to start negotiating from a much higher figure."

"Yes, well you did say that. Fine, the moment there is something new, you must call me."

Littlejohn interrupted the call abruptly and hung up the phone.

Somehow he must meet with the brother of Eric Hargrave. Somewhere, he might be able to find unequivocal proof that he was right and that the museum was wrong. A list, or a reference, an invoice maybe. Hargrave was, after all, a vain fool who ended up telling the world what a bloody genius he was. A man like that kept records! The first time they had met, he had disliked Eric Hargrave. Too bloody smooth an operator, he thought.

The train jolted Giulia from her sleep. Passengers were already standing, ready to leave the compartment. Through the window she read the sign "Victoria Station", black letters against a white background. The man with a laptop was staring at her curiously but when she turned her head towards him, he averted his gaze and looked down. He was older than she had first thought, maybe in his thirties; the bleached hair made his face look younger.

Giulia stood up and walked slowly off the train. Still dazed from her sleep she reached the newspaper kiosk and bought the Evening Standard. The front cover showed a photograph of Tony Blair, the Prime Minister, in the House of Commons. Under his picture was a provocative headline suggesting he was the cause of deep divisions in the Labour Party. In the bottom corner of the front page an advertisement promised you could win a studio apartment in Chelsea if you read the Evening Standard often enough to collect coupons, send them in, and enter a draw.

Giulia folded the newspaper and strode towards Hyde Park. The walk made her feel good. The temperature was cool, and the rain had stopped falling. She passed by an Italian restaurant with red and white chequered curtains and stopped. No one was waiting for her at her flat; she would eat before going home.

After having ordered a pasta dish and a glass of white wine it suddenly hit her. In fact, it was staring her in the face. The front page of the Evening Standard had triggered her memory. She pulled out her mobile phone and called Bernard Hargrave's number.

"Mr. Hargrave? Hello, it's Giulia. I am sorry to call you so late."

"It's perfectly all right. Is anything the matter?"

It was just before nine o'clock and most of the retirees in Sussex were ready to go to bed, Bernard Hargrave among them.

"No, I'm fine. I just arrived in London and remembered something important."

"Hmm," Bernard muttered.

"Was Eric's studio emptied as well as his apartment?"

"What studio?"

"Are you not aware that Eric rented a small studio where he liked to work during the day?"

"A studio, you said? No, nobody mentioned any studio to me. How odd that nobody said anything."

"I know it was in Trastevere. Eric told me he walked to it every day."

Bernard repeated several times that nobody had mentioned any studio to him.

"I am planning to go to Rome next week. If you agree, I could ask where Eric had his studio and who might have the key."

Although he seemed guarded and cautious by nature, Giulia felt that Bernard had started to trust her. From remarks he had made, he was at odds with his siblings over what to do with their brother's legacy. He clearly felt he should be in control, but his family was no longer happy to let him take decisions now that they understood the value of their brother's estate.

Bernard's hesitation did not escape Giulia.

"Err, well, yes, it is a good idea. But, you have been so helpful as it is and we wouldn't want you to go too much out of your way."

"It's no trouble really. I'll give you a call from Rome as soon as I find anything out."

Chapter 12

Spring seemed to have come early as Giulia sat on the hotel roof terrace, enjoying the early afternoon sun. Large terracotta pots planted with different coloured roses, forsythia bushes showing little yellow flowers, and heavily scented lavender plants marked the boundaries of the restaurant. On the northern side, the *cupolas* of the two churches in Piazza del Popolo stood out against the gardens of the Villa Borghese. The southern side of the terrace was level with the top of the trees that lined the Tiber river. She had called everyone she thought would know where Eric's studio was, but had found out nothing. The answers varied from "He mentioned it but, no, I don't know where it is" to "I had no idea he rented a studio."

Giulia ordered a capuccino and a glass of water. Slowly, she leaned against the high backed chair and looked up at the sky through her sunglasses. The thought that Bernard Hargrave knew Eric was renting a studio and had lied to her crossed her mind but she quickly dismissed it. Why would he have lied?

"*Ecco il suo cappuccino, Signora.*" The waiter smiled at her.

"*Grazie, molto gentile,*" she replied.

As soon as clouds hid the sun, the temperature dropped significantly. Giulia shivered and put on her coat. From one of its pockets she pulled out a crumpled visiting card. It was Inspector Conti's. Giulia believed that most things happened for a reason and she toyed with the card in her hand. After a moment's hesitation, she decided to call the police inspector.

Conti said he would be glad to meet with her later in the afternoon. And yes, of course, he knew that Eric had rented a studio. Giulia smiled. She looked at her watch and stood up. Things were looking up.

The man who stood on Bernard Hargrave's doorstep meticulously adjusted the scarf tied around his neck. He felt uncomfortably out of place, although his origins were not too dissimilar from that of the Hargraves. His mother had been a nurse in a primary school and his father a post office employee in the Midlands. To disguise his working origin he had changed his first name from Leslie to Tarquin while at university.

The door was pulled open by a puzzled Bernard who asked the stranger whether there was anything he could do for him.

"I believe there is something you can do for me, Mr. Hargrave."

Hargrave's puzzled look remained unchanged. He said, "Yes?"

"You see, I am an art historian and I would be delighted if you would answer a few questions about your late brother."

"Well…," Hargrave started, at a loss for words.

"If you would let me in, I could explain to you what I am looking for," the man suggested.

Bernard was hesitant, but the calm demeanour of his well-dressed caller reassured him. Besides, he was curious to know what the man was after.

The visitor stepped into the house and apologised for having come unannounced.

"Allow me to introduce myself, Mr. Hargrave. My name is Professor Littlejohn. Professor Tarquin Littlejohn."

"Oh yes, you called a week ago," Bernard said.

Remembering the arrogant tone of Littlejohn, he stiffened and wondered whether it was such a good idea to have let the visitor in. He pointed at the sofa and reluctantly invited Littlejohn to sit down. The living room was orderly, but a faint smell of curry or Chinese food hung in the air.

Littlejohn pulled out a visiting card and handed it to Bernard. Shiny embossed letters stood out against a parchment-like paper.

"Mr. Hargrave, I knew your brother very well. We were, I dare say, good friends and his passing away was very sad. I know how close he was to his family and how difficult it must be for you. Please accept my sincere condolences."

Bernard frowned slightly at the suggestion that Eric was close to his family but thanked Littlejohn. Unconsciously, he passed his fingers over Littlejohn's card, feeling the texture of the paper and of the letters. Littlejohn went on to recount how he had met Bernard's brother and how they had struck up a friendship from their first meeting.

"Eric was very talented and surprisingly erudite, considering he was not a scholar. Imagine how paradoxical it was for me to ask for Eric's views on Italian renaissance drawings! After all, I am the one with a doctorate in art history and was curator of several important museums in London and in the United States!"

Littlejohn noticed that Bernard enjoyed the compliments paid to his late brother and went on for a while, selecting stories that emphasised the high regard in which he held Eric. It was also apparent that Bernard did not have any knowledge of art or the art world and stories quickly became imaginary.

Bernard Hargrave started to feel guilty about his initial antipathy towards his unannounced guest. He had obviously been close to Eric; the passing comment about how close Eric was to his family was forgotten.

"Professor Littlejohn, can I offer you a drink?"

"It is very kind of you but I wouldn't want to impose."

"You are not imposing. I will have a gin and tonic myself. Would you like one, or a whisky perhaps?"

Littlejohn said a gin and tonic would be fine and watched his host leave the room to fetch two glasses and some ice. The house was small and did not appear to have a cellar. Littlejohn wondered where Eric's belongings were stored. He had noticed a garage door, on the side of the house.

One gin and tonic followed another in relatively quick succession and Bernard looked more relaxed. Littlejohn felt confident he had overcome the first barrier. It was time to come to the point, and Bernard provided him with an opening.

"So, when did you see Eric for the last time, Professor Littlejohn?" Bernard asked.

"A few years ago. He came to Los Angeles for the opening of his art exhibition." Littlejohn paused. "He stayed at my place for a couple of days, in fact," he added, lying shamelessly.

"Oh, you live in Los Angeles?" Bernard sounded impressed.

"But we wrote to each other and spoke on the phone quite often," Littlejohn continued. "In fact I had recently sent him a copy of an interesting drawing to ask for his, er…shall we say, professional opinion. The drawing was allegedly by Michelangelo but I had reason to believe it might have been by a follower of the Old Master. The Museum was very upset when I questioned the drawing's authenticity so I sent Eric a copy in absolute confidence. No one was to know about it. The Board of Trustees of the Museum would be incensed if they knew I had sent Eric a copy."

"And what did Eric say? Did he agree with you?"

"Well, that is the thing. Eric did not answer me. He died before he could answer."

"Oh, I see."

"Now I am no longer able to consult with Eric," Littlejohn concluded, then as if an after-thought had struck him, he added, "I wonder if you could tell me whether you found my letter to Eric on this matter, or perhaps the drawing I sent him! Maybe he had written down a few notes for my attention but did not find the time to mail them."

"Er…I am not sure where to look and…well…what to look for," Bernard Hargrave retorted.

"I would be glad to help you look through Eric's notes and documents."

"Well, I don't know really…I could not decide alone…there is the rest of the family to consult with of course."

Littlejohn straightened up and looked at Bernard with new intensity.

"Surely you understand that Eric would not have wanted to embarrass me. Think of what could happen if the drawing or my letter were seen by the wrong people!"

"No, no, of course I understand what you are saying, but still… I am not sure I can help you at the moment."

The suave tone of Littlejohn suddenly disappeared, as though the effort of containing himself was finally too demanding.

"Mr. Hargrave, are you saying you are refusing to let me recover what is rightfully mine?" Littlejohn asked.

Eric's brother was taken aback by the sudden underlying aggressiveness in Littlejohn's question. "No, no. That is not what I mean."

"Frankly, I do not understand your reluctance to give me a straight answer. My request is quite simple: there must be a drawing that belongs to me among Eric Hargrave's papers. I demand to have this drawing back! And the easiest way is for us to go through his papers. It would take an hour or two at the most."

"We have not gone through all the boxes and it is possible that the drawing is still in Rome and we will have to wait for some news on that," Hargrave replied trying to remain calm, recalling the information Giulia had given him that Eric had a studio in Rome. He recovered some of his composure and stood up, to signify the end of their conversation.

Frustration was plain to see from Littlejohn's grimace. As he got to his feet, the phone rang, startling Bernard. He hesitated, his glance moving anxiously between his guest and the phone. Littlejohn was quick to take advantage of the distraction and called out exactly at the moment Bernard lifted the phone receiver.

"Do you have a bathroom I can use before I go, Mr. Hargrave?"

Bernard indicated the first floor, his back turned to Littlejohn who crossed the living room in three strides. He was at the foot of a carpeted flight of stairs that led to the floor above. To his right was a door to the kitchen and a few metres further another that probably led to the garage. Quickly he climbed the stairs and found himself on a narrow landing in front of four more doors. Without hesitation, he grabbed the handle of the first to his right that opened to a large cabinet with a boiler and cardboard boxes covered by thick layers of dust. The next door was that of a bathroom with striking bright orange and blue tiles. In front of him, the master bedroom door was slightly ajar. He pushed it open. The only significant pieces of furniture were a double bed, two side tables and a clothes cabinet, unlikely to conceal what he was looking for. He closed the door quietly.

Downstairs, Bernard put down the phone. Realising that his guest was alone on the first floor he decided to follow. Littlejohn opened the last door. Despite the drawn curtains there was enough light in the guest bedroom to see removal boxes piled on top of each other with the markings of a removal company clearly printed on their sides. Stacks of old books were lined up against the wall, under a window. Quickly Littlejohn closed the door and turned around to face the stairs. Hargrave was halfway up, but gave no indication he had noticed what his guest was doing. When he saw Littlejohn he backtracked down the steps. Without saying anything, Littlejohn walked downstairs, past Bernard, to the front door, his thoughts still on the guest bedroom that was filled with books and papers that must have been Eric's.

"Mr. Hargrave, you have my card. I will be in Cambridge for the next two weeks. Call me and let me know when I can go through your brother's papers. If you deny me this, my lawyers will make sure I have access to them anyway. But remember, I hold you personally responsible for my drawing. If it is not found, I will sue you and force you into bankruptcy."

Bernard stood transfixed both by Littlejohn's threatening words and his cold stare. The door slammed shut before he could even think of an appropriate reply.

Chapter 13

Alberto Conti looked at his watch and saw he was late. After a last glance at the letter on top of his desk, he shrugged, picked it up, folded it in four and slipped it into the pocket of his jacket.

An unshaven young man with curly hair appeared at the door of Conti's office. He was sweaty and his face slightly flushed.

"*Inspettore,* have you read today's *Il Messaggero?*"

"No," he replied. He did not have time to read a newspaper during the day and he wished the young policeman would find something else to do and get out of his way. Conti did not like small talk. He did not discuss soccer results with his colleagues on Mondays; he stayed out of political debates and only listened to gossip if it was relevant to one of his cases. In fact, he was so quiet that his colleagues referred to him as *il muto,* the mute. He knew it, and he did not care.

Conti lifted his jacket from the back of a chair and put it on. He felt for the keys in his right pocket and looked at the young man.

"I am going out and you are in my way."

"*Scusi.* But there is an article in the *Messaggero* about the dead Englishman. Maybe you want to read it?"

"What does it say?" Conti asked, suddenly interested.

"It says the investigation is going to be closed. It says the police believe it was an accidental death."

Conti shook his head and pushed the young man aside to close the door to his office. As he walked away he mumbled something unintelligibly; the young policeman was not sure, but thought the *Inspettore* had said "A lot of crap, as usual."

Once outside the *Commissariato,* Conti lighted a cigar and, standing between two parked cars, hailed a taxi. A battered Fiat stopped almost immediately and the inspector climbed in, slamming the door.

The taxi driver looked at his reflection in the rear view mirror and frowned.

"No cigar allowed in my taxi."

Conti glared at him and rolled down the window. He drew on his cigar, inhaling the smoke and let his arm hang outside.

"Good. Now the cigar is out. Hotel Locarno. Quickly."

The driver shook his head and drove off, to weary to argue with his passenger. Conti sat back, expressionless, occasionally putting the cigar in his mouth, blowing out the smoke through the window, not always successfully. Their eyes met in the mirror, but the taxi driver looked away.

Giulia had returned to her room because the inspector was late, so he had to call her from the reception.

"*Signora*, I am here. I will wait for you at the entrance."

No apologies for being half an hour late, no good afternoon. Giulia remembered the two times she had met the policeman, first at Eric's funeral, then in a café in Trastevere. Introvert, she remembered; direct as well, to the point of rudeness. As she walked down, Conti was standing in the lobby, oblivious of his surroundings, the *Messaggero* open in his hands, a half-smoked cigar between the fingers of his right hand. His mouth was frozen in an expression of disapproval.

Giulia slowed down as she approached him. He looked up and nodded to acknowledge her presence. Then, somewhat out of character, she thought, Conti took her extended hand and held it.

"I am sorry I am late. I hope you are not in a hurry," he said slowly releasing her hand.

Giulia said it was not a problem, that she did not have plans for the afternoon.

"Do you mind walking?" he asked.

"Why not," she answered.

He led her towards the Tiber.

"Where are we going?" Giulia asked.

"To Trastevere."

"It's quite a long way."

"If you prefer we can take a taxi. But I usually prefer to walk."

They walked side by side in silence, under the giant plane trees that lined the bank of the Tiber, until they reached the Ponte San Angelo, the spectacular bridge of angels.

"We can stop for some coffee, if that's okay with you?" Conti said, pointing to a bar to their left.

Giulia agreed and followed him inside. The waiter placed two espresso cups on the granite counter and pushed a silver sugar container toward them.

"My doctor says I drink too many *espressos* and smoke too much. But I need them to work," the police inspector explained without smiling.

"Did you read the *Messaggero* today?" he asked.

"Yes, I did."

"Then you have seen the article about Hargrave. And that the investigation is going to be closed?"

"Is it true?" Giulia asked incredulously.

"No, the journalists have to write something, and they pick up on anything they hear that can sell their paper. Many times they are not even credible sources," he explained.

"We still do not know who he was with for dinner that night and we also do not know what happened between the time he left the bar and the time someone called emergency to report his accident. We have also not been able to identify who made the call," Conti continued.

Giulia noticed that the barman was also listening to the inspector although he pretended not to.

"It also took a long time before Eric was attended to in hospital."

"You mean he might have been saved, had he been treated immediately?" she asked.

"I don't know. The hospital says no of course. They don't want to take the blame."

"Is a blow to the head the cause of Eric's death then?"

"Yes, but we do not know if he was hit and pushed or he simply fell."

"Didn't the autopsy answer these questions?"

"The autopsy was not conclusive, and here lies the problem."

Conti finally took notice of the eavesdropping waiter with a frown. He paid for the coffees and with a gentle nudge to Giulia's back, directed her towards the door.

They crossed the street and the bridge and passed in front of the grim façade of the Ospedale Santo Spirito and continued their walk towards Trastevere. The pavement was narrow and uneven because of protruding roots of the trees that lined the Lungotevere. Some ten metres below them the yellow waters of the Tiber licked the banks Romans used as a promenade in the summer. Giulia had to walk faster to keep up with Conti's pace. His stride was steady and purposeful, sidestepping obstacles yet slowing down to let people pass. As if reading her thoughts, the inspector half turned towards her and apologised for walking too fast.

"It's the only exercise I get, you see. Walking! I sleep little, work too much and drink too many espressos."

Giulia noticed the ring on his left hand.

"Is that what your wife says?" she asked him.

He looked at her quizzically but continued walking.

"I am not married."

"But you wear a…" she left her sentence unfinished.

He shook his head slightly and said, "I am not married anymore," and lengthened his stride noticeably. He had obviously no intention of talking about his private life.

Conti briefly looked up at the barred windows of the Regina Coeli, the notorious prison for hard criminals and Giulia wondered how many of its occupants the inspector had helped put behind its walls. They continued on until they reached the Piazza Trilussa passing the small shops of artisans, pizzerias and bars, on their way to Santa Maria in Trastevere. "We'll be there in a few minutes," Conti said.

After a couple of right-angled turns, Conti stopped in front of a tall building at the corner of two streets. The façade was one of the few that had not been repainted and cracks in the plaster let the brickwork show. The entrance was humid and cold, and the steps uneven, worn in the centre, by centuries of use.

"It is on the third floor," Conti said. "Hold the ramp, it is not well lighted."

"*Inspettore,* what are we doing here?" Giulia asked.

The Italian raised an eyebrow and pushed the door open. "You wanted to see Eric's studio, no?"

Conti unlocked the door and switched on the light. A strong smell of turpentine, oil paint and mould pervaded the room. He opened the windows to let in some fresh air.

"May I look around?"

"Go ahead, we've checked the place out for fingerprints and did not find anything useful. When we first came the cleaning lady was here, and she said the place was in a mess, but then she added it always was in a mess."

The room was square with windows on two of the walls. The wooden beams of the ceiling had been painted white and the old red bricks made up the uneven floor. A door led to a little room which contained a loo and a small sink.

On a kitchen table, pushed against the wall, a dozen glass jars of different shapes and colours stood, filled with tubes of paint and brushes. Paper, a stone mortar, acorns on a plate, more tubes of paint, stained rags, and other objects were haphazardly strewn. Shelves lined one of the walls, bare except for a catalogue that lay open on a marked page showing a photograph of an oil landscape by Claude Lorrain and a book Giulia picked up on Canaletto, in which various pages had been marked and annotated.

She felt Conti studying her actions with a feigned lack of interest. Impulsively, she asked the inspector whether she could take the two books.

"Why not?" he replied.

There was nothing else of much interest. Two chairs stacked against the wall, and an easel in the middle of the room.

The easel, Giulia noticed with curious interest, stood empty.

Chapter 14

"Were you present at Eric's book launch in Milan?" Conti asked Giulia.

Giulia nodded, her mind going back to that eventful night and a hint of a smile appeared on her face. Conti watched her, waiting to hear more. Finally, Giulia spoke.

"It was surreal. One moment Eric was giving a lecture on Old Masters, recounting anecdotes about this or that artist, explaining that he had dedicated his life to their study and everyone seemed… in fact…quite captivated by his words. Suddenly, someone interrupted him from the back of the room. Then, several people started to speak at the same time. It was not clear who was shouting at whom. I believe there was some pushing and shoving, chairs were overturned. The whole thing ended in chaos."

"And Eric? What did Eric do while this was going on?"

"At first he tried to respond but no one could hear him so he gave up. He then turned to talk to the representative of the publishing house sat beside him."

"Do you know what caused the confusion? Who was the first person to shout?"

"I was close to the front but on the side and I couldn't see very well. It came from a group of people who stood at the end of the room, well-dressed, middle-aged men."

"What did they shout?"

"*Ladro, bugiardo, disonesto,* and other insults."

"And Eric did not reply or defend himself?"

"He said that he was not dishonest and that he was not the one who claimed his drawings were originals but the experts. And then, he must have recognised the person who shouted. You could see it on his face. He said something like 'we know each other don't we?'" Conti looked up with interest.

"Someone from his past. Ah, *interessante!?* Do you know who it was?"

Giulia shook her head. "They could have been people Eric had sold drawings to in the past. Several people shouted they would sue him, send him to jail."

"But the people, those who accused him, maybe were not completely innocent either?" Conti suggested. "And maybe they decided to make sure Eric would not speak, using force instead of the law."

"The book launch was several years ago, and if somebody had wanted to kill Eric he would not have waited for so long," Giulia retorted.

"Ah, but maybe you forgot about the book. The book he was writing and he just finished."

How did Conti know about the book, Giulia pondered. She hesitated before answering, carefully choosing her words. "I didn't know that was public knowledge. He mentioned it to us, in fact he was coming to London to discuss it. But we never got the manuscript," she said.

"Some people knew about the book! Two of his friends we interviewed mentioned it. One of them volunteered Hargrave had hinted it was going to be more sensational than his first! These things get around."

"I suppose it is possible," she conceded.

"In my job there are almost never coincidences. Instead there are connections you must find, links between events and people that allow you to understand what happened to whom and why."

"There were journalists in the room; maybe they can identify the people who attended the book launch," Giulia suggested.

"I talked with one of them and he gave me some names. And of course, he phones me every other day to get information about my investigation in return."

It was easy for Giulia to understand how an investigation could take over the inspector's life. Every detail must be analysed, every lead must be pursued. What did he say? He worked too much, slept too little. Could this have been the reason for the breakdown of his marriage? A relationship with a man such as Conti would definitely be a difficult one. But what choice did he have? As if reading her thoughts, the inspector said, "There is no peace until a crime is solved, and then of course…there is another one!"

Chapter 15

"Christopher, you have not been listening to me, dear."

Through the window of his art gallery, Christopher Donovan saw that his visitor had arrived and stood in front of the door, mopping his forehead with a handkerchief. The art dealer turned his attention to the blond woman who stood between him and the door.

"I have, I have, but I have an appointment now."

"I can wait until you are finished…" she suggested.

"No you can't. And I don't know how long it will take. Go without me."

The woman looked annoyed and sighed. "I understand when I'm not wanted. Fine, I will buy this dress alone then."

"Yes, you go ahead," the art dealer told his wife absently, his mind already focusing on the impending encounter. Did he have some of Eric's drawings exhibited? He quickly surveyed the walls and saw none.

Donovan's wife put on her coat and retrieved her Gucci handbag from the desk. When she reached the first floor landing she turned to her husband and smiled sweetly, "Actually I might buy more than one dress, just to be sure. Bye!"

It was the dealer's turn to sigh as his wife left.

Donovan's visitor straightened his tie, using the shiny brass plate with the gallery name as a mirror, and tugged at the collar of his shirt. Startled by the sudden opening of the front door, he stood in front of it, rooted to the ground.

"Would you mind, sir?" the elegant blond woman said.

He stepped aside, mumbling an apology, and let her pass.

The muffled voice of Christopher Donovan emerged out of the intercom system.

"Mr. Hargrave?"

"Er, yes, it's me."

"Please come up, we are on the first floor."

Bernard Hargrave pushed the heavy front door and let himself in. He was far from confident that this meeting was a good idea but on the other hand, Donovan had represented Eric in the United Kingdom for almost two years. He was someone who would know the value of the paintings they had recovered from Eric's flat in Rome.

The art dealer was younger than Bernard had expected. Eric's brother was not sure what to make of Donovan's black leather trousers. But then, what did he know about dress codes in the art world? He accepted the glass of water offered to him and sat down in a straight-backed chair, in front of the desk.

"Ah, thank you."

"It's a great pity that Eric died so suddenly. He still had so many projects, so much work he wanted to do!" said Donovan.

Bernard nodded, thanked him for his condolences and listened to the recounting of his first meeting with Eric.

"I was in Milan for an auction and found out he was launching his book in a gallery I knew of, so you could say I was there by accident. Eric was introduced by someone from his publishing company and asked to say a few words. He spoke for fifteen minutes. He was witty. I remember how he started." Donovan paused, smiling. "He said that in ancient Greece two painters were competing for the title of best artist and were asked by the City Council to each produce a masterpiece. The pieces were brought to the judges, hidden by a cloth. They would be unveiled and the judges would then decide who the best was. The first artist uncovered his work. He had painted a wonderful scene with a majestic temple sitting on top of a hill with warriors returning from battle and beautiful young women welcoming them with fruits and wine. Everyone in the audience gasped and said 'this must be the best painting they had ever seen.'

The second artist then lifted the cloth draped over his work. It showed a bowl of inviting cherries resting on a stone. The composition was good, but it was too simple and there was no way he would win. Suddenly, a bird swooped on the painting and tried to pick one of the cherries. They looked so real, the bird kept pecking at the painting. One of the judges stood up and declared the second painter the winner. He had to be the best painter as even one of nature's creatures could not distinguish between his work and reality."

Bernard Hargrave listened attentively. Donovan was a good storyteller.

"But then it turned nasty. Journalists wanted to ask Eric questions but there were several art dealers in the room who started to shout that he was a crook, another that he should be sent to jail. There was a scuffle and Eric had to leave through a back door. I caught up with him outside. He appeared unruffled by the commotion."

"And was it then you asked to represent him in London?"

"Not at that time. We met later to discuss it. I was fond of Eric, you know."

Bernard had seen a letter written by his brother two months before his death in which he had broken his agreement with the art dealer. He was not sure this letter had been sent and found no reply from Donovan. It was probably wise not to mention the letter, he thought. After all, he needed Donovan's help.

Bernard explained that paintings and drawings by Eric had been brought back to England and needed to be valued – "for insurance purposes," he added cautiously.

Donovan said he would be glad to help but would of course first need to see the works. Eric's brother looked unsure of himself.

"Eric did wonderful drawings but also some less good ones," Donovan explained.

"Drawings, for instance." Hargrave tried a new approach. "You had several exhibitions of his work. What kind of price did they sell for?"

Donovan got up and fetched the catalogue of Eric's last exhibition.

"One to two thousand pounds on average, but somehow the sale was disappointing. Less than half sold."

"Ah, and what would be the value of a painting then?" Eric's brother pursued doggedly.

Donovan looked up and stared at his visitor for a moment.

"Eric was described by the media as the most prolific forger of the century. If Eric's claims are true, he produced over one thousand drawings in the manner of Old Masters. Again, if his claims are correct, his works are in private collections and museums in more than a dozen countries and exhibited as works of Rembrandt, Leonardo da Vinci, Piero della Francesca, Durer, Piranesi and many more. He has laid no claims to oil paintings however!"

"But he also did oil paintings and watercolours, didn't he?"

Donovan shrugged. "Yes, and he did a few commissions."

"Commissions?"

"Someone asked him for a specific painting in the style of a specific painter. In fact…" Donovan hesitated but continued, "in fact he was painting a view of Venice for a client and did not deliver it, although he must have finished it before his demise."

Donovan stared hard at Hargrave making him feel uncomfortable. Bernard looked down and shifted in his chair.

"The disappearance of this painting is a big problem for me and I would like to have it. A large canvas, about one by one and a half metres. It is a view of a church and the canal from the side of the square of San Marco. Easy to recognise! Not so easy to lose."

Bernard Hargrave assured his host he had not seen the painting and that he would let Donovan know if he found it. Donovan explained he had paid Eric a substantial advance for it above the money he paid him every month.

"If the painting is not returned I will lose money and credibility with an important collector. In fact, if you tell me it is not among Eric's possessions I will have to go to the police and file a complaint!"

"A complaint?" Bernard looked alarmed.

"Yes, declare it stolen and request an investigation."

Bernard assured him again that he had not seen the painting and would inform him if he found it.

"Giulia is in Rome now looking for my brother's studio. She may find it there. You see, we did not know he had a studio as well," Bernard volunteered.

"Giulia?"

"Yes, Giulia Vasari. She was a good friend of Eric's. A charming woman really. She lived in Rome for many years you see. And she speaks Italian of course." Hargrave spoke haltingly, vaguely aware that he was possibly saying too much.

"If this…if you find Eric's studio and the painting of Venice is there, let me know immediately. I know the right people who can arrange transport."

Donovan suddenly stood up, placing his palms face down on his desk.

"Mr. Hargrave, it was a pleasure meeting you."

Bernard stood up slowly, understanding he had just been dismissed.

"Mr. Donovan, do you still have any of Eric's drawings?"

"Some, not many. In fact, not enough to cover the money Eric owed me," was the surprising answer.

"Eric owed you money?"

"Oh yes. According to our contract, I paid Eric four thousand pounds every month and in return everything he produced would be mine; drawings, paintings, books. Everything!"

"Oh, I didn't realise what the arrangement was," Bernard blurted out.

"Since sales were poor, I didn't recoup my investment in Eric and therefore he owed me money!"

The news was clearly a shock to Bernard whose hopes of hearing that he was sitting on a fortune in works of art were being dashed.

"He was writing another book, I believe," Hargrave volunteered, hoping to arouse Donovan's interest.

"Really? What about?" Donovan bluntly asked, his thoughts still on finding out the whereabouts of the missing Canaletto.

"I'm not sure. Giulia did not really explain."

Chapter 16

Giulia and Conti sauntered through the maze of narrow cobbled streets of Trastevere. Restaurants opened their doors, bars turned up the volume of their music and the streets filled with people. Two Africans overtook them, burdened with heavy rucksacks, leaving in their trail the faint but distinct smell of marijuana. She looked at the inspector who returned her stare and smiled.

"Twenty years ago thieves and artists without money lived in Trastevere. Today, it is very popular and you are more likely to bump into actors, writers, lawyers! People with money. People like these two Africans who just passed as well, but they sell pirated cds not drugs. So…"

He shrugged his shoulders to indicate that the police had better things to do than to chase the sellers of pirated cds. They eventually stopped in front of an art gallery, adjacent to a wine bar and the workshop of a furniture restorer. The gallery's name was *Tela e Carta*, Canvas and Paper. Through the front window Giulia could see a row of prints and drawings on the walls. Each corner of the vaulted brick ceiling was illuminated as were the exhibits. In the middle of the gallery a man was looking at the floor, his back turned to the door.

Conti pushed the door open and held it for Giulia, who stepped in. The man at the centre of the gallery turned around slowly, theatrically. She recognised him instantly. He was tall with thick wavy white hair and an aristocratic bearing. The man frowned imperceptibly before an obsequious smile crossed his face.

"*Signora, che piacere rivedervi,*" How nice to see you again. "Giorgio Monticello, do you remember?"

"I remember you," Giulia said in English.

"It was at the funeral of Eric Hargrave. *Si. Che tragedia!*"

He took Giulia's hand and held it between his while he looked into her eyes.

"I am glad you have come here, *Signora*. My gallery is not very big or famous but Eric was a friend and I showed his work many times."

Giulia said nothing. Friends of Eric's seemed to come out of the woodwork wherever she turned. Alberto Conti stood two steps behind her, waiting patiently to be acknowledged. Monticello looked at him eventually and greeted him without releasing Giulia's hand.

"*Inspettore Conti, buona sera a Lei.*"

The gallery owner finally released Giulia's hand.

"I want to show you something very interesting. Very beautiful."

Monticello pulled out a large cardboard portfolio from the bottom drawer of an antique chest and opened it in front of her.

"Look at these. Eric did these engravings to illustrate poems of Ovid about wine. Bacchus, the god of wine, is the central figure in all the plates. We exhibited them here."

Giulia studied the engravings one after the other. Bacchus being fed grapes by nymphs, Bacchus, on a chariot, Bacchus, a mischievous smile on his face, tripping a young woman while supported by two youths. The engravings were in an unusually large format, each picture in sanguine red. Giulia found them beautiful.

"Unfortunately, I have only two sets left," Monticello stated, ready to discuss prices if necessary. The gallery owner liked to claim he could instantly spot the potential buyers, those who might buy and the "tourists" who would waste his time. Of course, this distinction was not important if the person entering the gallery was a beautiful woman!

Conti told the gallery owner they had just visited Eric's studio in Trastevere.

"His apartment you mean," Monticello corrected him.

"No, no, his studio. The place where he worked."

"He worked at home, I thought."

Monticello looked genuinely surprised that Eric had a studio. Giulia wondered why he should be. If, as he claimed, he had known Eric for years, he must have been aware that Eric usually worked in his studio and not at home.

"Are you from Trastevere, Signor Monticello?" Giulia asked.

"*Si*, I live two blocks from here. And my parents were both from Trastevere. You know, Trastevere is like a village," he said. Giulia shot a quick glance at Alberto Conti who seemed not to notice.

"Signora, if you have time I could show you Trastevere. We have the oldest pharmacy in the world and the night life, it is very animated. Everyone comes to Trastevere in the evening!"

Giulia thanked him for his offer and forced herself to smile. From the first time they had met, Giulia had disliked Monticello. There was an arrogance in his manner she found irritating.

"Signor Monticello, since Eric and you were practically neighbours, you must have met him often?"

"*Si, si,* of course. We had coffee together often, but Eric, he preferred wine, red wine you know."

"It is strange that he never mentioned his studio, don't you think?" Giulia asked candidly.

Monticello quickly glanced towards the inspector, who was absorbed in an engraving before answering.

"Yes, it is strange. Or maybe he mentioned 'my studio' and I thought he wanted to say 'my apartment' . I did not pay attention probably."

"Must be the explanation," Giulia said dubiously.

"Signor Monticello, how much is this picture?" Conti asked, cutting into the exchange between Giulia and the dealer.

"*Inspettore*, normally I sell the whole set, but okay, for you I can make an exception if you really like it."

The policeman held the picture of Bacchus fed grapes by two nymphs.

"I do like it," Conti continued.

"Normally, it is one million lire but, for you, half a million will be the price. But, *Inspettore!*"

"*Si?*"

"Do not tell anybody I gave you such a big discount. Everybody will come and ask me for the same thing!"

Conti assured him he would not tell a soul and, to Giulia's surprise, paid for the engraving and asked for it to be wrapped. While Monticello looked for a piece of cardboard to protect it, Giulia told Conti she didn't realise he was an art collector.

Conti gave her a half smile and replied, "It's never too late to start."

They declined Monticello's invitation to join him for an *aperitivo* and left the gallery once the dealer, who had clasped Giulia's hands again, finally released her.

Conti and Giulia reached Piazza Santa Maria in Trastevere in a few minutes. The mosaic of the Basilica's frontispiece was brightly lit and a young crowd was huddled on the steps of the fountain, at the centre of the square. A young gypsy girl, in open sandals despite the cool air, offered them a rose but the inspector waved her away.

"I can take you back to your hotel," he said, "but I would prefer it, if you would have dinner with me."

Giulia, who half expected the invitation, accepted.

The Taverna dei Noantri was located at the edge of the piazza. It was brightly lit, an arresting contrast with the street, and its walls were completely bare. Giulia and Conti sat in the main room, close to a large stone fireplace that could have been used to roast an entire pig. Shortly after they had been seated, a burly man in white overalls rushed out of the kitchen and went to embrace the *inspettore*. They greeted each other, the cook made a joke about Lazio's last match and Conti asked how his brother was. The cook then greeted Giulia.

"He is a good man," the cook said tapping Conti's shoulder.

"Do not stay here or the food will burn," the policeman pretended to scold him.

"What are you saying? The food never burns in Noantri. You know that very well, *inspettore*."

Giulia was aware that some of the theatre was produced for her benefit, but it was also apparent that the cook genuinely liked Alberto Conti.

"You come here often then," Giulia stated rather than asked.

"No, not really. I have not been here for months."

"The cook seems to like you!"

Conti shook his head sternly.

"No, he is afraid of me!"

Giulia looked surprised. "Why?"

"I put him in prison," Conti answered very seriously.

Giulia raised her eyebrows, not sure what to say. Then the inspector looked at her and smiled.

"I was joking, Claudio is a school friend."

She returned the smile. There was a lighter side to the inspector, and she wondered whether the dinner invitation had been purely motivated by police duty. The unmistakable voice of Luciano Pavarotti suddenly made the loud speaker above their heads vibrate. Conti smiled: "One of our national treasures, you know."

Claudio returned with two appetizing plates of *antipasti* and a chilled bottle of white wine from Orvieto, ready to take their next orders.

"You didn't like Signor Monticello, I think?" Conti asked.

"Not very *simpatico*," Giulia commented, "and I am sure he did not tell the truth. If he knew Eric well, he must have known Eric had a studio."

The inspector nodded in agreement.

"And he lives in Trastevere, which means Eric could have met him the night he was taken to hospital."

"He could have, but I cannot see why he would want Eric dead. He was buying his works and selling them in his gallery. No more Eric, no more works to sell."

"Where was he the evening Eric had the accident?"

"At home, and without an alibi," the inspector answered.

A waiter filled their glasses with wine and asked if everything was okay. When he withdrew, Conti spoke again. "What were you looking for in the studio?"

Giulia hesitated before answering. Then she explained that a gallery dealer in London had ordered a painting of Venice in the manner of Canaletto from Eric and had asked for her help to locate it. She also explained that she thought that Eric's manuscript would be there.

"Ah yes, that. Can you tell me what it is about?"

"He claimed that drawing was really a language and that if you knew how to read this language, you would recognise which artist had drawn which picture. He called it *The Language of Line*." And there would be drawings to illustrate his theories. Including ones that now hang in private collections and museums all over the world."

"So, if you could recognise the artist's 'handwriting', you could find out if it was, let us say, Canaletto or Eric Hargrave who had made the drawing!" interjected Conti.

"In a way, yes."

The inspector twirled his fork in the middle of a mound of *spaghetti ai frutti di mare* and lifted it to his mouth.

"Such a book would upset a lot of people, I think."

Giulia nodded.

"There is a long list of people who were not happy with your friend when he described his life and claimed he produced one thousand Old Master drawings. Only a few have been attributed to him since the book came out. What about the rest?" Conti asked more to himself than to Giulia and suddenly changed the subject. He told her stories about Trastevere. He explained how so many

Etruscan antiquities found their way from unexplored graves close to Tarquinia to the lucrative Swiss market. He drew Giulia into telling him about the years she had spent in Rome. She spoke of a period of her life she usually preferred to avoid discussing. Conti listened and did not comment. He had turned out to be an entertaining and perceptive dinner companion. They finished their coffees and stood up to leave to the final strains of *Il Maestro's* last song for the evening, *Volare*.

Chapter 17

The Alitalia flight to London was not full; there was an empty seat beside Giulia. She declined the meal but asked for a cup of coffee, which she placed on the tray in front of the empty seat. It had been a busy week in Rome and Giulia, always glad for an excuse to return to the Eternal City, already felt a twinge of nostalgia, having to leave yet again. But she had managed to fit in everything including some spare time to relax and even do some shopping.

Both Monticello and Conti had called Giulia at the hotel. Monticello wanted her to know that he was interested in buying any works by Eric Hargrave and asked her to let Eric's family know of his interest. She was quite sure she had not told him she stayed at the Locarno Hotel and wondered how he had found out. Conti's call had been brief. He wanted to thank her for joining him for dinner and made her promise to call if she found out anything about the missing Canaletto or Eric's new book. Giulia found Conti intriguing. One minute he was rigid and focused on his investigation, the next, he seemed open and calm. Had he used the investigation as a pretext to call, or was she just another link to his investigation?

She pulled out the book from her bag and opened it on her lap. Its title was *Canaletto and England*. British Gas had sponsored an exhibition in Birmingham in 1973 and the hardback catalogue had been published for it.

The book was badly stained, its cover torn and its spine broken. Several pages were marked with yellow post-it papers. The first one showed a view of the *Molo* in Venice, looking east; the second, a view of the *Riva degli Schiavoni*. Had Eric used these pictures to paint a view of Venice in the style of Canaletto, Giulia wondered. Page 74 was a view of the Thames. In the margin, Eric's neat handwriting had made his intention clear. It said "reference for handling of paint on ground and figures". The last page he had marked was annotated with only one word: "sky".

Giulia remembered one of Eric's confessions. He had explained that he did not make any copies but created new compositions in the manner of the Old Masters. He combined scenes from different paintings into one, changed the perspective, and worked in new elements. "In fact, you could say that I improve on the existing works or complete them. I create something a Tiepolo or Rubens could have painted but did not!" Giulia remembered him saying with a glint of mischief in his eyes. He genuinely admired Old Masters and meant it when he said he had dedicated his life to their study. While other students at the Royal Academy in London fashionably expressed the newest trends and drew abstract compositions, Eric obstinately followed the path Rembrandt, Michelangelo, Bellini and the other Masters had trodden before him. His fascination for Leonardo da Vinci's powerful portraits, for Piranesi's intricate scenes or the *pentimenti* of Italian Renaissance drawings had left him at odds with the art establishment from the beginning. He must have regarded the recognition of his extraordinary skills following the publication of his autobiography as a 'revenge of sorts'.

"Take Leonardo da Vinci's famous painting of the *Last Supper*, for example. There are two preparatory drawings known and both are at the Venice Academy. Leonardo probably did more for such a project. He must have studied different perspectives, examined different positions for the main characters, considered facial expressions, gestures. So, if I set out to 'imagine' a preparatory drawing Leonardo could have made, do I copy?"

Giulia had smiled and said it was hard to fault his logic.

"So when an art expert says he has discovered a new study by Michelangelo and if he asks me what I think, I smile, and I say: 'It could be. Who knows?' But he claims he is the expert, not me. I am only a draughtsman."

More than once, Eric had said that he lived in the wrong century, only to add that he was not sure what century he would have chosen anyway. Giulia often wondered whether he regretted having written his autobiography which had placed him in the limelight. A few months before his death he had told a friend, "Don't be surprised if one day I am found dead in the streets of Rome." Had it been a premonition? Did he feel threatened by someone in particular? When it was repeated to her, Giulia thought about it a number of times without coming closer to an answer. When she told Alberto Conti, he had not seemed surprised. Death threats, of course, were a part of his job.

The stewardess announced the imminent landing at Heathrow. Giulia closed the book and put it back in her bag.

Bernard Hargrave paced the living room and repeated his question for the fifth time. "Who did this? What did they want from me?"

The two English police officers looked at each other with raised eyebrows and bored expressions. The younger one took Bernard by the arm and stopped him.

"Sir, you must calm down. There is no point in worrying about it. The locksmith will be here in half an hour to change your garage door lock and our team will look for prints. Why don't you make a nice cuppa and sit down for a while?" he smiled encouragingly.

Eric's brother nervously walked towards the kitchen. The two constables heard him mumble to himself as he rummaged through a drawer, and one of them called out.

"After all, they did not take anything. You are lucky. Last week an old lady got robbed a few blocks away at gunpoint! They took cash, her television and her car. Can you imagine? They rob her and ask her for the keys to her car to get away!"

Bernard did not answer but returned with three mugs on a tray which he offered to the policemen.

"I must call Giulia. I must let her know," he said more to himself than to his guests.

"Who is she, your sister?"

"No, no. She's a friend. Giulia Vasari. She was a friend of my brother's."

The older policeman took out a notebook and asked him to spell Giulia's name and took her telephone number as well.

Bernard Hargrave's call reached Giulia as she entered her apartment, on her way back from London airport. She told Bernard that she had been taken to Eric's studio by Inspector Conti and aside from painting material, a few brushes and an easel there was not much else.

Bernard cleared his throat before interrupting her.

"Er, Giulia, I am afraid there have been some developments," he started.

"Yes?"

"An awfully unpleasant thing happened. My house has been

burgled. In fact, I am now with two policemen."

"Oh. I am sorry. Are you all right?"

"Yes, thank you. But it is a bit of a shock when you come home and find that someone has been through your personal things."

Bernard's voice trembled slightly as he went on to explain that the robber had broken in through the garage, and ransacked both bedrooms.

"Did they take anything?" Giulia asked.

"Not at first glance. I am not sure…I don't think so."

"When did it happen? Where were you?"

"I was in London this morning to meet with Mr. Donovan. The robber must have waited for me to leave and gone in while I was away."

Giulia suppressed the thought that Donovan knew Bernard would not be at home and could have organised it. Donovan was a rogue but she did not believe he was a criminal.

"Did you tell the police about the visit of Tarquin Littlejohn?"

"No. Do you think I should?"

"Anyone who wanted something from you could be a suspect, I guess. It is up to them to try and find out."

Bernard put one of the policemen on the line. Giulia answered his questions and said she could meet them if necessary. She put down the receiver and frowned. She would call Alberto Conti later to tell him what had happened. Now, all she wanted was a nice, long hot shower.

As the water ran down her body she closed her eyes and thought of her visit to Rome, of the missing manuscript, and of the missing Canaletto. What was the real purpose of Monticello's call? Surely he could have called the Hargraves himself. She remembered what Inspector Alberto Conti had said: there were still gaps in the investigation and although there were a number of suspects, no one could be charged. Giulia remembered their walk from the hotel to Eric's studio, she remembered his buying one of Eric's prints, and then the relaxing dinner in Trastevere. She opened her eyes, pulled herself away from the stinging water and adjusted the shower head to soften the flow. To complicate matters even further, Bernard having been burgled was not good news at all. She sighed and turned off the water before stepping out of the shower onto the white marble floor. She took the towel off the heated rack and wrapped it around her body. She shivered; the temperature in London was definitely not that of the Italian capital.

Chapter 18

Bernard Hargrave regretted having accepted Giulia's suggestion that they meet at the Royal Academy as soon as he stepped onto the Brighton to London train. The rowdy group of teenagers with brightly dyed hair reminded him that he was about to enter a world he found oppressive, an environment in which he felt insecure.

The noise and confusion of central London left him dazed and drained for several days and he swore every time he returned home from such a journey, that he would avoid another one at all costs. But here he was for the second time in two weeks.

He allowed himself the luxury of a taxi between Victoria Station and Piccadilly. He passed under the arch that led to the courtyard of the Royal Academy and sat on a stone bench. In front of him water spouted from a fountain and ran along cobble-stones. To his right, by the main entrance of the museum, two fluttering banners advertised the forthcoming annual summer exhibition.

Giulia Vasari materialised in front of him and smiled. She said she hoped the trip had not tired him and he heard himself answer that he was fine because he had taken a taxi from the station.

"Good. Would you like to visit the Academy or shall we have some lunch?" she asked.

Bernard said he was not hungry but would not mind drinking something warm.

Richoux was the closest café to the Royal Academy. With its round marble tables, its pale green wood panelling and gilded mirrors, it seemed to come straight out of a Victorian illustration. They ordered tea and sandwiches, and while they waited to be served Giulia told Bernard about her trip to Rome, the visit to Eric's studio, and the encounter with Giorgio Monticello.

Bernard felt his agitation ebbing away. He said he remembered Monticello.

"He was at the funeral and introduced himself. Very polite. Quite helpful if I remember well."

Giulia kept her opinion of Monticello to herself.

"Any news on the break-in?" Giulia asked, showing concern.

"You know I am going to be seventy this year and I've never had to deal with a situation like this," he started. "The funny thing is the burglar does not appear to have taken anything."

"Did you say he searched your house?"

"Everything was ajar, thrown around. All of Eric's boxes were opened, drawers pulled out, the desk, the cabinets…everything."

He drank some tea and his hand trembled a little.

"It might have been a good thing you were not at home."

Giulia did not share her suspicions with Bernard. He was still visibly shaken by the thought that his house had been broken into. Whoever searched his house had not found what they were looking for. She realised that either Donovan or Littlejohn could have been behind it.

"I talked to this…Donovan while you were in Rome and I could not get any information out of him. He claims Eric owed him money and accused me of keeping a painting he had paid Eric for." Giulia was listening intently.

"A painting of Venice, a large one. But I don't have any such painting in my possession. We didn't see it in Eric's apartment either." Bernard's voice was shrill.

"And there was nothing in his studio," Giulia added.

"Who could have it then? Bernard asked. And before Giulia could even answer, "And do you know what I think?" Bernard continued.

Giulia shook her head.

"I think he was accusing me to confuse me! To prevent me from asking him to show me his accounts with Eric."

Bernard started to stutter, "but…I..I..I..will show him that…that I am not easily fooled. I will sue him!"

Giulia tried to reason with him, to explain that he was likely to spend more money than he would recover, but gave up after a few minutes. Bernard Hargrave was agitated and clearly did not want to listen. His brother was a famous man, who had sold hundreds if not over a thousand drawings to numerous museums and at auction; his autobiography had been on the bestsellers list. He clung to his conviction that Eric had left a substantial inheritance, somewhere, the way a drowning man hangs on to a buoy.

Later that day, Giulia decided to surprise Donovan at his gallery. Although she found Bernard's avidity embarrassingly transparent, he was no match for someone like Donovan, nor Littlejohn, for that matter.

The door of the gallery had been left open, so Giulia entered and climbed the single flight of stairs. Donovan was staring at a computer screen and did not see her right away. A line crossed his brow that made him appear older than he was. He was uncharacteristically clean shaven, wore a tie and a conservative grey suit. Giulia was used to seeing him in brighter shirts and tight fitting pants, sporting a carefully groomed stubble. He looked up, startled. She stepped into the room, a half smile on her face.

"Are you dressing like a banker these days?" she teased him.

He quickly looked up from the screen of his laptop and pressed a key before folding the screen. Standing up he replied that he had not heard her enter.

"Look, if you are busy, I'll leave. I just came in to say hello."

"No, stay," Donovan quickly responded, "Make yourself comfortable," he said as he disappeared into the next room.

Giulia walked towards the window that looked out onto the street.

Donovan returned with two balloon glasses of white wine, handing one to Giulia,

"*Gavi de Gavi*, I believe you will like this one," he said.

Giulia took a sip and smiled appreciatively.

"Do you offer white wine to all your visitors these days?" she asked.

"Only if they are as attractive as you."

She ignored the flattery and took another sip.

They now faced each other, Donovan half sitting on the table he used as a desk. Giulia noticed a notepad beside his laptop covered with numbers. She guessed he had been in the middle of doing accounts when she had unexpectedly turned up.

She raised her glass. Donovan's gaze shifted from the young woman's face down to the curve of her neck, and stopped at her breasts. Giulia lowered her glass, their eyes met, and Donovan made no effort to hide the fact he was staring at her.

"I was in Rome," Giulia started, knowing it would catch his attention. Donovan looked up.

"Came back yesterday, in fact," she continued.

"Well, what were you doing in Rome?"

"Looking for Eric's studio."

Giulia placed her glass on the desk.

The dealer waited, his eyes still fixed on Giulia.

"I found it, but unfortunately, there was not much inside."

Donovan did not react the way she had expected him to. He did not ask about the painting in the style of Canaletto but just continued to stare at her. Feeling exposed, she crossed her arms in front of her chest.

"Are you interested in what I'm telling you?" she asked.

Donovan put his glass down close to hers. By doing so he had moved closer to Giulia.

"I am always interested in what you have to tell me," she heard him say.

Before she could step away, he had taken hold of her right wrist, unclasping her arms gently, and pushed her hair away from her face. He bent towards her and kissed her lightly on the lips. Despite her misgivings, Giulia found him attractive and did not turn away. He kissed her again, this time more intensely, and Giulia found herself responding to him. The sudden buzz of the front door startled him. She gently pushed him away.

"Saved by the bell, I guess," Giulia said relieved. She was not ready for this.

The dealer looked out through the window and pulled it open.

"I'll join you in half an hour, don't wait for me," he hollered.

A woman called out something back from the street.

"Your next victim?" Giulia asked.

"No, my wife."

"Preliminaries out of the way, let's talk business, Christopher," Giulia started.

He raised his hand in mock surrender.

"Ok."

"There was no Canaletto in Eric's studio, and Bernard Hargrave swears he has no painting of Venice."

"And you believe him?"

"I do. His house was broken into, he is very nervous and I don't think he lied to me. I also told the inspector in Rome that a painting was missing. He may be able to help."

"What inspector?" Donovan snapped.

From a corner of Giulia's mind alarm bells rang, telling her that he may have had something to do with the break-in at Bernard Hargrave's home.

"The police inspector in charge of the case who let me into the studio."

Donovan clenched his jaw, making an effort to contain his feelings.

"You had no right to tell a policeman or anyone else about this painting," he hissed.

Giulia hit back instantly, "You asked me to help and you didn't say it was a state secret. But if you don't need my help, do it on your own. I'm sure the Hargrave heirs will be delighted to help you."

Donovan was taken aback by her sarcasm.

"For all I know you did not intend to sell this painting as a Hargrave but as a Canaletto."

Donovan protested and said it was not the case.

"Maybe Eric never even started it!" she exclaimed.

"He did."

"How can you be so sure?" she continued.

"I went to see him and I even took a photograph of his work in progress."

"For your buyer, I guess?" Giulia asked, her tone slowly losing its sharpness.

"Yes," Donovan answered curtly.

"Why didn't you show me the photo? At least I would have known exactly what I was looking for?"

"Well, yes… but I didn't have it with me when we spoke about it."

Giulia turned around and crossed the room to the door in a few steps. As she started to go down the steps, she looked back over her shoulder.

"Thank you for the wine and good luck in your hunt for the 'lost Canaletto'," was her parting shot.

Donovan was furious and frustrated. He kicked a leg of the table and the two glasses of wine smashed on the floor.

Giulia closed the door and strode towards Oxford Street. It was obvious that the dealer was going through a tough period with money troubles. The Canaletto, and probably some other deals that were going badly at the same time? One of Donovan's clients once hinted that Donovan had a "habit". She wondered whether his sudden changes in mood and his money problems were connected to this.

It started to drizzle and people walking by picked up speed to avoid the impending rain.

Giulia, deep in thought, continued to walk at the same pace.

Chapter 19

The week that followed Giulia's visit to Donovan's art gallery was uneventful. She took long walks in Hyde Park, visited a few exhibitions and saw a few friends.

London, in fact the whole of England, was preoccupied with the mad cow disease scare and beef had been banned for health reasons until investigations could be completed. The threat of more bomb attacks still hung in the air.

Giulia was not any closer to finding Eric Hargrave's manuscript than she was to discovering who was in possession of his Canaletto painting. She leafed through pages of the book on the Venetian painter she had picked up in Eric's workshop but it yielded no clues. Her call to Bernard Hargrave to inquire about his health was equally unproductive. Eric's brother had sounded distant and cautious as if he was no longer sure he could trust Giulia. She avoided Seldom House and no one at the publishing firm made contact with her either. She wondered whether there was any point in continuing to work for the publishing company, but as the positive and negative arguments balanced out evenly, she postponed the decision to a later day. Her introspection did nothing to help cheer her up.

She missed Robert. Her father's death when she was seven had been traumatic, and her mother, feeling lonely and needing help in raising her and her younger brother, had married not long after. Giulia never got along with her stepfather, and neither really did her mother, and the tumultuous years that followed were only made bearable by the summer months Giulia and her brother spent in Argentina with their maternal grandparents.

So, when the phone rang, and Alberto Conti on the other end of the line sounded glad to hear her voice, she kept their conversation going past the subject of Eric, enjoying the exchange with this intriguing man.

The phone rang almost immediately after she had put the receiver down. Victor Edelman's voice caught Giulia by surprise.

Firstly, because he never bothered to put in a call himself and always asked his secretary to do it; and secondly, he sounded unusually calm and composed, taking time to inquire after her health and her trip to Rome. Giulia's instinct told her this was not a social call.

"Victor, I know you're beating around the bush. Want to tell me the reason for your call?" she asked abruptly.

"Aside from asking how you are, you mean?"

The sarcastic tone was more in keeping with his character, Giulia thought.

"Yes."

"Well, I was calling to let you know that I have found Eric Hargrave's manuscript and thought you might be interested!"

Giulia was momentarily stunned.

"So, are you interested, or not?"

Edelman obviously relished the moment.

"Of course! Where is it?"

"The art dealer, Donovan, the one who represented Eric in London, called. He has the manuscript and is prepared to let us have a look at it."

"Donovan? How could he have Eric's book?" Giulia questioned in surprise.

"I don't care how he got it. The point is, he has it," came Edelman's quick reply.

"And he offered it to you?"

Giulia was not sure she believed it.

"Yes, he did. In exchange for a favour!"

"But the book rights are not his to dispose of. They belong to Eric's heirs!"

"I didn't say he wanted to sell the book rights, did I? I said he had the manuscript and was prepared to give it to us...provided we help him find something he is looking for!"

"What?" Giulia shouted down the line, although she already anticipated the answer.

"A painting. He is looking for a large painting and he believes you can help him find it."

"This is ridiculous. I don't work for the lost art squad. I have no idea where his painting is. And if Eric's manuscript is with him, I wonder how he got his hands on it?"

Edelman was losing patience.

"I told you I don't give a monkey's ass how he got it. The fact is he will let you see it now, and consign it into your hands, as soon as his painting has been found."

"I hear you," Giulia interrupted Edelman.

"Good. So this is what I want you to do: I want you to call Donovan, go and have a look at the manuscript. Read the darn thing, and come back and tell me about it. Then I want you to find his goddamn painting. It is really quite simple."

"I'll call him and let you know."

"Call him now," was Edelman's stern command.

Giulia shook her head in exasperation before putting the phone down.

Donovan shrugged away Giulia's accusations.

"Look Giulia, it's nothing personal. I felt you were not telling me everything you knew…so I offered Edelman a deal!"

"And since when did you have Eric's manuscript?"

"It came into my possession recently."

"When?" she insisted.

"When is not important. The point is that I have it."

"You sound just like Edelman," she scoffed.

"We understand each other," Donovan said simply.

Giulia's annoyance was visible. To divert the confrontation, she asked him for some water to drink.

Donovan returned from the adjoining room with a glass of water in one hand and a stapled hand-written manuscript in the other. He placed both objects on his desk, directly in front of Giulia, and stepped away.

"I have to check my inventory in the backroom so I'll leave you for a while. When you are through, call me," he said.

Giulia nodded and without touching the glass of water, she picked up the manuscript. The document, fifty or so pages, was a photocopy, but Eric's handwriting was recognisable. He had given the book a title, *The Language of Line*, and in the long introduction, he explained what led him to deduce that drawing was a language and the lines used in drawings, its words. Fascinated by Old Masters, he had intuited that the characteristics of each draughtsman were identifiable; the nature of their lines, their shapes, the way they held their writing instruments, whether they glided over the parchment or dug into it; the flow itself of a drawing formed the syntax which in turn revealed each artist's own style, his handwriting. Eric went on to explain how he had studied cuneiform, the alphabet of the Sumerians, as well as the antique Egyptian hieroglyphics to search for parallels with drawings.

The conclusion of his introduction was in itself a fascinating proposition.

"I believe," he wrote, "that I have unlocked the mystery of the language of line. In fact, it is not so much a mystery but rather a series of logical deductions and accurate observations that will allow the reader to identify the author of most drawings without fail."

Giulia wondered whether Eric suggested that his own hand, borrowing the style of the Old Masters, could also be identified in the drawings he had made. There would be mixed reactions in the art world if this treatise became public. On the one hand, it could help the art expert in making correct attributions but, on the other, the dealers and auction houses who had handled Eric's drawings would have no interest in finding out which drawings were by Eric.

The spectre of multi-million dollar lawsuits and ruined reputations loomed large over the world of experts and dealers.

Chapter 20

Tarquin Littlejohn threw a log into the fireplace, sending red sparks bouncing against the charred plate that refracted the heat. He glanced at his work and turned to look at himself in a mirror. A bottle of scotch and two glasses stood on the dining table beside a silver ice bucket. He poured himself a generous helping of whisky and made himself comfortable in a leather armchair. The journalist was late, he thought, looking at his watch again.

Jack Goldman, the California lawyer who represented him, had suggested that Littlejohn give an interview to relate his version of the disagreement with the Silverstein Museum. "It will increase the pressure on the Board of Trustees," he explained. "The last thing they want is publicity. But you must not speak to one of the major newspapers; choose a regional or local paper, one in Cambridge."

"Why not give an interview to the Times or the Independent?" Littlejohn had asked.

"Because there is no need to apply too much pressure. I will make sure the Board gets a copy of your interview. The lawyers will complain officially but will not be able to do anything. Believe me; they understand that we could give your court case a lot more publicity through national media in England, and in the States of course."

Gruffly, Littlejohn had agreed.

"And please do not go into details regarding the legal action. We want to send the Museum a warning, not give away everything. We need to save ammunition!"

Littlejohn resented the lecture and said he understood perfectly well what the object of the exercise was. Yet, he begrudged having to waste his time talking to a provincial journalist who would not appreciate the difference between a Rembrandt and a Rubens.

The doorbell rang. The journalist was half an hour late. Littlejohn downed the rest of his glass and went to the door. The young man who stood in front of him could not have been more than twenty-two or twenty-three. His blond hair was unruly and his cheeks, reddened by the cold, made him look like he should still be in school.

"Doug Stewart, nice to meet you, sir," the young man said cheerfully.

"That would be Professor to you, sit down over there," Littlejohn commanded. "You are late."

"Sorry, I had difficulty finding your…"

"Whisky?" Littlejohn interrupted him.

"Yes, please. It's suddenly quite cold outside," the young man said rubbing his hands together. He then opened a shapeless satchel and pulled out a notepad and a small tape recorder. Littlejohn frowned.

"No taping. You will have to take notes," he snapped.

The journalist acquiesced and stuck the tape recorder back into the satchel.

"No problem," he said nervously.

Littlejohn pushed a glass in front of the journalist and took a sip from his.

"Do you know anything at all about art history, Mr. Stewart?"

"Yes, I studied art history here at Cambridge."

Littlejohn arched his eyebrows.

In the background classical music drifted intermittently from another room, but the walls absorbed some of the passages so that it was not possible to recognise the piece.

"I have a degree in English Literature, but I took a course on art…." the young journalist continued.

"As I suspected, you know nothing about art!"

"Well…" Doug Stewart started.

"Here are the rules, Mr. Stewart. I will tell you who I am and I will tell you a story. You will write it down and only question me if you do not understand me. No 'off the record' comments will be provided. Am I making myself clear?"

"Crystal clear, sir, I mean Professor."

Littlejohn started to tell his story. He explained that he had worked with the Victoria and Albert in London and the Louvre in Paris, lectured both in London and New York and written numerous publications on art history.

"Sotheby's and Christie's call me when they need to authenticate a major work and museums ask for my expertise before buying an Old Master drawing."

"You specialise in French and Italian Old Master drawings then!" Stewart stated.

"I am an authority in French and Italian Old Master drawings, the Renaissance period in particular," Littlejohn corrected him.

"Like which Old Masters, for instance?"

Littlejohn sighed.

"Artists like Michelangelo, Tiepolo, Piranesi, Watteau, Boucher and Poussin."

"Okay, got that."

"You could write that I am a recognised expert in drawings and that because of this, the Silverstein Museum in Malibu approached me in the early nineties. I accepted to work for them and became curator of the Department of Drawings at the start of 1993."

The young journalist wrote in longhand, Littlejohn noticed, and not very fast. He paused to give him time to finish writing.

"Professor, can I ask why you moved to California? I mean, most drawings are found in Europe, aren't they?"

Littlejohn glared at the journalist: "The Silverstein is probably the best museum in the States and they have strong financial resources. They intended to double the size of their drawing collection and could not do so without somebody like me."

The ringing of the phone startled Littlejohn. Irritated by the interruption, he stood up to answer the call telling the journalist to stay where he was.

"Tarquin Littlejohn," he barked into the receiver. "Who is this?"

"My name is Giulia Vasari. I am a friend of the Hargraves, and of Eric, in particular."

"Yes?"

"I understand that you visited Bernard Hargrave and enquired about a missing drawing," Giulia replied.

Littlejohn looked over his shoulder, wondering whether he should continue this exchange in the journalist's presence. The young man seemed to be absorbed in his own notes, and not paying any attention.

"What if I did?"

"Well, Bernard gave me your number and suggested I call you. It would be useful if you could let me know what you are looking for, as I am helping the Hargraves sort through Eric's things."

"Not now. It is not a good time. Give me your number, and I will call you back."

Giulia ignored his request.

"Oh, by the way, Mr. Littlejohn, Bernard's house was burgled not long after your visit," Giulia dropped casually.

"What? I hope you are not suggesting that I had anything to do with this. This is a ridiculous insinuation. You don't know who you are talking to!" he said, his voice rising.

Littlejohn mumbled something unintelligible and put down the receiver.

Littlejohn returned to his armchair, sat down and stretched his right leg. He looked at the empty glass beside him and noticed that the young man's was still full. "Don't you drink whisky?"

"Yes, yes I do," Stewart replied without touching his glass.

Littlejohn stood up to fetch the bottle of whisky and placed it on the coffee table that separated them.

Doug Stewart cast a glance at the room and noticed the faded flowers in a vase at the far corner and the layer of dust on most of the furniture. There is no woman in this house, he thought to himself.

"A beautiful house you have here, Professor."

"I am not here very often. It's too bloody humid."

"It's certainly a different climate from Malibu," Stewart added with a smile.

Litttlejohn nodded suddenly feeling weary. The house stood about thirty metres from the river and humidity made the cold weather colder. He poured himself another whisky, hoping it would restore some warmth.

"The milestones in the career of a curator are the major exhibitions, the catalogues he produces and, of course, the artworks he acquires for the Museum. At first, everything went well at the Silverstein. I organised several major exhibitions in the first couple of years and prepared an inventory of all the drawings we had. We also acquired a number of important pieces that occupy a prime position in the Museum."

Littlejohn took another gulp of whisky and Stewart wondered whether the man was an alcoholic.

"Then it all started to go wrong. The budget was sliced and funds reallocated to other departments; an exhibition on Florentine drawings was postponed and the Silverstein refused to publish the catalogue I had worked on for almost two years!"

"What happened?"

"Let us say that what I discovered in their collection caused some problems and rather than face these problems they tried to blame me and to say my judgment was erroneous!"

"Oh."

"I quit and am now suing the Museum for breach of contract and fraud!"

Doug Stewart stopped writing and reached out for his glass.

"What did you discover, Professor?"

Littlejohn paused.

"I found out that several of the drawings bought by my predecessor were forgeries."

"Important drawings?"

"Yes, they were."

"And…I suppose the Museum had paid a lot of money to acquire them!" Doug Stewart stated.

"Obviously," came the smug reply.

"And you believe they wanted to cover this up and, let us say, made your life difficult or put pressure on you to prevent you from making your discovery public?"

"Exactly!"

"Very interesting."

Littlejohn stood up and turned his back to the sofa on which Doug Stewart was seated. He rearranged the logs in the fireplace. The heat warmed his face, his hands and his chest, yet his shoulders and back remained tense and frozen. Instead of turning around to warm his back, he stayed in the same position, facing the fire, reflecting on the phone call he had just received. Did this woman really suggest that he broke into Hargrave's house? Who was she anyway? Vasari? Was it her real name or a joke?

Doug Stewart looked up from his notes.

"Professor, can I ask you a few questions?"

Littlejohn asked him what he wanted to know without bothering to turn around.

"How much did the museum pay for these drawings you claim were forgeries?

"A lot of money, even for a rich museum like the Silverstein."

"Can you give me an approximate figure?" he insisted.

"I have already answered you," Littlejohn snapped.

The journalist found it unnerving to question a man whose back was turned to him but plucked up the courage to go on.

"Do you know who was responsible for these forgeries? I mean they must have been pretty good to have fooled the museum?"

"I have a fair idea who it was, yes."

Doug Stewart had not really expected an answer but as long as the Professor was willing to speak, he was willing to listen and take notes.

"Who was the forger?"

"Someone called Eric Hargrave."

"The one who published his autobiography a few years back?" Stewart shot back.

"That one, yes."

"And...er...are you sure? I mean...couldn't it be...?"

Littlejohn finally turned around. His face had turned red from close exposure to the fire but to the journalist he looked enraged.

"I am the expert! And when I say it is by Eric I know what I am talking about, damn it!"

Doug Stewart stared at Littljohn, frozen and open-mouthed.

"Now finish your whisky and go. The interview is over."

Littlejohn walked stiffly to the low table, picked up the bottle of whisky and left the room without looking back.

Chapter 21

The *Commissariato* in Trastevere occupied the three floors of a dilapidated building in a street perpendicular to the busy road of viale Trastevere, and would have been inconspicuous but for the flag and the shield that hung over the main entrance.

Inspector Conti spent as little time in the police station as he could, blaming the dust from the ongoing building works for his smoker's cough, and explained that he needed to walk in order to stimulate his thought process.

The *Commissario Capo* had heard what he called Conti's justifications for absenteeism one time too many and looked up in exasperation.

"I don't care if you need to stand on your head to get your brain working, *Inspettore*, but you must file your reports like everyone else, and I doubt you can do it while walking around the block!"

"The reports," Conti nodded.

"Yes, the reports! And I would like to know how far we have got on the burglary of the residence of *Cavagliere* Spada."

"Not very far really."

"Not very far, is how far exactly?" the commissioner inquired with exaggerated politeness.

"I have been investigating the death of Eric Hargrave, the *Inglese*," Conti replied.

"So what I have heard is true," he said more to himself than to Conti.

"Hargrave was drunk, he fell, hit his head against marble steps in Piazza Trilussa and died in hospital after a surgical intervention failed to repair the damage caused by the fall. There were no witnesses and the medical examiner confirmed it was an accident. There is no Hargrave case," his chief stated.

"Except that there was a witness who called the emergency number but disappeared, and that the examiner's report says that the fall could have caused the fracture and therefore death, implying it was not the only possible explanation," Conti retorted, contradicting his commanding officer.

"And what is your explanation, *Inspettore* Conti?"

"He had drunk a lot of wine, but then he was used to it as the examination of his liver showed, and statements from friends and neighbours confirmed. But this does not rule out the possibility that he could have been hit. And, if you add the fact that he was a well-known forger whose autobiography caused a major scandal and made him a lot of enemies who wanted him silenced, I believe, there is cause for an investigation."

"What evidence have you obtained?"

"Nothing conclusive yet," Conti admitted, knowing that he had just provided his boss with the argument he was looking for.

"Look, nobody is interested in finding out whether Hargrave was murdered or fell down in a drunken stupor. Write a short report. That closes it. Death by accident. And get moving with the Spada case, which the mayor of Rome calls me about nearly every day!"

Conti stood up, taking the *Commissario's* raised tone of voice as a sign that their conversation had come to an end.

"Why don't you ask Alberti or Lupa to investigate the Spada burglary?"

"Because I asked you, not Alberti, not Lupa!"

Lupa and Alberti had more seniority than Conti but had not solved a case in over ten years and were the target of most jokes at the *Station*. If you wanted a case buried and archived, you suggested that it be given to Lupa and Alberti.

"Cavagliere Spada is very close to the mayor, Conti!"

"I understand."

"So, you will write your conclusions about the *Inglese* and have your report on my desk by the end of the week. Clear?"

Conti shrugged but did not answer. He let himself out of the *Commissario's* office. He wondered why the *Commissario* was so insistent on closing the case.

On the ground floor Conti stopped at his desk and checked his in-tray perfunctorily. The computer screen was gathering dust and reflected the three open windows behind Conti's back, momentarily transporting him out of the room, away from the cacophony of ringing phones, shouts, doors being slammed, mixed with the sounds of heavy traffic from outside. The inspector had his own office, but it was, together with the bathroom and another large common room, currently under refurbishment. He suspected that his chief secretly enjoyed having told him that he would have to share an office with two junior inspectors until his office was ready. Conti had said nothing. This would be another good reason to step out for one of his brisk invigorating walks.

He unlocked the right hand drawers of his desk, pulled out the top drawer and extracted a file marked "Hargrave". Slowly and methodically he went through each sheet, occasionally jotting down a couple of words on a yellow writing block.

He looked at the list he had produced, tore off the page, folded it and inserted it into an inside pocket of his jacket. He needed a smoke and had no intention of returning to the *Commissariato* that afternoon.

The two young inspectors stood by his desk and asked him whether he wanted to join them for a *panino* and coffee. He said he did not have the time.

Conti had circled Saturday on his desk calendar and could not recall why. After checking he still had cigars, he stood up, cast a last glance at his calendar and left the station. He climbed up the Gianicolo hill until he stood directly above the Spanish consulate and lit his Tuscan cigar. Ahead of him, the Vittorio Emmanuele building on Piazza Venezia stood out, in the middle of a forest of spires, domes and red-tiled roofs. Mussolini used to stand and make speeches from the balcony of one of the palazzi that stood at a right angle to the monument.

He suddenly remembered why he had circled the Saturday. It was his son's birthday. He had not seen him for several weeks, which was not unusual as he lived with his mother. Conti felt a pang of guilt. He would have to buy something for his son, and make time to meet up with him.

Sitting on the edge of a banister, his thoughts refocused on the Hargrave case and the *Commissario's* comments. Strictly speaking, his chief's question was relevant: aside from finding out that Hargrave had many enemies what had he established? He unfolded the sheet of paper he had taken from his desk and reviewed his notes.

It had taken several weeks of canvasing the bars and restaurants in Trastevere and across the Ponte Sisto to establish that someone, whose description matched Monticello, had dinner with Hargrave the night he fell. The gallery owner had reluctantly admitted it was true, but vehemently stated they had parted ways just after ten o'clock in Piazza Campo dei Fiori as Hargrave needed to get up early the next morning. According to Monticello Hargrave had no more than his usual bottle of Chianti over dinner yet he was found intoxicated several hours later. Where had he gone after dinner if Monticello had told the truth? No one remembered seeing Hargrave in any of the bars the police visited.

Conti had doubts about Monticello's character but could not find a credible motive for the dealer to want Hargrave dead. In addition, the Indian cook of a nearby restaurant had reported seeing someone matching the forger's description in Piazza Trilussa arguing with a younger man. The cook said it was pouring and he had only glanced in the direction of the Piazza, but he seemed a credible witness.

Conti was convinced that forgeries were at the centre of Hargrave's death. But, was it because he was soon to reveal more about his nefarious activities or because of a deal that had gone wrong? Did Donovan and the lost Canaletto have anything to do with Hargrave's death? He pulled out one of his cigars and lit it carelessly. The flame consumed only its lower half and he had to use his lighter a second time until it burnt evenly.

In his book Hargrave mentioned the names of the London auction houses and galleries that had bought his works but only alluded to his dealings in Italy, yet, as Giulia had told him, several people had threatened him publicly during the launch of his book in Milan.

And Giulia Vasari? She seemed to be the link to many of the characters and was a valuable source of information. She had told him of her conversation with Hargrave the night he fell, revealed that Donovan was looking for his Canaletto, and was present in Milan during the book launch She had told him about her meeting with the Hargraves in Brighton, not to mention that she was also looking for the book Hargrave had intended to publish.

Then there was the matter of the younger man seen with Hargrave. Could it have been someone he had picked up on his way home? Did they stop at a bar and have a few drinks before heading back to Hargrave's apartment only to get into an argument at the Piazza? Eric still had his wallet and money on him when he was found unconscious.

Finally he had jotted down that Hargrave's keys were missing. Nothing appeared out of place when they searched the apartment for clues, but then, they did not know what they specifically should be looking for.

To finance his lifestyle Hargrave needed to complement the regular monthly payments from London with "commissions" from new customers or from dealers he had worked with in the past. Here, of course, lay the main difficulty: How was he ever going to be able to identify who was dealing with Eric? Maybe Eric's boyfriend? He had only made the most fleeting of appearances since Eric's death and swiftly disappeared to Canada.

Conti asked himself how much time he still had on this case if the *Commissario* put more pressure on him to drop the investigation.

Would Giulia Vasari be able to help, he wondered.

Another reason to telephone her.

Chapter 22

Tarquin Littlejohn stretched out his tall frame as he stepped out of a rented car in front of Bernard Hargrave's house. The cool sea breeze caused him to shudder. I should be in California, he thought, not in this pathetic excuse for a seaside resort.

Bernard Hargrave had been reluctant to meet him again but could find no good excuse to give Littlejohn, who was determined to see him.

Littlejohn was what Americans would describe as a self-made man. Born in the Midlands to a working-class family, he excelled in school and earned a scholarship to read English Literature at Oxford University. His aristocratic bearing was not enough to mask the origin his accent betrayed and he was mocked by his fellow students who sarcastically called him 'Lord Tarquin'. Littlejohn shrugged off the jibes and perversely seemed to encourage them, by becoming even more aloof and distant, if that was possible. While at Oxford, he made no attempt to join societies or clubs and instead sought out the most obscure thesis subjects, and by the end of his first year, a few of his tutors had taken to calling him 'Lord Tarquin' as well.

He took a keen interest in the history of art and worked his way to a postgraduate course discovering that he had the ability to discern painting styles and spot weaknesses or inconsistencies in a work of art, the way others realised a mathematical equation to be imbalanced.

His progression at the Victoria and Albert was regular rather than spectacular until the departure of the curator of Italian and French Old Master drawings propelled him to the forefront of the art establishment.

He was not liked by his peers but the Board of Trustees acknowledged his talent and was comforted by his aristocratic bearing. So much so that they brushed aside rumours of improper conduct a junior female staff member was alleged to have reported against him.

After so many years playing the part, Tarquin Littlejohn had convinced himself he was in a class of his own and only lowered himself to cajole and plead with the Hargraves because he had no choice.

A flash of annoyance crossed Littlejohn's face when Bernard Hargrave's sister greeted him at the door. He had specifically requested that the encounter be kept private.

"You must be Professor Littlejohn," she said without smiling.

"Yes," he answered and stepped in without waiting to be invited.

Despite Bernard Hargrave's distrustful manner, Littlejohn succeeded in establishing a basis for dialogue. Sensing that Bernard and his sister were nervously waiting for him to lead the discussion, he started by saying he was sorry for his directness and lack of sensitivity the first time they had met. "Too many years in America, I am afraid, may have rubbed off on me."

Bernard Hargrave shifted uncomfortably in his chair but his half-nod could have passed for an acknowledgement of the apology.

"Americans are very direct and go to the point without preamble," Littlejohn continued. "In the beginning I was not too comfortable with this, but I eventually learned to adapt and accept it as being their way. Nothing wrong with it."

Littlejohn told them that he had been in charge of the Drawings Department at the Victoria and Albert in London before becoming the curator of the Silverstein, one of the richest American museums in California.

"I knew your brother long before he published his autobiography," he lied, "and although we were of course on different sides of the art world, if you allow me to put it this way, I had great respect for his skills and his knowledge."

Eric Hargrave's sister nodded in approval. Bernard appeared lost in his thoughts and stared at a point somewhere over Littlejohn's shoulder.

"On a number of occasions we had…let us say…dealings with each other. And in particular, when I discovered what I believed to be forgeries in the California museum. I suspected that several drawings acquired before my arrival had been done by a much later follower of the artist they had been attributed to."

Littlejohn made up his story as he went along, adjusting and embellishing it according to the reactions he received from the Hargraves. Remembering that Eric had written that he was not close to his family, Littlejohn felt that there was little chance that they could disprove what he told them. In any event, none of his lies were questioned and he went on weaving his tale with impunity.

"The Museum tried to cover up my findings and hide the fact that they had paid several million dollars for forgeries."

"Why?" asked Bernard.

"Because the shareholders and benefactors would ask for an investigation and people would lose their jobs, money might have to be returned; this kind of thing was best swept under the carpet. At least, this is what the Museum management thought."

Littlejohn cleared his throat, satisfied to see that Bernard's interest had been awakened.

"In any event, as I told you before, I sent a drawing to Eric to ask for his opinion. First I sent him a copy of the Silverstein's Michelangelo drawing, but it was not of a good enough quality so…" he hesitated, "I asked him if he could duplicate it; if he could make a new drawing similar to the copy I sent him to prove my theory that he was the author. He received a generous advance for the drawing and it was to be delivered to me before the end of last year. Unfortunately, he died in tragic circumstances before he could hand me his drawing and before we could discuss the all-important question of attribution. So you see, if this drawing or even the exchange of correspondence were to fall in the wrong hands it would be most detrimental to my case, and would not go down well for Eric either!"

Bernard frowned, unsure how to react to this admission.

"You told me you had sent a copy to my late brother. Now you say you commissioned a copy?" he enunciated carefully in disbelief.

If Littlejohn's rivals were to describe him in one word it would be: self-important. Yet, in the situation he now found himself in, Littlejohn had little choice but to submit to Bernard Hargrave's pointed question with good grace.

"I admit that I was less than forthcoming but you surely understand how delicate this matter is and I saw no need to further complicate the situation with too many details."

Hargrave agreed it was a sensitive issue.

"But we are honourable people, and we would not keep something that does not belong to us," Hargrave protested.

"This is what I can see now," Littlejohn replied. His grimace resembling more a wince of pain than a smile.

Eric Hargrave's sister was more willing than Bernard to accept Littlejohn's tale.

"What does this drawing look like exactly?" she asked.

"It's a sheet of studies with a Madonna and Child in pen and brown ink. The paper it is drawn on is slightly larger than a normal A4 sheet but irregular in shape and one corner will appear badly damaged."

The Hargraves glanced at each other without comment.

"I am prepared to make a contribution to the Eric Hargrave foundation for the return of this drawing."

Bernard looked over to his sister, again seeking support. She shrugged her shoulders imperceptibly and looked away.

"We have not yet completed the inventory of our late brother's possessions, you see, and we have not found a drawing such as the one you have just described."

Littlejohn's jaw tightened but he kept his impatience under control.

"I will be glad to help you finalise the inventory. I have time this afternoon."

"Er, well we also have not received everything yet. The second batch of boxes is due to arrive in a week's time…" Bernard hesitated.

The curator stood up abruptly and towered over the Hargraves.

"I need this drawing before the end of the week. If it has not been returned to me by then, my lawyers have been instructed to follow up and take legal action."

Before letting himself out, he reminded the Hargraves that he needed their answer by Friday. Bernard sank into his armchair and said nothing.

In the evening, Alberto Conti called Giulia at home under the pretext of asking her if there was any news on the missing manuscript. She said that it had mysteriously appeared in the possession of Donovan and that Donovan refused to explain how he got it. He was holding on to it until she could come up with his missing Canaletto.

"Giulia, are you coming back to Rome soon?" Conti asked a little awkwardly.

She said she was not sure.

"And I just talked to Bernard Hargrave's sister. He has been hospitalised after suffering a heart attack," she added.

"When?"

"This afternoon."

Giulia repeated what Eric Hargrave's sister had told her about the visit of Littlejohn.

Conti listened with great attention.

"This drawing by Michelangelo that Littlejohn claims is a forgery, how much do you think the Museum in California paid for it?"

Giulia explained that there were very few Michelangelo drawings in circulation and that the museum must have paid between five and ten million dollars.

"Hmm…" Conti said, "That could explain why Littlejohn will go to some lengths to get it back."

"In fact," Giulia added, "I called Littlejohn the other day, on the request of Bernard. I told Littlejohn Bernard had told me about the missing drawing and it irritated him to learn that yet another person knew about his missing drawing."

The concern in Conti's voice was apparent. He said to Giulia, "Be careful. We don't know enough about Littlejohn, and we don't know what he is capable of. I wouldn't want anything to happen to you."

Chapter 23

One wall of the Boardroom was lined with framed front book covers of the bestsellers, and winners of the Nobel Prize, Pulitzer and National book awards published by Seldom House in the United Kingdom and in North America over the last twenty years. At one end of the room, as if they still presided over the publishing house, were the portraits of the two founders. At the other end were two black and white photographs – a view of New York's skyscrapers taken during the early thirties and a view of London from the same period.

Giulia sat behind the long modern design glass and steel conference table, her back turned to the window. She looked at her watch. Edelman was late. She went over the notes she had taken in Donovan's gallery, trying to recollect as accurately as she could what Donovan had said, and reviewing the notes she had taken to explain the contents of Eric's manuscript to Edelman.

Victor Edelman rushed in, with two executives from New York and his own personal secretary in tow.

"Right, Giulia, this is Max from Legal and John from Finance. Let's hear it. How is the book?"

Giulia stood up to greet them, ready to face the barrage of questions she knew would come once she gave her views to Edelman. The Vice-president of Seldom House walked over to the side table and poured himself and the others some before joining Giulia at the table.

"I have read some of it. In my opinion it is a fascinating book from a scholarly point of view but of little commercial potential."

Edelman adjusted his tie over his bulging stomach and rebuked Giulia with a certain casualness.

"Leave the commercial judgment to me and tell us what the book is about. What does it say? How long? Any illustrations?"

Giulia explained Eric Hargrave's theory, quoting from his introduction to the book.

"Sounds great. A recipe on how to spot forgeries!"

"Well, not exactly. It's designed to teach the reader how to recognise drawing styles, how to interpret the lines and spaces. It's both a treatise and a manual depending on how it's read. It's for the art expert, the art student who wants to understand the work of others and learn to really appreciate drawings."

Edelman frowned, looking puzzled.

"Can you give us an example?"

"The book explains that the lines in a drawing can be deciphered as one does a language. Eric argues that a line has movement, rhythm and tempo. It can be straight, long or short, drawn quickly or smoothly etc. Any drawing can be broken down into a series of elements, the lines, which are combined in a certain order that identify the author's style."

The publishers waved her on impatiently. "This is all quite technical. Does he give examples?"

"Yes, he does. He explains for instance, that an artist like Rubens had a workshop where he employed painters to produce some of the work given to him. Rubens did his best to suppress the individual characteristics of his assistants and to force them to adopt his style. Despite this, several individualistic draughtsmen like van Dyck and Jordaens did go on to pursue their own styles."

"Does Hargrave refer to his own work?"

"He does, constantly, but there lies the problem; the illustrations are missing and without them the book loses much of its interest."

Edelman turned to the man from Legal who looked nonplussed.

"There must be a way to transform this book into a viable commercial project," Edelman interjected.

"Well, maybe there is, even if it's not what Eric may have intended." Giulia paused, looking at her notes. "In his conclusion he sends the reader on a mission. Eric challenges the reader to identify which drawings used in the text to illustrate his arguments are his. For this, he refers the reader to a list of illustrations that support his theories," Giulia paused, looked up at Edelman and continued. "Eric claims that more than half of the drawings in this list are by him."

Giulia saw the transformation on Edelman's face. This he could understand.

"And the list?" he excitedly asked.

"The list is missing as well."

"Fuck it, I knew you were playing us, Giulia."

"I've told you exactly what I've seen and what I think. The list must exist. It could be with Donovan, it could be with the Hargraves. After all, he finished the text and wrote a conclusion. He also wanted to see me about the book's publication."

John, from Finance, smiled and pushed his glasses up his nose with the index of his left hand.

"Do you think you can find the list, Giulia?"

"I'll do my best."

Edelman cut in, "This is a priority for all of us. I will talk to Donovan myself, in case he's the one who has the bloody list."

Giulia pointed out that Bernard Hargrave had just been taken to hospital and that she could hardly ask him about the list now.

"He has a sister as well, doesn't he?"

"Yes, but it is he who manages the estate. I'll try and speak to him soon and if he is able to talk, find out if the original manuscript and list have surfaced.

Edelman nodded and stood up unceremoniously.

"Give us a call the minute you hear anything."

"Will do," Giulia promised.

Chapter 24

Alberto Conti tightened his safety belt and picked up the Alitalia magazine from the pocket in front of him. He nervously flipped the pages and tried his best to ignore the instructions broadcast by a loudspeaker. Flying always made him anxious and a bit queasy; the idea of being cooped up in a plane for one and a half hours without being able to draw comfort from one of his Tuscan cigars increased his uneasiness.

The middle-age stewardess stared at him sternly.

"*Signore*, no smoking please."

Conti looked up with a frown.

"I am not smoking. The cigar is not lighted."

"I must ask you to put it away," the stewardess insisted.

"I will put whatever I want in my mouth," Conti replied stubbornly.

The pilot chose this precise moment to announce that they were entering a zone of turbulence and asked everyone to make sure they had their safety belts on.

The stewardess mumbled to the next passenger row something about how *prepotente* some passengers could be. The inspector continued to chew on his unlighted cigar and looked out through the round windows. They would land in Turin in half an hour where he would continue his journey by car.

The plane lurched forward, sending the glass of red wine of Conti's neighbour crashing between their seats. The man apologised.

I'll take the train back to Rome, Conti thought to himself, as he brushed some of the spilt wine from his trousers.

Earlier in the morning, Conti had received a call from Val d'Aosta where the local *carabinieri* had intercepted a smuggler as he was about to cross the border into Switzerland. The man denied that he was doing anything illegal, as could be expected, and insisted that the large canvas in the trunk of his station wagon was a copy. The local *carabinieri,* who sensed that things were not quite right but felt they did not have the expertise to recognise a copy from an original, had called the office of the *carabinieri* that specialised in the recovery of lost and stolen artworks. The call had been put on hold, then the line had cut off. They tried a second time, with the same results. They then thought of checking the details on the man's driving license which instigated the call to the police in Trastevere. The call reached Alberto Conti whose interest was aroused when he heard the suspect's name. Conti asked the *carabinieri* to describe the subject of the painting in question and when he was told it was a view of Venice, he instructed them to hold the painting and the man until he arrived.

He was picked up at the Turin airport by a *carabinieri* in civilian clothes who drove like a maniac and reached their destination with time to spare. Conti extricated himself from the Alfa Romeo and asked the driver to show him the way. In sharp contrast to the Roman *Commissariato* office, the *carabinieri* station in Aosta was as antiseptic as a Swiss clinic and any noise was swallowed by the wood panelled walls and a thick green carpet. The officer on duty took over the guided tour and unlocked a room in which a large painting leaned facing the far wall.

"The smuggler had this painting and various terracotta figurines in his possession when he attempted to cross the border," the *carabinieri* explained. Conti turned the painting around and leaned it back against the wall. The columns that guarded St. Mark's square and the *Chiesa Santa Maria della Salute* were easily recognisable. The perspective suggested the artist had stood on the *piazzetta*, in front of the Ducal palace, a little closer to the column of San Teodoro.

"Hmm, beautiful, quite beautiful," Conti murmured.

The *carabinieri* officer asked him if he was an art expert.

"No, I am not," Conti answered without looking up from the painting.

The painting was not signed, but this did not prove anything. As far as he was concerned, Conti could have been standing in front of a genuine Canaletto, no less inviting and vibrant than those he had seen in the National Museum.

The *carabinieri* rubbed his forehead and asked whether they should release the man they had detained.

"No, don't release him yet. I need to talk to him first."

Giorgio Monticello thought himself sophisticated and a man of consummate good taste. He enjoyed being the centre of attention and took great pains to dress and act as if the world was a stage and he the star attraction. His abundant white hair reached his shoulders, his fingernails were carefully manicured. His limp was the justification for the silver-pommeled cane he carried at all times. His art gallery in Trastevere did not claim a prestigious address as it would have if it stood on Via dei Coronari, for instance, but he explained that artists lived in Trastevere.

At the moment, however, Monticello was not quite as self-confident as he had tried to appear when the *carabinieri* asked him to park his car on the side of the road for a routine control, just before the Swiss border. Not being able to demonstrate that the painting he was transporting was not a genuine Canaletto he was now forced to wait for an inspector who would examine it.

To his surprise, it was the familiar face of Inspector Conti that first appeared through the door of his holding cell, in mid-afternoon. His puzzled look was plain to see and Conti did not waste any time demanding an explanation.

"Signor Monticello, who painted the view of Venice if, as you claim, it is not a genuine Canaletto?" Conti asked without wasting any time.

The art dealer felt trapped, without time to collect his thoughts, unsettled by the appearance of the Roman inspector.

"Well, it is not by Canaletto. So why should it matter who painted it?"

"It does matter, believe me," Conti said calmly.

Monticello remained silent, hoping that the inspector would pass on to the next question, but Alberto Conti just stared at him. After a few seconds, the art dealer sighed.

"If I can prove who painted it, you will have to release me, right?"

Conti's gesture could have passed for an acknowledgement.

"It is a copy, painted only a few months ago. In fact, the painting is still fresh in the right hand corner."

"To me it looks like it was painted in the mid-1700s" retorted Conti.

"Well, it is a copy and I am not breaking any law," Monticello insisted, doing his best to sound firm.

"We will get back to the painting later. You also had with you a box of stone and terracotta figurines?"

The dealer nodded.

"If I am not mistaken they are Egyptian, Roman and Etruscan pieces?"

The dealer acquiesced reluctantly.

"Can you explain the origin of these pieces? Who did you buy them from? And can you prove they were not dug up illegally in Tarquinia, for instance?"

Monticello remained quiet.

"Unless you would like to claim that the Etruscan pieces are copies as well, you were smuggling these antiquities into Switzerland!"

The dealer explained lamely that he was carrying the figurines for someone else.

"Which would make you an accessory and party to the smuggling act. Makes no difference to me."

Conti paused and lighted the Tuscan cigar slowly and carefully.

After a couple of puffs he hunched forward and glared at the Roman dealer.

"I have a theory. Maybe you can tell me if my theory is correct!"

Conti inhaled tobacco and blew it slowly towards Monticello.

"My theory is that an Englishman painted this copy in Rome recently and probably showed it to you in his workshop. Since the untimely departure of the artist you…let us say, borrowed the painting, and along with the painting various stone and terracotta figures…"

Monticello's face betrayed his confusion and he wisely chose to keep his mouth shut. It was becoming warm in the room and he undid the top buttons of his shirt.

"Seeing you do not deny my version I assume I am correct."

Monticello's mind worked furiously to find a plausible counter-explanation. He cursed the fact that, of all people, Alberto Conti was the one interrogating him.

"You are really faced with a dilemma, Signor Monticello. If you admit you took the painting from the dead Englishman, you could be accused of theft. If you argue it is an original, you could be accused of smuggling a part of our national patrimony abroad. And if you say nothing you leave it to the police to choose what offence to charge you with!"

Monticello had his back to the wall and realised that the truth was probably preferable to making up an explanation that Conti was unlikely to accept.

"Eric Hargrave painted this view of Venice in the manner of Canaletto, yes, and I...borrowed it...to...let us say, I wanted someone's opinion about its quality. But I would have brought it back to Hargrave's studio," Monticello tried to defend himself.

Conti raised his eyes and shook his head.

"And the collection of antiquities was also borrowed from Hargrave, Signor Monticello?"

"Yes."

"At least this part is clear. Now what is not very clear to me is the exact nature of your relationship with Eric Hargrave."

"He was an artist, I have a gallery and as you know I am exhibiting a series of lithographs he made...inspired by Ovid's poems."

Conti said he remembered the lithographs and, in fact, had recently bought one himself.

"Monticello, tell me one thing. If the Canaletto was, in fact, by Canaletto, how much could it be sold for in...say, Switzerland?"

The art dealer looked alarmed.

"I was not trying to sell it..."

"Just answer my question. How much would a Canaletto fetch in the art market in an auction then?"

Monticello hesitated.

"A few million dollars probably," he offered.

"A few? How many, two, three, ten? You must have a better idea than I. After all you are the art dealer!"

"Well, then, four to six, I would say."

"Hmm..." Conti rubbed his chin slowly. "Signor Monticello, are you aware that there is an ongoing investigation into the death of Eric Hargrave?"

The dealer nodded, not sure where the interrogation was headed.

"Mr. Hargrave may have fallen in the streets of Trastevere, unless he was hit and killed by someone. In fact, the investigation is a murder investigation."

Monticello turned pale.

"A few million dollars could be a motive, wouldn't you agree?"

"I have absolutely nothing to do with his death. I took this painting after his death," Monticello said in protest.

Conti stood up slowly and pushed the chair away from the table.

"Here is what we are going to do, Monticello. First, you are going to sign a statement concerning the origin of the artworks you were transporting. Once you have done that you and I are going to take the train."

"The train?"

"Yes, back to Rome. Unless you have an objection."

Monticello slowly shook his head, resigned to his fate.

Chapter 25

Conti stood in the arrival hall of Fiumicino airport with his hands crossed behind his back. He observed others who, like him, were expecting to welcome someone. Women eagerly awaiting a returning boyfriend or husband; an elderly couple nervously consulting their watch and each other, a couple of Asian nuns, serious and silent; an anonymous group of people clustered around two pillars and behind a barrier, focused on the sliding doors that opened and closed, impatient to catch a glimpse of whoever they were waiting for.

The police inspector, self-conscious, stepped away from the group and strode to the entrance of the bar. He figured there was enough time for another espresso.

When he called Giulia to suggest she come to Rome and see the painting in the style of Canaletto confiscated from Monticello, he was surprised that she had instantly agreed to fly to Italy. He heard himself say he would pick her up at the airport as if it was the most natural thing to suggest and Giulia thanked him.

"Are you not going to offer me a coffee, inspector?"

He turned around to see Giulia smiling at him.

"You are early, no?"

"The plane landed twenty minutes ahead of time," she said.

The inspector moved forward impetuously to hug her, but then thought better of it. Giulia put her right hand on his left arm and kissed him on the cheek.

"I would like a cappuccino, thank you."

On their way to the city centre, Conti recounted the arrest of Giorgio Monticello at the Swiss border and the confiscation of the canvas as well as various antiquities. No, he explained, Monticello was not in police custody but the artworks were at the *Commissariato* and the dealer had been told not to leave Rome for the time being.

"Do you think Monticello had anything to do with Eric's death?" Giulia asked.

"He knew Eric, he did business with him and stole a painting and a collection of statues from his studio," Conti shrugged. "The question is: did he steal because he saw an opportunity to earn some money or did he kill to be able to steal from him?"

"For a painting?"

"If Monticello could fool someone into believing the painting was a Canaletto he could make a lot of money, right?"

Giulia nodded.

"I met Monticello and I did not like him. I found him too suave and devious, but to kill someone!"

"Devious? What does that mean?"

"Oh, someone you cannot trust. Someone who is after something."

Conti stole a glance at Giulia.

"Maybe he was trying to impress you," he suggested.

"Maybe he was. And maybe it's unfair of me to even judge his character with the little I know of him."

"I think you are a good judge of character," Conti countered.

Giulia said nothing and looked ahead. Traffic was flowing along the pine-tree lined Via Cristoforo Colombo and Conti drove skilfully. In minutes they went past the Terme de Caracalla, turned left between Circo Massimo and the Palatine hills to finally reach the Tiber behind the Bocca della Verita. The trees that bordered the Lungotevere were starting to show their first leaves.

"Yes, spring is here." Conti said, as if he had read her thoughts.

"I'll drive you to your hotel first and after that we can go to the *Commissariato*. Is that okay with you?"

"We can go directly to the *Commissariato* and I can take a taxi from there to the hotel. I don't want to take too much of your time!"

Conti said he would be happy to drive her to the hotel after they had viewed the painting, and turned onto the nearest bridge in the direction of Trastevere.

The air was crisp and the sky was cloudless, the sun already warm. Giulia felt at home in the Italian capital although on reflection she decided that "home" was maybe a substitute for comfortable. Where was home really? Was it New York where her mother still lived? Was it Argentina where she used to spend summers visiting her maternal grandparents? Or was it London?

She was brought back into the conversation when Conti lowered the volume of the radio, and asked for the second time.

"What's on your mind?"

Giulia smiled apologetically.

"Sorry, my mind was elsewhere. I didn't hear what you said."

"You did seem far away," he agreed.

"I was wondering what feeling at home meant," she said.

The inspector looked at her quizzically. "It is where you belong, I would say."

"Maybe that's the question I was trying to answer. Where does one belong? Where one was born? Where one lives? Where one works? Where is home for you, inspector?"

"Alberto, please call me Alberto."

"So, where is home for you, Alberto?"

"Rome, for sure."

"Why?"

"I just do not see myself anywhere else."

"My friends say I am lucky because I get to travel, because I live in exciting cities, because I meet writers, famous people. At first, I would disagree with them. I used to think that people who led restless lives were often people who were either running away from something or looking for something. But now…"she tilted her head upwards, "now I go along with them, I no longer argue."

"When one has too many choices, sometimes, it can be as difficult as not having any choice at all," Conti said.

Giulia agreed.

"Well, here we are. The *Commissariato* of Trastevere!" Conti pointed out a building a few metres away.

Giulia admired the large canvas with a view of Venice that to her looked very much like an authentic Canaletto. She unzipped her bag and pulled out the book entitled *Canaletto and England* that she had picked up in Eric's studio and opened it to the pages Eric had earmarked. Alberto Conti went to fetch a thick book that he had brought in entitled *Il Settecento Veneziano* and opened it to several pages he had identified that featured Canaletto's paintings of the *Molo*, or waterfront from the *piazzetta* near San Marco and where the two columns of St Mark and St Theodore stood. The paintings hung in the Hermitage of St. Petersburg, The National Gallery in Milan, and with the National Trust in Staffordshire. They put their findings side by side and together discovered how Eric had used three separate versions of Canaletto, injected his own ideas, arbitrarily moved one of the columns and produced the Canaletto that stood staring them in the face. Eric had chosen to include the two most famous buildings in Venice, the Doge's Palace and the church of Santa Maria della Salute, together with the Riva degli Schiavoni which was popular with English clients of the time. He must have had an English client in mind, Donavan's mysterious customer, when he painted this one, Giulia thought.

"Very clever. So nobody can say it is a copy as it is not a copy!" Conti exclaimed.

"And Monticello admitted it came from Eric's studio?"

Conti said he had.

"So what are you going to do with Monticello?"

The inspector made a face.

"Let him sweat. What I really want from him is information for our investigation into Eric's death. I will probably offer him a deal. No prosecution, if he tells me what I want to know."

"And the painting?"

"The Hargraves are the heirs. They decide what happens to the painting. If they want to sue Monticello, they can; if they do not, the Roman prosecutor could decide to anyway."

Conti agreed to let Giulia take a picture of the canvas and of the statues. He understood that the painting was most probably what Donovan was looking for but he repeated that he could not release it for the time being.

"It is my weapon for now," Conti said apologetically.

"And the statues, do you recognise them?" he added.

She looked at them but said she was not sure.

"They could have been Eric's. He had a collection in two cabinets but I never looked at them closely. This Sumerian tablet though, is very familiar."

She pointed to a flat grey stone carved with cuneiform scratches.

Conti picked it up carefully.

"Did Hargrave really learn to read this?" he asked.

Giulia said he did.

Conti shook his head.

"Interesting. Quite amazing really."

Slowly he repacked the box and replaced the protective bubble wrap over the canvas. He signed the log book and took Giulia's arm.

"And now, allow me the pleasure of taking you to dinner," he announced.

Giulia did not protest and, like two amateur art investigators, they both walked out with their reference books, triumphant smiles on their faces.

Chapter 26

Giulia was in no rush to get back to London. The telephone calls that she needed to make she could as well do from Rome. She asked to extend her room reservation at the Hotel Locarno another night and rebooked her flight back to London to leave on the Sunday instead. For the time being, more things were happening in Rome, she reasoned; Eric's Canaletto had turned up, clues to the original manuscript and the missing list would most probably be found in Rome, and of course there was Conti's investigation into the death of the "Prince of Forgers" as the local press called Hargrave.

Anything could happen in the next forty-eight hours!

She picked up the notepad beside the phone in her room and scribbled four names,

Bernard, Edelman, Chris and Marisa.

Giulia first called Bernard Hargrave at the hospital. The news was encouraging. The heart attack had been mild and he expected to be released in a few days. He insisted on telling her about Littlejohn's last visit and the latest version of his story, which was now that he had commissioned a drawing from Eric. Giulia said it sounded like Littlejohn was in a bit of a panic and there was probably more to the story than he was willing to admit. She told Bernard not to let it get to him. He had been straightforward from the start with Littlejohn, and with regards to any agreements between Littlejohn and his brother.

They talked a bit more and no, Bernard was not aware of the whereabouts of Eric's last manuscript and the news of its appearance in the hands of Christopher Donovan was as puzzling to him as it was to Giulia.

"Eric had the original manuscript and was bringing it to London to show to me. So someone must have taken his notes either from his apartment or his studio," Giulia suggested to Bernard.

Her conversation with Victor Edelman was brief and to the point. The Vice-president of Seldom House, in an unusually elated mood, was all compliments and encouragement. The fact that he was off to the airport for a weekend in Lisbon with someone who did not sound like his wife telling him to hurry in the background, may have had something to do with his friendly disposition.

"Great, I knew I could count on you. Please call Donovan and tell him you have the Canaletto. All you have to do now is to get your hands on that missing list and we are in business. Got to go. Enjoy Rome!" So unlike Pit Bull, Giulia smiled to herself.

Christopher Donovan sounded as tense as Edelman was relaxed, making an effort to conceal his agitation. Yes, things were fine, his business was fine, his family was well.

"I am in a hurry, Giulia. What is the purpose of this call?" he snapped.

"I wanted to talk to you about Eric's manuscript."

"Some other time maybe? Call me back around six," he suggested.

"And also about this painting you said you were looking for," she dropped casually.

Donovan was quiet for several seconds.

"Wait a minute," he told her.

She heard footsteps and a big door being slammed.

"Do you know where the painting is?" he asked.

"The Canaletto you mean? Or to be precise the painting in the manner of Canaletto?"

"Yes, that's what I mean."

Giulia described the oil painting that was in police custody at the station of Trastevere and Donovan confirmed it was the one he was looking for.

"So, do you have it? When can I have it?" he asked impatiently.

"One thing at a time, Christopher. I know where it is and who has it. It is in safe hands for the time being. And by the way, I noticed that Eric had used an old canvas, could be 17th, 18th century," she guessed, "what do you think?" she asked, trying to provoke a reaction from Donovan.

He did not make any comment.

"What I really would like to know is who gave you Eric's manuscript?" she continued.

Dovovan sighed.

"There are important drawings and attachments missing. Without them, in fact, the manuscript is incomplete. So I'd like to know how it got to you and find the missing parts."

"If you give me the canvas, the manuscript is yours. Let's leave it at that."

"The manuscript is not worth much to Seldom House without the attachments. The Canaletto however is worth a good deal of money to you, so you are not quite in the best bargaining position I believe."

Donovan hesitated before speaking, "Let's meet and I'll tell you how I got it in exchange for the Canaletto. Can you drop by the gallery this afternoon?"

Giulia told him she was in Rome and would only be back in London in a few days.

"I cannot wait until Monday. I'll meet you in Rome," he blurted out.

Giulia was caught off guard but quickly recovered her composure.

"I won't be in Rome during the weekend. I am going to visit friends in Umbria." It was a half-truth. Alberto Conti had invited her to his place in Umbria but she had graciously declined, unsure about how she felt, and had anyway been booked to fly back to London before then.

Donovan insisted, but Giulia did not relent.

She heard male voices, loud in the background, as Christopher agreed to meet her in London the following Monday.

"Look, this changes everything. I have everything under control now," Donovan pleaded with the two men.

One of the men rubbed the back of his head. He was the one who did the talking.

"You must come with us now and explain it yourself. We have been asked to collect you and you are coming with us. We are not interested in your explanations. Save your breath."

The second man stepped forward, ready to force Donovan if necessary, but the dealer raised both hands.

"I'm coming. Just let me switch off the computer."

The client who had ordered the painting in the style of Canaletto was not a tolerant man and had refused Donovan's suggestion to reimburse his deposit. He wanted the Canaletto and nothing else. Donovan had assured him that he would find the missing painting but the buyer was getting impatient and had sent two thugs to pick him up. A thought crossed Donovan's mind: did the buyer intend to put it aside and resell the painting as an authentic

Canaletto in a few years and at a huge profit? He cursed himself for not doing a background check on his client. But at least he was now confident he could recover Eric's painting. Donovan sat back against the car seat and did his best to look unconcerned.

"April showers" was an understatement. Rain was beating down on Rome, and the yellow ochre of the buildings that lined the Piazza di Spagna reflected in the puddles of water that had quickly formed. Two carabinieri took shelter under the awning of a shop, but kept their eyes on the motley crowd and stared unashamedly at the women.

Giulia needed a break from everything and who better to take her mind off things but her good friend Marisa. Marisa had been her cheerful self on the phone and agreed to meet Giulia for lunch in a restaurant close to the Spanish steps.

They met at the crowded entrance of the *trattoria*, shook their umbrellas and warmly embraced each other just as the waiter came and led them to a table for two by the window.

They chatted animatedly about Marisa's husband who was working on a project in the Middle East, and about their daughter, Alessia, who had just turned thirteen and was proving to be a handful. They commented on the new mayor of Rome who threatened to turn the *centro storico* into a pedestrian zone and the former mayor who wanted to run for President. Marisa happily chatted on and Giulia tried to keep up with her friend but found herself drifting in and out of the conversation.

Realising she had been talking incessantly, Marisa put her hand on her friend's and leaning over said to her, "I am sorry, I talked and talked and I didn't even ask you how you are doing? I tell you every detail about my family life and you haven't told me about yourself! But you are looking well, so things must be all right?"

Giulia smiled at her friend and told her she was fine and that her new life in London kept her busy, but admitted to still missing Robert. They talked about Eric Hargrave whom Marisa had met at one of Robert and Giulia's dinner parties, and Giulia mentioned the police inspector who was in charge of the investigation.

"This Conti, how is he? Good-looking?"

"Early forties, tall, dark and well, almost handsome. Very direct, cautious, taciturn."

"Is he married?"

"Divorced, I think."

"And you like him?"

"Not the way you mean Marisa, but I enjoy his company."

"Great, then why don't you both come to dinner at my place tonight?"

"Another time maybe," Giulia said. "You must have already made plans for this evening."

"We have a few people coming over for dinner. And both Lucio and Alessia would be happy to see you. Can't say I'm not curious about your police inspector either. So, we'll wait for you at eight!"

"I can't just call him and invite him for dinner at your place."

"Giulia, if you won't, I will. Now, what's his number?"

And before Giulia could say anything more, Marisa had pulled out her phone, waiting for Giulia to dictate Conti's number.

After a brief exchange, Marisa, poker-faced, announced, "He'll come and pick you up around half-past seven," then handed the phone to Giulia smiling. "But he wants to say hello to you first."

Chapter 27

As he waited for Giulia, Donovan reread the introduction of Eric Hargrave's manuscript. He doubted Eric's claim to have deciphered what he called *The Language of Line*. In reality, the dealer had only skimmed through the manuscript, found it too technical and realised it was hardly a commercial text. He understood that without illustrations and references the manuscript was unlikely to be published.

Donovan remembered the day he had offered Eric Hargrave an exclusivity contract in exchange for a monthly stipend of four thousand pounds sterling. The artist had agreed without hesitation and offered to sign the contract then and there but Donovan had insisted he showed it to a lawyer before proceeding.

"So all the drawings I make from the time we sign this agreement will be yours?" he enquired politely, and Donovan explained it was what the agreement said and added, "At the end of the year we will see how many of your works I have sold and for how much. I will be entitled to keep fifty percent of the sales. The amount I pay you every month will then be deducted from your fifty percent share. The difference will be yours."

Eric had nodded, "It is quite generous of you. Thank you."

The first months had been uneventful. Eric produced the drawings he had promised and the dealer prepared the exhibition. A week before the opening he received an incredulous call from a representative of the British Association of Art Dealers who asked him without the usual reserve you would associate with the representative of such an established body, if he realised the trouble he was getting into by arranging an exhibition of Eric Hargrave's works. Donovan recalled the exact exchange of words as if it had just taken place.

"Mr. Donovan, I am told you intend to arrange an exhibition of works by Eric Hargrave. Please tell me this is not the case."

"You have been informed correctly. The opening is scheduled for next week."

The BADA spokesman continued in a rather patronising tone.

"Mr. Donovan, you are surely aware that Mr. Hargrave claimed he forged hundreds of Old Master drawings and could end up in jail at any time. If you associate your gallery with such a person of questionable morality you will only jeopardise your own reputation. I am sure you understand this."

Donovan, who had always felt marginalised by the British art dealers' community, reacted calmly.

"I represent Eric Hargrave and will exhibit his work. Although his drawings are done in the style of various Old Masters, he lays claim to each drawing. As to his going to jail, I doubt it. No one has yet attempted to take legal action against him despite the publication of his autobiography!"

"But the man is a criminal!" the spokesman shouted into the telephone.

"I will show his work," Donovan retorted.

The spokesman was left at a loss for words and instead repeated "the man is a criminal!" Donovan said, "I heard you the first time."

"Mr. Donovan, if you go ahead with this exhibition you will bring your profession into disrepute and your own reputation will be seriously damaged."

"I hear you," Donovan replied coldly.

"And BADA may decide to exclude you from our association!"

"Are you threatening me? Are you trying to blackmail me?" Donovan asked, slightly louder than he intended.

"I am only a spokesman, Mr. Donovan, and as such, I can only point out the risks of persisting in exhibiting Eric Hargrave. I am not threatening you."

"Good. In fact, I am giving an interview to the Times this afternoon. I will suggest they ask you for your opinion."

"That would be unwise, Mr. Donovan."

To which the gallery dealer replied mockingly, "What you should do is actually come and see the exhibition rather than give me lessons on morality. You may learn a thing or two about Old Masters' drawings."

That phone call had been only the first of a series. Several colleagues and friends pointed out that Donovan was gambling his career and reputation and asked whether it was worth it. Others supported the challenge he was taking on. He answered with confidence, unruffled by the criticisms and concerns. Obviously, he was well aware of the risk he was taking but, since he believed the publicity would do him more good than harm, did not alter his plans and opened the exhibition on time.

Donovan recognised Hargrave's talent and, like Hargrave, enjoyed a jab at the establishment.

Although the show had been only a limited commercial success, the St. George's Fine Art Gallery had certainly become more prominent. Donovan had made enemies but also gained new clients. Some shared his admiration for Hargrave's skill; others were more mercantile in their approach.

Eric had turned out to be less and less reliable. The new commissions he was given took longer and Donovan believed, without being able to prove it, that the artist continued to accept other projects not channelled through his art gallery.

The financial results at the end of the first year left Donovan with a deficit and when Eric asked how much he would be receiving at the end of their first year, the gallery owner replied curtly that he should be asking Eric for money and not the other way around.

Eric who had drunk too much at the time the conversation took place, laughed as if he had found Donovan's retort humorous.

Then, halfway into the second year of their arrangement, Donovan considered breaking their agreement. He postponed the discussion with Eric for several months, waiting for him to deliver the unfinished commissions, and in the end simply cancelled the monthly cheques. He subsequently received a letter from Eric stating that if payments were not resumed he was no longer beholden to respect the terms of his agreement with the gallery.

When Eric died suddenly, he left an important commission unfinished and left his heirs with the responsibility of discussing whether the contract between Eric Hargrave and the St. George's Fine Art Gallery had been breached or not.

Giulia was dressed conservatively, in a black pinstripe suit and white shirt. Although the meeting had been set up to discuss the exchange of Eric's manuscript for the painting in the manner of Canaletto, the dealer looked forward to seeing the young woman for reasons that had nothing to do with the deal. As soon as she entered, he locked the front door and pulled a chair out for his visitor saying, "So that we are not disturbed this time."

Giulia was about to answer but decided to ignore his ambiguous remark.

Donovan knew that Giulia possessed a sharp business mind as well as good judgment, and quickly realised that she was also focused and in control of the situation. She coolly dismissed his attempt at being flirtatious.

"Christopher, we have business to discuss, that's all. Don't play childish games."

Donovan made a face and raised his hands in resignation.

"Okay, fine with me."

Giulia wasted no time and asked him how he had obtained Eric's manuscript. He refused to answer the question, insisting it was unimportant.

"Did you read the manuscript?" she asked patiently.

"I skimmed through it," he admitted.

The young woman looked him straight in the eye.

"Then you know what is missing?" she continued.

"Missing?" Donovan tried to stall.

"The illustrations are missing. And in particular, a list of drawings he refers to in the last chapter."

This time, Donovan looked genuinely puzzled. He had not read anything about a list and he said so. Giulia smiled a little condescendingly.

"He only refers to the list in the last couple of paragraphs. I guess you did not read it through."

Donovan looked at her with renewed respect. She had spent less than half an hour going through the handwritten manuscript the last time she was in his gallery, and yet identified the essence of the book as well as what was crucially missing.

"I have no chance of finding the illustrations or the list without knowing how the book got to you."

Although Donovan acknowledged her argument, he stubbornly refused to explain himself.

"Look, I cannot tell you where it came from. Let's say 'I plead the fifth amendment' as you say in the States."

Giulia glared at him. For a brief moment she considered telling him that the Italian police might want to ask him the same question, but she held back.

"If I tell you where the Canaletto is, you then give me the manuscript. Is this our agreement then?"

Relieved that Giulia was dropping her line of questioning, he confirmed it was indeed their agreement.

"It is with the Italian police at the *Commissariato* in Trastevere."

The air of disbelief on Donovan's face was quickly replaced by a hard stare and clenched jaw.

"How the hell did it end up at the police station?" he snapped.

"No idea," Giulia lied. "It may have been confiscated by the police, but under what circumstances, I am not sure."

So violently did Donovan fiddle with his pencil he snapped it in half.

"And how did you come about the painting, may I ask?"

Giulia shrugged. "The police wanted to ask me some questions and showed it to me."

"But why you? What questions did they ask you?"

"I was at Eric's funeral and they had found correspondence between Eric and me at his apartment."

"What exactly did they want to know?"

"If I knew Eric's friends, who he saw often. They put a few names to me; some I had heard of, others were complete strangers. I was not really able to help too much in that area."

"Are you sure the painting they are holding is…is mine? I mean, by Eric?"

"I believe it came from Eric's studio," Giulia replied calmly, selective with the information she volunteered.

Donovan suddenly looked under a lot of strain and repeated his question: "What did they want to know?"

Giulia made a face and raised her right hand palm up to signify she had no answer.

"I was allowed to take a photograph of the painting," Giulia said as she reached into her bag. She handed the picture to Donovan.

The print was not of a very good quality and the flash had bounced off the top right hand corner, creating a white blur that masked part of the painting, but Donovan nodded and said it was the one he was looking for.

"You could try and claim it from the police in Rome, although…."

"Although?"

"Although you should probably get in touch with Eric's heirs first. The police are likely to give them the painting."

Donovan stretched and swept his right hand through his hair.

"Oh, shit! I'm not exactly popular with that bunch."

"I'm sure they can be reasonable, if you are."

He looked out the window, weighing up different options in

silence. Then he turned back to face Giulia, his face devoid of expression.

"Now that you know where the painting is, can I please have the manuscript?" she asked calmly and matter-of-factly.

Donovan chuckled and shook his head.

"You have been very clever Giulia, but I am not sure you are telling me the whole truth, so maybe I should hang on to it for a little while longer."

Giulia was taken aback, not expecting Donovan to go back on his word. After all, there was nothing he could do with the manuscript and Giulia was not in a position to deliver the painting to him, even if she wanted to. She glared at him icily.

"I guess it was wrong of me to assume you would behave like a gentleman," she said.

He shook his head, and smiled. "Let's just say that there are a few things I need to check out first before I give you the manuscript. If what you have just told me is correct, the book is yours."

"I've told you the truth. I've told you what you wanted to know."

He shrugged. "I'm sure you did, but you can't blame me for wanting to check. Is Eric's brother aware of the painting's location?"

Giulia pushed back her chair and stood up. She was furious and allowed her emotions to dictate what she was about to say.

"Christopher, I will expect you to hand me the manuscript this week. It will give you plenty of time to check that what I have told you is correct. If you don't, I will do everything I can to delay the return of your "Canaletto". I believe it is a lot more important to you than the manuscript is to me."

His smile enraged Giulia.

"And before the painting is returned to you I will make sure that it is well photographed and documented. It will make a great news item. 'The last masterpiece by the Prince of Forgers,' don't you think?"

The smile vanished from Donovan's face, and Giulia knew she had made her point.

He went over to the door, unlocked it, and held it open for Giulia to leave.

As she brushed against him on her way out, he grabbed her right arm with force and coldly said, "If I see anything in the press, I will burn the bloody manuscript, rather than give it to you. Be warned!"

Chapter 28

It was not the Roman Colosseum and it was a different kind of battle, but the atmosphere was tense and the two Roman gladiators were Conti and his chief.

As of late, Conti's presence was enough to put the *Commisario* in a bad mood and he would have liked nothing better than to exile him as far from Rome as he could. The island of Pantelleria, halfway between Italy and Libya, was probably the most distant location he could think of, and would do just fine. But the inspector seemed to ride his chief's anger as a surfer rode a wave; the more agitated and angry his chief was, the calmer Conti seemed to become.

The inspector had been pursuing his investigation into the Hargrave case obstinately, against the order of his superior. Instead of working on the robbery case of the *Cavagliere* himself, he had appointed two junior investigators to do the job.

"Conti, I, assign inspectors to a case, not you. Who do you think you are?"

Conti did his best to look surprised. "I did not assign them, *Capo*. I only asked for their help since I am quite busy. After all you did ask me to help train them, didn't you?"

"Don't try to twist things around, you're not a lawyer, you are a cop and you are supposed to follow direct orders!" the *Commisario* shouted, hitting the desk with the palm of his right hand to emphasise the words "direct orders".

"Well, you asked me to look into the robbery and I am doing just that," Conti protested.

The *Commissario* was at a loss for words and looked away in exasperation.

"Anyway, as I was saying, we have questioned Monticello, the owner of an art gallery in Trastevere, who stole a painting in the style of Canaletto done by Hargrave. He was caught trying to bring the painting into Switzerland. He has a motive, he knew Eric and, we know, was with him the evening before his death."

His chief looked at Conti reluctantly. As it happened, his mother was Venetian and the mention of Canaletto, who was known above all for his views of Venice, caught his attention. He asked about the painting and insisted on seeing it at once. Conti complied graciously and led his chief to the depository where the painting was stored. The *Commissario* thought himself an art expert and inspected the painting, its frame, noted the various stamps and faded labels on the back of the artwork before pronouncing his verdict.

"I am impressed," he said.

He then took another look at the painting, searching for a signature, finding none.

"Are you sure this is by Eric Hargrave?" he asked sternly.

The inspector explained that it was, based on not only Monticello's statements but on the information Giulia had given him.

"He was talented, that I have to admit," the *Commissario* said.

This would be a good time to ask, Conti thought.

"In connection with this ah…painting, I would need to talk to Hargrave's heirs since they are now the rightful owners, being the beneficiaries."

Still admiring the painting, his chief absent-mindedly agreed to Conti's suggestion.

"And of course it would be a good idea to speak to Mr. Donovan who ordered this painting from Hargrave," Conti continued. In the absence of a reaction he went on. "And the best way would be for me to make a quick trip to London…this week."

At first he thought that the *Commissario* had not been listening as he had merely mumbled something that sounded like "of course". But the *Commissario* finally looked away from the splendid view of Venice, glanced quickly at Conti and shook his head.

"Twenty-four hours in London is all you get. And when you come back, I want signed statements that prove this painting was done by Hargrave."

Conti was about to point out that he was hardly in a position to force anyone in England to make a statement but did not want to give his Chief a reason to change his mind. Instead, he pointed to the auction stamp on the back of the painting.

"He must have used an old canvas and probably an old frame as well, which is why it would be easy for someone to be fooled," the *Commissario* said more to himself than to Conti.

Conti only called Giulia when he arrived at Fiumicino. She

promised to make contact with Bernard Hargrave and to accompany him to Brighton. Conti also asked Giulia to arrange for an appointment with Donovan after the visit to Brighton. He stressed that it was imperative for him to meet with the gallery dealer. Giulia said she would ring him and let him know that they would be paying Donovan a visit. Conti thanked Giulia and was pleased that she sounded glad at the prospect of seeing him.

He looked at his watch, and took his place in the queue at the Alitalia check-in counters.. His gaze fell on an elderly English woman who was constantly looking behind her, her eyes moist. He strained to see what the woman was looking for and noticed a younger woman with a toddler in her arms, both blowing kisses in the woman's direction. Directly in front of him, a young Italian couple appeared to be in the middle of a heated argument. Behind him stood a corpulent businessman, who alternated between mopping his forehead and looking at his watch. He could have been Middle Eastern or Sicilian. The passenger-gazing had momentarily allayed Conti's fear of flying.

Once Conti had his boarding pass he strode directly to the security control and then to the boarding gate. He still had forty minutes to wait and looked around nervously. At the bar he bought *Il Messaggero* and ordered a coffee and an *amaro*. Conti worked methodically and the more time he spent on the case related to the mysterious death of Eric Hargrave, the more he was convinced that foul play was involved. He was of course aware that the odds in favour of his finding the culprit, or culprits, were not stacked in his favour. There were too many possible suspects for him to reasonably expect to find who was guilty, but as he had often noticed, the most obvious theories, the people closest to the victim usually provided the clues he needed. The names of Monticello and Donovan were linked by their interest in the "Canaletto", the painting that could have provided a motive. But murder? In the case of Monticello it was theft, in the case of Donovan he was not sure, but suspected the he might have intended to pass the painting off as a genuine work by the Venetian painter. If he had provided the 18th century canvas, Eric would have understood his intention, and maybe wanted to renegotiate his fee. Aware that his theory concerning Donovan was speculative, Conti intended to find out the truth from Donovan. Obviously, he was out of his jurisdiction and would need Giulia's help. He felt uncomfortable about getting her more involved than necessary, but she had offered to help, after all.

The flight to London arrived on time. He walked down to the Heathrow Express train which reached Paddington Station in twenty minutes. From there he took a black cab to the Kensington Close Hotel, off South Kensington High Street. He had not been in London for at least ten years but little seemed to have changed. More people perhaps, more foreigners like him on the streets, pockets of newly-built or rejuvenated luxurious housing with shabbier dwellings a few blocks away; but still the same incredibly busy feeling of a city that woke up early and went to sleep late.

The hotel had known better days and its clientele consisted mostly of tour groups that passed through the lobby and the restaurant in successive waves. Conti's room was oppressively small and its only window looked into a yard at the back of the next building. He wondered why the backs of most buildings in London were so neglected, the bricks streaked with black watermarks, drainpipes hanging loosely, broken windowsills and windows obscured with grime, while their façades were painted white, and brass plate addresses religiously polished, gleamed like mirrors.

London also brought back memories he would rather not remember. It was in a hotel room close to the busy shopping area of Oxford Street that his wife had told him she was thinking of leaving him; that he was always too busy for her for and for their son. The fact that she had chosen to tell him on the second day of their first vacation outside Italy in three years had then seemed incongruous. She had chosen a time when none of his defences were in place. He could hardly run away and pretend an emergency required his attention at the *Commissariato;* he was forced to face his wife for another two days.

Only when he was back in Rome did he allow himself to look back at his marriage. Conti realised that there were plenty of clues had he wanted to see them. He provided well for the family's needs but late nights at work, and weekends spent on a case, kept him away from them. There had been some heated arguments followed by periods of silence which Conti did not take too seriously. Filippo felt the absence of his father, and his wife sought comfort elsewhere. When she finally told him she was no longer in love with him and was seeing another man, a policeman, and, when he pointed out that it would end up the same way, she laughed. She said she had no intention of "ending up" with him. At which point Alberto Conti packed a suitcase and moved out.

It was a bitter separation and the aggressiveness with which his wife's lawyer had argued the divorce left him even more wary and taciturn. She had subsequently married a wealthy lawyer, who brought her several rungs up the social ladder, and, she now frequented the kind of people she had always aspired to rub shoulders with. Therefore, Conti could not understand why his ex-wife was still being vindictive ten years later.

He still had time to spare before his meeting with Giulia. He took a hot shower and put on a new shirt. She said they could meet at a restaurant on the rooftop of the Oxo Tower Wharf building. The concierge said he would need, at most, half an hour by taxi.

Chapter 29

The restaurant and brasserie of the Oxo Tower commanded one of the most spectacular views in London. On the tenth floor of an office tower block on the river Thames, it overlooked the lighted outline of the London Bridge to the right, Saint Paul's Cathedral, and several glass and steel structures from the City and Westminster and Big Ben to the left. He was about to step out onto the terrace to get a better look when he saw Giulia's reflection in the five metre floor to ceiling window.

He turned towards her, about to offer his hand, but she kissed him on the cheek and smiled.

"Tonight, you are my guest."

Conti protested, saying there was no way he could accept, but Giulia insisted.

"I will feel very uncomfortable if you don't allow me," he started to say.

Giulia gently interrupted him and said, "In London, it is not unusual for a woman to invite a friend for dinner."

"I guess in Rome it is different," Conti sighed.

They stepped out onto the terrace where Giulia pointed in the direction of the dome of St. Paul's and said they had the same view from the rooftop of Seldom House, but of course, from a different angle.

Giulia had been lucky to get a table for two by the window, a last minute cancellation they told her over the phone. The fact that Giulia had been a guest at the brasserie on several occasions, entertaining Seldom House clients, could have helped.

The waiter came with two glasses of champagne and Giulia asked Conti whether he was familiar with London, and before he knew it, he found himself telling her about his last visit, many years ago, with his ex-wife and the divorce that followed.

"Let's hope you take back better memories of London this time," she said.

"It already is, thanks to you," Conti said raising his glass. "To you, to me, to us."

Giulia raised her glass but wondered about the ambiguity in those six simple words.

They ordered their starters and a bottle of white wine, followed by Dover sole with chickpea, chorizo and squid, an unusual combination but an interesting and pleasing flavour Conti had to admit.

"Giulia, have you told the Hargraves about the Canaletto?"

"Yes," she said.

"How did they react?"

"Bernard did not say very much, even when I told him Donovan had a claim on the painting."

Conti looked at her, noticing her hesitation.

Giulia continued, "I also told Donovan. He was clearly unhappy that the painting was still in Rome, and at a police station!"

Over dessert and coffee they shared stories, laughed at jokes, exchanged views, and talked about themselves, like two carefree spirits with all the time in the world. Many of the tables were being cleared and Conti noticed that they were among the last customers in the restaurant. It was well past midnight.

"I didn't realise it was so late," he said.

Giulia said she always slept late but agreed they should leave.

"I'll pick you up at the hotel at eight and we'll drive straight to Brighton to meet Bernard Hargrave," she said.

"And the rest of the brothers and sisters?"

"Bernard is really the one who has taken charge. If he agrees, the others tend to follow. He's just out of hospital and is still a bit weak."

"You don't mind driving me there? We could take the train if you prefer?" Conti offered.

"I don't mind, and I am starting to like Bernard Hargrave, so I'd like to see how he's doing."

"What kind of man is he?"

"Very quiet and unassuming but also a bit of a control freak. He's retired, was an accountant or a civil servant I believe."

"Married?"

"A widower. He lives in a modest terraced house. Two of his sisters live in the area. Bernard is very cautious, very conservative, and I suspect, he will be intimidated by the presence of a policeman."

Conti smiled and held her hand for a few seconds.

"And are you intimidated by a policeman?" he asked teasingly.

She smiled at him sweetly without answering his question.

"I hope you enjoyed the evening." she said as she released her hand from his and retrieved her credit card from the tray.

Bernard Hargrave was on his own when Giulia and Inspector Conti arrived at his home in Brighton. He explained that his sister had to attend some social function and would be back later in the afternoon. Giulia inquired after his health and offered to prepare tea, which he was grateful to her for, and she went into the kitchen while the two men sat opposite each other in the living room.

"Mr. Hargrave, I want you to know that I am not here on official business. I mean, I cannot question anyone and any statement you make to me would not be accepted in Italy. But I thought it was a good idea if we met and I could tell you at what stage we are at with the investigation," Conti said.

"Thank you for being candid, Mr. Conti."

"No problem."

Giulia interrupted them with the teapot and mugs. She poured three cups and sat down on a leather chair between the two sofas.

"I believe that your brother, Eric, may have been killed. Perhaps it was an accident but one thing is sure, he had enemies."

Conti paused. Bernard nodded gravely.

"We have many possible suspects so the investigation could take some time. And there are some other characters I still have to identify who may be involved," Conti continued.

"I will be glad to help if I can, of course. Eric's death was very traumatic to all of us."

"Do you know Signor Monticello?"

Bernard nodded, remembering having met him at Eric's funeral in Anticoli.

"Has he spoken to you since the funeral?" Conti asked.

"No. Why do you ask?"

"Well, Signor Monticello apparently visited your brother's studio in Rome and stole a large oil painting. He also had various art objects, statues, tablets, that he intended to smuggle out of Italy and into Switzerland."

"My God! Are you sure?"

Conti gave the details of Monticello's arrest and summarised his interrogation.

"Monticello will be prosecuted for attempted smuggling, of course, but I would like to put him under more pressure."

"Do you suspect he had something to do with Eric's death?" Bernard looked shocked.

"He was possibly the last man to see Eric alive."

Eric's brother sat back and rubbed his forehead slowly.

"Are you all right?" Giulia enquired.

He nodded.

"It is just...there's so much to take in and deal with. Eric's death, the articles in the newspaper, some people...I am not sure who to trust."

"I told the inspector about Littlejohn's call and visit. I hope you don't mind," Giulia intervened.

"No, no, of course I don't mind."

"It is possible that Monticello stole more works from Eric, and Littlejohn's Michelangelo drawing could be in his possession."

"You think so?" Bernard asked Giulia, but it was Conti who replied.

"We're not sure, but if you ask the police to investigate, I will be able to obtain a search warrant and check."

"Of course, of course. What should I do?"

Conti explained that he should write a letter to the Trastevere *Commissariato* requesting an investigation and describing the works thought to be lost, including the drawing Littlejohn claimed.

"This Littlejohn was a very unpleasant fellow," Bernard stressed.

Conti cast a quick glance at Giulia and asked for a description of the drawing.

Bernard gathered his thoughts together and spoke slowly, "Littlejohn describes it as a sheet of studies with a Madonna and Child. The Madonna looking down at the Child, and the Child looking up at her." Bernard paused trying to remember what else Littlejohn had said. "Ah, yes, he also mentioned two sketches of an infant in the top right hand corner of the drawing. And on the back there was a sketch of a seated male figure in the centre of the sheet." Bernard smiled, pleased with himself for having remembered the last detail.

"How big is the drawing?" Giulia asked.

"Twelve inches by eight if I remember right," Bernard answered.

Conti looked up, unfamiliar with measurements in inches.

"About thirty by twenty centimetres," Giulia clarified.

Alberto Conti wanted to ask about Eric's friends, about his will, the works that were missing but Bernard was visibly tired and Giulia suggested they go.

On the drive back to London Conti was silent. Giulia asked him whether something was disturbing him, and whether her suggestion to leave Bernard's house was premature. Conti unconsciously felt for the piece of paper he had in the pocket of his jacket. Bernard's handwritten request to carry out further investigations on Monticello.

"No, no," he replied. "I'm sorry if I gave you that impression. I'm just thinking of what I have to do when I get back to Rome."

When Giulia had phoned to make the appointment with Donovan she had only mentioned that there was a new development with his Canaletto and had to see him urgently. He said he would wait for her in his gallery and she could hear the eagerness in his voice.

Traffic was fluid and they were in Mayfair in good time. They went straight to Donovan's gallery and rang the bell. Donovan's face dropped when Giulia introduced Conti, but he regained his composure quickly and asked the Inspector how he could help.

"We found a painting in the possession of an Italian smuggler. The person who was stopped at the Swiss border claims it was painted by Eric Hargrave. Since you have been Eric's dealer for several years I thought you might be able to identify the painting in question."

Donovan shot an angry glance at Giulia.

"Do you have a photo?" he asked.

Conti pulled out a photograph from his coat pocket and placed it on the dealer's desk. Donovan looked at it, but did not pick it up.

"It was painted by Hargrave. It is a work commissioned by one of my clients and Eric was paid for it. I am glad to see he had finished it," he added sarcastically.

Conti studied the dealer's reaction carefully.

"I will need a written statement from you that confirms you commissioned Mr. Hargrave to do this painting."

Donovan shrugged. If it was the only way to retrieve the Canaletto, he had no choice. He wrote a few lines on his gallery's stationery, signed and stamped it. He handed it to Conti.

"When can I have the painting?"

"We will contact Eric Hargrave's heirs to let them know when the painting will be ready for shipment to England. It will take a week or two I believe."

Donovan was about to protest that he could not wait that long, but thought better of it.

Chapter 30

Monticello's apartment was on the top floor, the *attico*, of an elegant building fronting the Ponte Sisto on the Lungotevere, with a large terrace and a view over the Tiber. The high ceilings, unusual for a top floor apartment, and large arched windows gave a feeling of space that even the multifarious pieces of antique furniture and artworks in the living room did not diminish.

Alberto Conti, however, was in no mood to appreciate the elegance of the art dealer's home. Still panting from the climb to the fifth floor, he had handed the search warrant to Monticello and stepped in without being invited, ignoring his protests. The apartment was large and he estimated that they would need a couple of hours to search it thoroughly. He did a quick tour of the place and then assigned different rooms to his team.

Monticello tried to reach his lawyer but only got a busy tone. He slammed the receiver down, and turned around to catch the inspector watching him with a frown.

"You'll have plenty of time to call your lawyer. We'll be here for a while," he announced drily.

Monticello bit his lip and turned away mumbling something about being harassed by the police.

"*Complimenti*, a very nice place. Business must be good," Conti commented before leaving Monticello alone in the living room.

One room, in direct contrast to the living room, was spartan in furnishings. Obviously used as an office by the art dealer, Conti noted. A sixteenth-century bookcase in walnut lined two of the walls, filled with art reference books. In the opposite corner of the study stood a massive desk made of dark exotic wood . The desk was orderly with a leather pad, a bronze pen holder and a matching lamp on top of it; one large oil painting occupied the white wall. The only other piece of furniture was a print cabinet.

Conti was struck by the marked difference of the two rooms and wondered which one of them would give him an insight into the mind of Monticello.

He sat behind the desk and tried to open the drawers but they were locked. He stood up, abandoning his attempt, and surveyed the books, at first simply taking in the wide range of titles, noticing that a vast majority dealt with Old Masters, then picking several volumes at random. An original of the "Stories by Italian Artists" by Vasari caught his attention. On the next shelf, an entire row was filled with treatises on sculpture and the shelf above held various histories of print-making and engraving. The library would have met with the approval of Eric Hargrave, he thought suddenly.

He did not have to ask the dealer to open the drawers of his desk as he was already standing in the study with a bundle of keys, looking ill at ease.

"What are you looking for?" he asked the inspector.

Conti shook his head, took the keys from Monticello and sat in front of the desk without answering him.

"If you tell me what you are looking for…you will not have to waste more time than necessary," Monticello continued hesitantly.

The policeman looked up sharply.

"Do you have more stolen artworks here, Monticello?"

"*Inspettore*, of course not!" Monticello protested, looking offended.

"There, you see! You cannot help me."

The inspector pulled out the first drawer and went through it methodically, placing each object on the desk before putting them back into the drawer. Once he was finished with the first, he proceeded in the same manner with the second, then the third.

Monticello stood there, at the centre of the room, transfixed, watching the systematic search.

Once he was finished with the desk, Conti transferred his attention to the library, lifting books, three or four at a time, to see whether there was anything hidden behind them.

After a while, the dealer seemed to come out of his stupor and pointed to a print cabinet that stood behind the desk. Conti turned and nodded.

"I will get to that in a moment," Conti said, refusing to be hurried or distracted in his methodical search.

Resigned to his present fate, Monticello's shoulders slumped and he left the room. Conti half smiled to himself knowing he was slowly breaking down Monticello's guard. He continued with his thorough search of the bookcase and, finding nothing, walked over to the mahogany print cabinet and carefully pulled out the first drawer.

Various folders were neatly stacked on top of each other with a label to indicate their contents. The hand-written labels read, *Roma antica*, *Vedute di Roma*, *Via Appia*, *Il Vaticano,* then various Italian cities from Ancona to Venezia. The second drawer shifted the focus from cities to plants and animals as well as medical and scientific objects. The prints varied in size and state of conservation. Many appeared to have been torn out of books, some were foxed or showed small holes bored by insects, and nearly all were annotated in pencil with a date and a provenance. Monticello obviously kept accurate records and was a man who liked precision and order, not qualities Conti had associated with him.

At the bottom of the third drawer a cardboard portfolio was simply marked with the letters, "O.M.". Inside, Conti discovered a dozen drawings on paper and vellum, unsigned and seemingly important. The inspector shook his head in disbelief. "O.M." for Old Masters. Not exactly the most cryptic description. But then, Monticello had probably not expected his apartment to be searched. Conti carried the portfolio to the living room where the dealer, who had finally reached his lawyer, was in the middle of an animated phone conversation. Conti carefully placed the portfolio with the drawings on the table, in front of Monticello.

The dealer instantly looked up and nodded before ending his conversation.

"Where do these drawings come from?" Conti asked.

"They belong to me," was all Monticello offered as a reply.

"You didn't answer my question."

"I don't have to," the dealer retorted.

Conti looked exasperated and flipped the portfolio open, lifting each drawing, one after the other, and repeated his question each time. Monticello, who was then under instructions from his lawyer not to answer questions, just shrugged his shoulders a couple of times.

The inspector closed the portfolio and glared at him.

"Are any of these drawings by Eric Hargrave?"

The question appeared to unsettle Monticello who started to answer, but thought better of it. Monticello's arrogance, bolstered by the conversation with his lawyer, irritated Conti and strengthened his resolve to discover what the dealer was hiding.

"With or without your lawyer, you will have to tell me where these drawings come from."

Monticello sat back in his chair.

"I've told you, they're mine, and that is all I am ready to say about them."

"Can you describe the drawings inside this portfolio?" Conti asked suddenly.

"Of course I can."

"Good, good. Because some of these drawings are being claimed by someone else."

Monticello frowned and reacted instantly.

"That's highly unlikely!" he exclaimed.

"Ah, it is not likely, you say! You probably think that Eric Hargrave hadn't shown them to anyone before you helped yourself to them in his studio?"

Monticello's eyes betrayed his growing contempt for the needling inspector; he had to hold back the urge to snap at him.

The doorbell rang, and one of the policemen walked to open the door to a small bearded man, out of breath, who introduced himself as *Avvocato* Ortolani.

He nodded at Monticello and abruptly turned to address Conti.

"I am representing the interests of Signor Monticello," he pronounced.

"Alberto Conti, criminal inspector," the police officer said in turn. "I guess you would like to see the search warrant."

The lawyer nodded and walked towards Conti, hand outstretched. With the other hand, he took the glass of water that Monticello offered him.

Conti looked at his watch and noticed that less than ten minutes had elapsed since Monticello had called the lawyer.

"Is your office in the building, *avvocato*?" he asked.

"No, I was in the area visiting another client," the lawyer explained.

"What is Signor Monticello charged with?" he then asked.

"Smuggling artworks out of Italy, and now most probably, theft."

"The smuggling charge I will not comment on, but theft? Theft of what and from whom?"

During the exchange Monticello affected to be an uninterested observer and took an exaggerated interest in the pattern of his shirt.

"Theft of drawings from Eric Hargrave's studio just after his death, or just before his death actually."

"And you can prove that these drawings belonged to Eric Hargrave?"

"Some of them, yes."

Monticello stopped studying his shirt.

"And how can you prove it?" the lawyer continued.

"We have a filed complaint from the owners, with precise descriptions of some of the works."

The lawyer stole a glance in the direction of his client who shook his head.

"If the owner is dead, how could he complain?"

"His heirs did…among others."

"Among others? Can you be more specific?"

"We can continue this discussion at the police station."

Conti turned to the art dealer and waited for him to stand up, which Monticello did rather reluctantly.

"But you assured me…" he started, looking at his lawyer.

"I will follow you to the police station, don't worry. I am sure we can clear up this misunderstanding in no time."

"Can't we clear it here?" he whined.

Conti grasped Monticello's arm firmly, startling him.

"You heard *l'avvocato*. Let's go."

Alberto Conti walked behind the art dealer. He noticed that Monticello was not using his cane as he descended the steps, holding on to the banister rail, his limp even more apparent. He seemed lost, an almost vulnerable figure, and looked nervously ahead. But Conti refused to be taken in. The dealer had struck him as a calculating con man, always searching for an angle for a way to obtain what he wanted by whatever means. And a good actor as well. But Monticello's luck seemed to be running out and as he slowly reached the bottom of the steps Conti was all the more aware of this.

Chapter 31

Although his reputation rested on the study of artists who lived hundreds of years ago, Tarquin Littlejohn demonstrated a strong reluctance to examine his own past, or even worse, to be questioned about it. His lawyers were told flatly that his family background was of no relevance to the court case and he refused to answer any questions in this regard.

Littlejohn fetched the bottle of malt whisky from the drinks cabinet and poured himself a generous drink. The bottle was almost empty and a second bottle, completely empty, stood to remind him how he had spent the last evenings.

In an alcohol fuelled moment of introspection, he allowed himself to reflect on the lack of recognition he had suffered in England. Twelve years at one of London's most prestigious museums had led Littlejohn to a confrontation with the Head of the museum, who had made it very clear he would progress no further. The stinging comments still rang in his ears. "We really appreciate your hard work and expertise, old chap. You have a good academic record, no doubt, but you lack social skills and contacts in the right places."

Littlejohn fully understood what he meant. He could choose a new name and affect an upper class accent but there was nothing he could change about the reality of his working class background.

The approach of the Silverstein Museum, almost two years later, had been the first good news in a long time. He grabbed the opportunity with both hands. When he moved to California, the art establishment was still fiercely debating Eric Hargrave's autobiography.

The Silverstein Museum was a landmark of the West Coast. Perched on a natural ridge at the foot of the Santa Monica mountain, the museum complex seemed designed to absorb the California sunshine, a museum for sun worshippers, rather than to house an impressive collection of classical sculpture and art, mostly from Europe, pre-twentieth century. On his arrival at the Los Angeles airport he was driven directly to the Silverstein Museum in the early hours of the morning. The sun was rising behind the 110-acre complex that seemed to grow from the hillside as the limousine glided along the San Diego freeway.

Tarquin Littlejohn acknowledged the philosophical challenges of contemporary art and modern architecture but enjoyed neither and his first impression of the Silverstein was critical; too big, too bright, too flashy, like a Hollywood stage set. He concluded, a bit prematurely, that the museum would overshadow its content. Even the cordial reception arranged by the Director of the Museum and two of the Board members from the Trust was overdone, he felt. Little by little, however, he came to change his opinion about the museum and its design. For instance, many of the Centre's walls were made of glass, allowing sunshine to illuminate the interior. But to avoid damaging the artworks, special filters cooled some of the glass panels on one floor while computer-adjusted shades on another regulated the intensity of light.

The Museum was composed of five pavilions interconnected by bridges and separated by courtyard spaces, fountains and vegetation. Because the complex could not be more than two stories high, all the buildings extended underground, where artworks could be stored or transported safely from one area to another.

Four collections were housed at the Silverstein: Greek and Roman antiquities, French decorative arts, photography and European paintings from pre-19th century. Littlejohn was offered the position of curator for the European paintings collection because the Trust wanted to expand its collection of Renaissance paintings and Professor Tarquin Littlejohn came with the best possible references, contacts with European museums and auctions houses where the most interesting works were to be found. While in London, his social standing had been considered a handicap, whereas in California, he was welcomed because of his knowledge and experience.

The Silverstein Trust was very well funded and supported his proposals enthusiastically. During his first years, he was responsible for several major acquisitions on behalf of the Trust, mounted two major exhibitions. and authored several publications on the study of Italian drawings, including Pontormo and Luisini. He also slept with two of his colleagues, several junior intern staff and the personal assistant of one of the other curators, drawing the ire of several of his colleagues and several counselling sessions with the Head of Human Resources who tried, in vain, to convince him that sexual harassment was a very serious legal matter in America and that he ought to exercise more restraint and discernment.

Littlejohn knew that his contribution was appreciated by the Board of Trustees and became more aloof in his dealings with his colleagues and employees. After three years in California, he had made several enemies and, although he appeared blissfully unaware of it, his tenure was the object of stormy discussions at meetings of the Board of Directors of the Trust, between those who disliked him on a personal level and the Directors who pointed at his achievements.

From the moment he joined the Silverstein he started to work on the compilation of Italian drawings held by the Museum that would be included in the production of an official catalogue about two years later. More than a mere list, museum catalogues are considered reference books of scholarly value and the curator is expected to comment extensively on the collection, shed new light on the work of certain artists and introduce original ways of presenting the artworks exhibited. Littlejohn scrutinised the drawings in the collection of the museum and in particular the Old Masters acquired by the curator who had preceded him, Christopher Gardner, who was now working for one of the major museums in New York.

In a letter he wrote jointly to the Director of the Museum and to the Board of Trustees in his third year with the Silverstein, Littlejohn unequivocally stated that at least half a dozen Old Master drawings in the collection were forgeries. He pointed out that four had been acquired by his predecessor and announced that he would change the attribution of these drawings in his catalogue. Needless to say his letter caused consternation among the Trustees and deep resentment from the Museum Director whom he had informed previously and who had asked him not to do or say anything until more analysis had been carried out.

Littlejohn could clearly remember his discussion with Tom Arnold, the Director of the Museum, and Mary Goddard who sat on the Board of Trustees and was the senior partner of a well-known law firm. Looking at the concern and embarrassment on the faces of Arnold and Goddard, Littlejohn failed to understand their reaction. Where he expected contrition and acknowledgement of his expertise he instead faced acrimony and legal censorship.

The discussion had started well enough, Littlejohn thought, with Mary Goddard acknowledging both his contribution to the Silverstein and his expertise especially in Old Master drawings.

"Tarquin, the museum is glad to have you and appreciates the honesty of your approach. If you have doubts about the attribution of some of our works it is indeed your duty to let us know."

Littlejohn nodded solemnly.

"This is exactly how I see it."

Goddard cast a glance at Tom Arnold as if giving him a cue, and Arnold cleared his throat.

"However, we have a dilemma on our hands, and now that you have officially written to me and the Board of Trustees, this dilemma could turn into a serious legal and financial risk."

Littlejohn understood exactly what the Director meant. If the museum published his conclusion on the six drawings, the reputation of his predecessor would be damaged and the Director himself would have to take the blame for using funds to acquire works that were not genuine. Tom Arnold had held his position for close to ten years and rumour had it that he and the previous curator, Christopher Gardner, were very close to each other.

"Risk or not, it is my duty to let you know what, in my expert opinion, I consider an undeniable conclusion."

"It certainly is your duty," the lawyer said.

"But maybe it is the conclusion itself we should talk about," Tom Arnold stated without looking up at Littlejohn.

The sun was setting and a golden hue brushed through the blinds of the meeting room, colouring a series of black-and-white photographs that lined the wall behind the Director and the representative of the Trust. Littlejohn sat facing them, his back to the sun, unsure how to take the Director's last comment.

"Are you questioning my expertise?" he asked almost in disbelief.

"Let us say that, before we reach a final conclusion, we should test these drawings and, get a second opinion. In view of the risks involved."

"I am certain of my conclusion. You employed me for my expertise and there is no one else in California who can give you a more qualified opinion."

Littlejohn's cheeks reddened slightly as he crossed his arms.

"This is art, not an exact science by any means and it is not unreasonable to discuss your opinion before accepting it as fact," Goddard intervened in an attempt to be conciliatory.

Littlejohn kept his arms crossed and said he was ready to discuss his findings with whoever, but he was not likely to change his mind.

Goddard and Arnold looked at each other briefly before the lawyer concluded their discussion.

"Tarquin, we must ask you not to communicate your conclusions with anyone else outside the people you wrote to for the time being. The Board needs to look at the implications before anything else. Do we have an understanding?" she said, looking straight into Littlejohn's eyes.

"Fine, I will wait, and hope that the author of the drawings will not claim them as his."

Mary Goddard, who was about to stand up, stopped and bent forward.

"Did I understand you correctly? Are you suggesting you know who did these alleged forgeries?"

Littlejohn shrugged, "I'll keep this to myself for the time being."

A few weeks later, however, he found out through the personal assistant of the curator for photography that Christopher Gardner had been at the museum. The young woman explained that he had been asked to look over some artworks the Silverstein Museum wanted to acquire. But Littlejohn instantly understood why Gardner had been summoned. He also realised that his troubles were far from over.

Chapter 32

Giulia Vasari was drinking a *caffe latte* at a café in Kensington and reading a newspaper when her mobile phone rang. Willie, Eric Hargrave's last boyfriend, announced without preamble that he had just arrived in London and wanted to see her.

The relationship between Eric Hargrave and Willie had seemed doomed from the start. While Eric was refined and scholarly, Willie had barely scraped through high school and spoke poor English. Eric's apartment in the centre of Rome was without a kitchen, badly heated and contained neither a radio nor a television but his bookshelves bent under the weight of rare art books and stone sculptures. Willie read the tabloids and comic strips, watched sitcoms assiduously and dreamt of setting-up a pig farm.

Yet, Eric and Willie stayed together for the last years of Eric's life. He installed a kitchen, bought a small television, and promised to help fund his pig farm. Willie cooked for him, bought gold trinkets whenever Eric gave him money and flew back and forth between Canada, where he hoped to obtain a residence permit, Rome, to be with his "big baby" as he affectionately called Eric, and the Philippines, where he dreamt of establishing his farm.

Eric's friends generally ignored Willie, treating him as just a passing infatuation, and Willie did not seem to mind. He often waited on Eric and his friends, sat back and paid no attention to anyone but Eric, who once told Giulia, "At my age and in my condition I should be glad that someone is still interested in me!" He was well aware that Willie was mainly interested in him because of what he could get from him, but accepted it nevertheless.

Giulia had not been particularly close to Willie but recognised that he had taken care of the artist in the best way he could. She expected him to be in some sort of trouble, probably in need of money, but was also curious to find out why he wanted to meet her. Perhaps, she thought, he will know something about Eric's book.

They had agreed to meet in front of Kensington High Street tube station, as soon as Willie made it from Heathrow airport. Giulia looked at her watch and figured she had an hour to kill. It was muggy outside and clouds threatened to break. She picked up her bag and left the café, walking briskly towards Kensington Gardens.

She strode along the Broad Walk of Kensington Gardens as far as Bayswater Road and turned round, deep in thought. Joggers ran past her in bright t-shirts pasted to their backs by darkened patches of sweat. Teenagers played football between the trees under the disapproving eyes of two mothers pushing baby carriages. Clusters of young people sat around a crate of beer while others stood arguing with each other. A world of mundane trivialities where lives crossed each other without having much effect on anyone else except perhaps at the precise moment that eyes met, a ball was kicked too far and bounced off a pram, or teenagers whistled at a young girl who walked past them.

Giulia reached the entrance of the tube station at the same time as the first big drops broke from the clouds and crashed onto the pavement. Willie emerged from the crowd with a bag slung over his shoulder and waved at her. He seemed lost and a bit hesitant. Outside, the storm had reached tropical proportions and sheets of water washed across the road in waves. She kissed him on both cheeks.

"Willie, it's quite a surprise to see you here in London."

"I need to talk to you, Giulia."

She smiled and suggested they run to the nearest café.

"Are you hungry?" she asked.

"Not really, but I would like a coffee."

They ran from the station and pushed open the door of a small Italian restaurant, both of them dripping wet. The waiter smiled and commented aloud, "The pizza here is so good people run to us! Welcome to Peppino's!"

Giulia and Willie sat at a table decked with a red and white chequered tablecloth that looked onto the street. Outside the rain continued to pour and the street was empty of people. The waiter brought two coffees and asked whether they wanted a menu.

"Now that we are here, I am a bit hungry. Will you share a pizza with me, Willie?"

"I don't know."

"Come on, we might have to stay here for some time unless you want another shower."

Willie made a face that could have passed for a yes.

Giulia was in no hurry to ask Willie why he wanted to talk to her. Instead she asked him about Canada, how he had spent the last few months and where he was heading. Willie was in his mid-thirties, dark skinned with a smiling face. Two thick gold chains dangled from his right wrist, and another hung from his neck. He looked tired, with bags under the almond shaped eyes that revealed his Asian background. He played nervously with his wristwatch.

After a few sips of the warm, soothing coffee, he settled down and became more communicative.

"I'm going back to the Philippines," he explained. "Canada's not for me. It's too cold."

"And what are you going to do now?" Giulia enquired, wondering if he intended to stay in London and maybe needed a place to crash.

"I'm flying back to Manila."

"And what about your farm?"

His eyes lit up.

"You remember? I will have a pig farm one day, you know!"

"I am sure you will. If you want it hard enough."

It was a bit like talking to a child, Giulia thought.

Willie seemed slightly embarrassed and looked down.

"I must tell you something Giulia. You were a friend of Eric's and you were always nice to me. The others are bad." He did not define "others" leaving it to Giulia's interpretation.

"Eric's family. He didn't like them. He wanted them to have nothing, but they got everything…everything. It's not right."

"It's the law, Willie. Since Eric did not leave a will his closest blood relatives inherited what he owned."

"What about me then? Do you think it's fair I got nothing?"

As he became more emotional, he lost some of his affectations. He raised his voice but his eyes were pleading for Giulia to agree with him.

Giulia sighed, "I agree it's not fair. Maybe if you talk to them they'll help you. They are not such bad people, just very different from Eric."

He crossed his arms and made a face.

"I will not talk to them. I have nothing to say to them. But Eric made a will. He showed me!"

Giulia frowned.

"Are you sure about this?"

"I am sure. It was in a black book that he took with him everywhere. He wrote important things in it and he said he wrote that I should be taken care of in the book."

"Where did he keep this book?"

"Not a book, you know. A notebook! A notebook with a black leather cover. He kept it in the drawer of his desk in Trastevere; in a locked drawer. He said many times that if something should happen to him I should take the notebook."

"You mean take it to a lawyer."

"He did not say. He only said to take it."

Eric's personal effects had been shipped to his brother's house in Brighton and it was possible that not everything had been checked. On the other hand, she knew that, while Eric was still in a coma in hospital, some of his so-called friends had entered his apartment, to search for a will.

"I can talk to Eric's brother," Giulia offered.

Willie's outburst seemed over. He rubbed his face wearily.

"Tired?"

"Yeah, a bit."

"When is your plane?"

"Tomorrow afternoon. But I'll have to get to the airport early as I left my suitcases in a deposit there."

She hesitated before asking, but felt compassion for the lover of her dead friend.

"Do you have a place to stay?"

Willie shrugged. Giulia offered to let him stay with her for the night and she noticed he was on the verge of tears.

When they reached her place he was wide awake and wanted to talk. He spoke of Eric's passion for the Old Masters, his unquenchable thirst for knowledge but also for wine.

"Many times I told him to stop drinking, and I even hid his wine bottles, but he found them anyway. I once tried diluting the wine with water, but when he found out he got very angry with me. Anyway, he went to the bar near the piazza where he did not have to pay."

Willie also said he did not like Rome, could not learn the language and found people noisy and chaotic. He preferred Canada, he explained, but it was too cold there.

"Eric always liked to joke. One day he told a journalist that he was not gay and had a son in London. He even showed him a photo but it was a photo of a friend's son who wanted Eric to paint his portrait."

Giulia smiled and remembered reading about Eric's alleged son in an English newspaper.

"Another time, he said, he had a brother who was an orthodox priest who lived in Rome."

"Well, he does have a brother who looks like a priest!" she laughed with him.

Willie spoke late into the night; about the launch of Eric's autobiography in Milan and of the group of angry Italians who shouted at him and threatened to take him to court. They were critics and art dealers who were upset that Eric's claims would bring the art world into disrepute.

"You know I was there, Willie?"

Willie ignored her comment and excitedly continued, "I am sure one of these people killed him! He said to me that if I stayed too long in Canada, I might come back to find him dead with his head broken. He said that! Really!"

"Well, the police are still investigating but they are not sure whether it was an accident or murder," Giulia said.

Willie became even more very animated. "Eric said he was going to give me enough money to start my pig farm. He said that if he behaved well, there would be a lot more money coming soon!"

"Did he tell you from where?"

"He said that he did something for an Italian customer, you know…something important," Willie said in almost hushed tones. "But that the Italian didn't want to pay enough money for it. So Eric said he was only giving him a photocopy until he got more money, and we laughed at that."

"A drawing?" Giulia was curious to hear more.

"I don't know, maybe, or a painting even."

"Do you know him?" Giulia asked.

"No," Willie hesitated, "Only that he owns a big gallery in Milan and he is a very rich man."

"Do you remember his name?"

"Something like Serra, no, more like Zenga I think."

Giulia reminded herself to tell Conti what Willie had just told her.

He spoke with admiration of Eric's trip to the USA and the fact that he was famous "even in California" but no, he did not know that Eric had been writing a new book before he died.

Willie was winding down after his third glass of cognac and started to yawn.

Giulia showed her guest to the second bedroom and went to wash the cups and glasses in the kitchen. Once she was finished, she sat on the sofa and stretched her legs. Could Willie have been mistaken and misunderstood Eric's comments about his notebook? Eric had his own way in dealing with practical matters. She remembered him stating that writing a will could hasten the inevitable. She remembered how he forgot to pay invoices, knowing a reminder would always follow. His line was cut off once a year, the building administrator had threatened to sue him for unpaid bills twice, and when the heating was switched off because he had not paid his gas bill he simply assumed the boiler had broken down and bought two electric heaters. Giulia and Robert had bought a second watercolour from Eric, a view of Rome from villa Borghese. When they picked it up at his apartment in Trastevere, and gave him the cash, Eric insisted on inviting them for lunch in a nearby restaurant, ordered the best wine available and left a generous tip for the waiter. "I don't like having too much money in my pocket. Money is meant to be spent," he said with a mischievous smile.

Chapter 33

It was evident that the ordeal of the few days days spent in jail had aged Giorgio Monticello, so much so that when he entered the interrogation room flanked by a policeman, Conti frowned and almost felt sorry for him. Gone was the arrogant look and the obsequious attitude; he now stooped, his bloodshot eyes suggesting he had not been sleeping well, and the effort he made to straighten up and look unconcerned when he saw the police inspector was short-lived.

Monticello sat at a table in front of Conti and kept his hands on his lap. He noted that the inspector was alone, which was unusual at this stage of the investigation where most of the evidence had already been collected and lay on the desk of the public prosecutor.

"Monticello, with the evidence we have against you, you are going to spend long enough in prison to either die there or go straight to an old age home on your way out."

Conti measured his words without aggression. Monticello looked up and said nothing.

"I have some questions, however, and depending on whether you answer them truthfully or not, you could end up in *Rebibbia* with the scum we hold there or in a less harsh environment."

Monticello nodded and suggested without conviction that his lawyer should be present.

"I have no tape recorder and no one is with me as you can see. We can consider this discussion an informal talk. If you prefer, we can make it more official and I will come back with someone from the prosecutor's office tomorrow. It is up to you."

Monticello shrugged which Conti interpreted as an agreement.

"The artworks we confiscated from you belonged to Eric Hargrave. According to your own statement you do not dispute this. Your lawyer argued that they were entrusted to you by the Englishman; however, you have not been able to substantiate this claim and we know that at least some of the objects were taken from Hargrave's studio and some from his apartment, after he was taken to the emergency unit at San Giacomo hospital.

Monticello started to protest but Conti raised his hand to indicate he was not finished speaking.

"What I would like to know is when you last saw Eric Hargrave, Signor Monticello."

"I've told you this already; we had dinner the night of his accident. We parted ways around ten as he had to get back early he said." Monticello looked utterly confused.

"Yes, you were seen having dinner with Eric Hargrave. But, you have presented no alibi for your whereabouts after dinner, and your apartment is not far from the place of the accident!"

Monticello felt Conti bearing down hard on him. Was he now also being accused of killing the Englishman?

"I have nothing to do with Eric's death, I swear!" Monticello frantically protested.

The inspector sat back and observed the accused with detachment.

"You have to believe me, inspector; I would never have harmed him. Despite what you think of me I am not a murderer. I am not a violent person, and besides I bought a lot of work from Eric. Why should I want to harm him?"

Conti did not believe the gallery owner was a murderer which is why he had staged the interview as an informal conversation, but he certainly was a thief. He had initially lied about meeting Hargrave on the evening of the 8th and it was very possible that the two had argued and that Eric had fallen or was pushed during an argument. If this was the case, Monticello could have been the one to call the emergency number, and of course left in a hurry, not wanting to be seen by the paramedics from the ambulance.

One thing troubled the inspector though: when did Monticello take the drawings and the artworks from Eric Hargrave? If he claimed he had taken them that fateful night, it would prove that he knew that Eric would not be returning home and so would incriminate him a little more.

Conti stared at Monticello and continued his line of question.

"What did you discuss over dinner?"

"He had agreed to exhibit lithographs and drawings in my gallery in March. The theme of the show was to be based on the Epic of Gilgamesh and he promised 25 to 30 images."

He hesitated, but Conti did not want to leave him any time to think or reconsider what answers to give.

"What did you argue about, Monticello?"

Instinct told him that a disagreement could have been the reason for the two men's encounter over dinner and he was right. The art dealer rubbed his temples and replied wearily: Eric had wanted to renegotiate the terms of their agreement; he suspected Eric had probably fallen behind in getting material ready for the exhibition.

"Why?"

"Because he was seen every day at the wine bar next to his apartment drinking until late at night. You see, his boyfriend was away and he was probably looking for company."

"So what exactly did you agree, or not agree to, over dinner?"

"I paid for dinner and I told him that when he delivered the first half of the drawings and lithographs I would buy two of them for cash."

"Was he happy with that?"

Monticello buried his face in his hands as he replied without looking at the police officer.

"He didn't disagree."

Conti considered Monticello's answer for a moment before pushing further.

"When did you steal the artworks from Hargrave, Monticello?"

There were no protests from Monticello this time and he slowly replied, "At different times. I called on him the morning of the 9th. His cleaner opened the door; Eric wasn't in. I said I would wait for him."

"Why?"

"To continue our conversation of the previous night."

"How long did you wait for him?"

"Not for long. A few minutes later there was a call from the Regina Margherita hospital saying that Eric was in the emergency unit in a serious condition and was being sent to the San Giacomo hospital for a brain scan. The cleaner was in a panic and didn't know what to do or who to call."

"What did you do then?"

"The cleaner did not have legal papers which is why he was afraid. So I told him to go home because the police might come."

"And he left?"

"Yes, right away. It was not the first time he had seen me in the apartment."

"I will need the name of the cleaner to verify your story," Conti said jotting down a few lines in his notebook, and continued, "So you were alone in the apartment and decided to help yourself?"

"No, no. I looked around to see what work Eric had done for the exhibition but I couldn't find anything. So…"

"So?"

"So I borrowed the key to his, well, studio," Monticello hesitantly continued, hoping Conti would not remember how he had lied to the Inspector and Giulia about not knowing of the existence of Eric's studio, "thinking that he had left his work there."

"Well then, what did you do next?" Conti prodded, making a mental note of Monticello's admission.

"I went to Eric's studio and found several drawings, a large oil painting that was almost finished, another one that was half done, but nothing for the exhibition. It appeared that he had not even started and the exhibition was less than two months away. I was furious."

The dealer seemed ready to confess to everything he knew in a hurry.

"I had both keys with me when I walked back to the gallery. The key to Eric's flat that the cleaner had left in his hurry to leave and the key to his studio. But I didn't take anything then, I swear. I was angry with Eric but he was in hospital so what could I do?"

His throat felt dry and he asked for coffee, but the inspector ignored the request and told him to continue.

"Later that day I phoned the hospital to find out how Eric was. It was difficult to get any news. They had moved him from one hospital to another and administration was the last to be informed.

"The next day, on the 10th, I was told he was going to have brain surgery. In the evening I found out that he was in a coma and that his condition was critical."

He stopped, catching his breath.

"Go on. You're doing fine," Conti encouraged him.

"That evening, I went to his studio and I took the drawings."

Including the drawing of the Madonna and Child commissioned by Littlejohn, Conti thought to himself.

"And the painting of Venice?" Conti asked.

"I took that as well."

"Where did you take them? To your apartment?"

"Yes, right away."

"What about Hargrave's collection of antiquities?"

"Well, I had left my phone number at the hospital. I told them I was a relative. So when he died, on the 11th, they phoned and left a message on my answering service. That's how I knew he wouldn't…"

Conti finished the sentence for him.

"…come back and accuse you of stealing from him. I see. And when did you go to his apartment?"

"Right away."

Conti frowned.

"I had a claim," Monticello protested weakly.

"You didn't have the right to go and take what you wanted. There are laws in this country. The family of the deceased have the right to inherit; not his business partner, not his live-in partner, nor his so-called friends," Conti said tersely.

"Eric was my friend and…he had said that he would burn down everything he had before he died. I didn't feel I was stealing from him…"

Conti studied his notebook and purposefully posed the next question to Monticello, "One of the drawings you stole from Eric was not an original but a photocopy. Why did you take it? Who was the drawing by?"

Monticello had to think for a moment before replying.

"The shepherds and a woman in front of a tomb. Yes, I realised it was a copy only when I got back to my apartment. I believe it is a preparatory drawing for a famous Nicolas Poussin painting in the Louvre Museum in Paris."

The inspector closed his notebook and got up slowly. He told the dealer that he would check his story.

"What will happen now?" Monticello asked weakly.

"There will be a trial. And even if you did not murder Hargrave you have plenty to answer for!"

"So you do believe me?"

"I will check. That's all I can say at this point."

As Conti was about to leave, he turned to Monticello and asked, "One last thing, and think hard before you answer, in what state was Hargrave's apartment when you visited on the morning of the 9th?"

Monticello paused before replying, "The cleaner had of course started to clear up before I got there, but everything looked normal. I remember the cleaner saying that Eric's bed did not appear to have been slept in that night so he was not sure whether Eric was out of town."

After he left Monticello, Conti decided to walk to the police headquarters. His informal interview was completely against regulations and if the prosecutor found out, or worse the Commissario, he would be in trouble. On the other hand, provided that Monticello had spoken the truth, he could at least eliminate one suspect from his list.

Conti was hungry and in need of a caffeine kick. But more than anything else, he wanted to light a cigar, which was the first thing he did. He stood under the shade of one of the bar's umbrellas. From where he stood, he could see half of the façade of the Basilica di Santa Maria in Trastevere, its mosaic frescoes shining like a beacon above the colonnade.

The waiter recognised him as he placed a cup of espresso and a tuna and tomato *tramezzino* in front of him. "Here you are, *Inspettore*."

Conti absent-mindedly thanked the waiter, and bit into his sandwich.

With Monticello scrapped from his list of suspects for the time being, his thoughts moved to the next step of his investigation and the trip to Milan. He wanted to talk to Enzo Zangara, the owner of two prominent galleries in Milan and Turin, and a very vocal critic of Eric Hargrave.

Zangara had attended the launch of Eric Hargrave's autobiography in Milan together with several colleagues. He was reported to have heckled and shouted that Hargrave should be thrown in jail, drowning the voice of the Englishman who had to retreat from the podium. Taking into account that the launch was a few years back, the inspector was not sure what Zangara would have to say but, if the art establishment had conspired against Eric Hargrave, or if some individual held a personal grudge, his visit might provoke some reactions that he hoped would shed some light on the direction his inquiry should follow.

Conti knew getting the *Commissario* to agree to this initiative would not be an easy task.

Chapter 34

Giulia met with Victor Edelman and Sebastian Greenwood in the office of Seldom House. She had not spoken to Greenwood since the Seldom House cocktails at the Grosvenor but expected that he had made progress in the development of a film script based on Eric Hargrave's life. Edelman was obviously supporting the project, which meant that he still had an interest in publishing Hargrave's book, *The Language of Line*. Giulia was not particularly in favour of the angle Greenwood was pursuing but knew that if it helped Seldom House sell books, Edelman was likely to throw the weight of the publishing company behind it.

The Vice-president of Seldom House and Sebastian Greenwood were already seated in the conference room when Giulia arrived. Edelman was laughing, probably at one of his own jokes, and Greenwood was smiling politely.

"Giulia, you remember Seb Greenwood, don't you?"

"Yes," Giulia smiled walking over to greet him.

Edelman turned to the film producer with a conspiratorial grin.

"Giulia Vasari is the secret weapon of Seldom House. She can edit, she has good commercial sense and (he emphasized the "and") she is able to charm any writer into meeting deadlines."

Greenwood smiled politely, as he was expected to. Edelman turned towards Giulia and then to Greenwood.

"Seb here has submitted his idea for a script based on Eric Hargrave's life. I find it excellent, and very clever. In principle, I have agreed to help him. I would like, no, in fact, not I, but we would like you to get on board and help with the development of his script. You could be the artistic adviser!"

"With credits when the film is produced, of course," Greenwood was quick to add.

"Before you say anything for or against the idea, you must listen to Seb's angle. Then we can talk."

She nodded cautiously, thinking how little Edelman really knew her; getting her name in credits was not at all on her wish list. But she was curious, and she suspected that Edelman's enthusiasm was forced and purely motivated by commercial interest.

She, however, had to remind Edelman that Eric Hargrave's book was incomplete, without illustrations or examples.

"Without these, no one will buy it, even if it is by Eric Hargrave," she added.

Edelman brushed the remark aside without a moment's hesitation.

"The book was lost and we found the manuscript. So now, the illustrations are missing and we will find them as well. Or we will find a way, one way or the other."

Giulia was not as optimistic but knew that Edelman was as stubborn as they come and would not admit, especially in front of the film producer, that his enthusiasm could be misplaced.

Edelman got up and moved away from the table. "I'll leave the two of you to discuss it. If you need me, I'll be in my office. Giulia, you know where to find me! No, Seb, you stay put."

But Greenwood was already following Edelman to the door to thank him. Giulia noticed he was taller than the publishing executive; he appeared to be in his mid-thirties but an almost complete absence of facial hair made him look much younger. He stooped slightly, and was neither aloof nor aggressive as some Oxbridge graduates might be perceived. She doubted he was much of a businessman and suspected it was family contacts that had made it possible for him to produce films. She decided to test her theory.

"Sebastian, do you think yet another film on Eric Hargrave is likely to interest many people? His autobiography caused a lot of controversy but that was a good five years ago!"

He smiled, glad to be able to explain his ideas and rise to the challenge.

"I think so. In fact, the BBC is interested."

While Giulia mused over this revelation, Sebastian started to explain what he had in mind. "Essentially, I want to show that Eric Hargrave's life was not dissimilar to that of Caravaggio. So, instead of starting with his death in a dark alley of Trastevere, I will start with the story of Caravaggio and progressively blend it with that of Eric's."

Giulia looked dubious. She knew that Caravaggio had a troubled history, got into fights and went to jail, but little else.

"First we start with Caravaggio, born in 1571 in a small village outside Milan. He has a troubled family history and is raised by relatives. Even as a child he constantly gets into trouble and when he leaves Piedmont for Rome at the age of 21 no one expects him to come to any good. Eric is born to a poor family, with a father who drinks, and an abusive mother. He sets fire to his school and is sent to an institution for delinquent children, to various foster parents, gets into all sorts of trouble until he follows his artistic calling and ends up in Rome."

Greenwood stopped to drink some water and Giulia intrigued, prompted him.

"And how did Caravaggio die?"

The film producer smiled and continued.

"Caravaggio flees Rome in 1606 after being accused of killing a man. He goes to Malta, then Sicily, before returning to Naples, from where he wants to return to Rome. In 1610 he paints several masterpieces for his protector in Rome, the Borghese. On his way back, he becomes ill and dies, or so the official story goes, at the gates of Rome, alone! However, Caravaggio had a lot of enemies: powerful people who wanted him dead, influential cardinals who found his paintings too provocative; one could say he made it back to Rome, only to be killed. Hargrave's death is also cloaked in mystery. Did he fall? Was he pushed? Was he hit on the head?"

Without pausing for Giulia's reaction, Greenwood continued.

"We will also focus on the spirit of the time, the renaissance artists working and living in Rome, and show how Eric and his lifestyle fitted in perfectly. And as Caravaggio's paintings, after his death, were safely delivered to his protector, here we can introduce Hargrave's posthumous book, *The Language of Line*, delivered and published after his death. A tribute to our very own modern renaissance man."

Sebastian Greenwood paused, and waited for Giulia to comment.

"I am not sure how much of Caravaggio's story you've made up to fit your idea, but it makes an interesting analogy. I guess Edelman liked the ending," she said with a wry smile.

Greenwood laughed.

"He loved it. He wanted me to make sure that Seldom House was mentioned as the publisher of the book!"

"There's still a lot of work to be done. Research, contacts etc. So Giulia, will you help?"

"I'm not sure what I can do, but yes, I'll be happy to help you, although as I told Edelman, the book without illustrations and examples is at best, of interest to art scholars, but not to the general public."

"Maybe they will be found," Greenwood suggested.

Giulia made a face.

"What about the police in Italy? Do they have suspects? Do they still think Eric was murdered or do they believe it was an accident?"

"I don't think they have reached a conclusion yet."

Giulia had to admit that Sebastian Greenwood was intelligent and likeable. She was glad Edelman had arranged the meeting. Her first impression of Greenwood was that he was an opportunist with little personality and more connections than talent. She had been quick to form an opinion and was pleased to be able to acknowledge her mistake and change her view.

They talked some more about certain details Greenwood wanted to include, and, agreed to sit together and review the first draft of the script within a week.

Giulia also reminded him that he would need the permission of the Hargrave heirs if he intended to use any part of Eric's autobiography and offered to intercede on his behalf once he was satisfied with the outline of the film script. Greenwood repeated that he was grateful for her help.

After leaving the offices of Seldom House, Giulia decided to call the Porters. Andrew and Clara Porter had been friends of Eric Hargrave for over thirty years and Eric often stayed with them, in their house in Islington, when he visited London. She wondered whether the Porters would not prove more helpful to Greenwood in the preparation of his film. They knew Eric a lot better than she did, and had known him a lot longer than she had.

Chapter 35

Littlejohn polished off two large whiskies before taking the train to London where he was due to meet one of his American lawyers in the afternoon, but the alcohol did little to calm his restlessness. When he had received the request to go over some of the finer points in his case against the Silverstein Museum he assumed the lawyer meant a few dates and facts needed to be checked. He was surprised to hear that one of the partners of the law firm would be coming to London to start the preparations for the trial. According to the last discussion he had had with them over the phone, the Museum was about to agree on a settlement out of court and a conclusion was close. Now he was told that his lawyers believed that the Museum would eventually settle but they might let the actual court case start to demonstrate how strong or how determined Littlejohn was and how far he might go.

Littlejohn had complained that his lawyers were misleading him; he reminded them that he was willing to go all the way and seek not only reparation but punitive damages. He received reassurance that his case was solid but, as he continued to moan and rant, it was suggested to him that his lawyers were working on a contingency basis and therefore would not go through the expense of sending someone to London if they did not believe it was necessary.

Littlejohn felt that the Dorchester was a much more appropriate venue than his own modest cottage. The thick carpets and opulent decoration would remind the lawyers that he was a man of a certain standing, of impeccable reputation and used to enjoying luxuries that the Silverstein was unfairly depriving him of.

Jack Goldman had come to London himself, not only because Littlejohn was a difficult client but also because an associated law firm he worked with wanted to see him to discuss possible cooperation on an international copyright infringement case.

Goldman was the same age as Littlejohn and a founding partner in his legal firm.

Despite the numerous offers from the east coast he had stubbornly refused to move to New York or Washington. Goldman was born in California of a wealthy family with political connections and links to the entertainment industry. He specialised in copyright and intellectual property law early in his career, assuming that the film and music industry would provide him with a lot of career opportunities. He was not wrong, but even he had not anticipated the goldmine Silicon Valley, with its software and technology companies, would represent.

The case against the Silverstein Museum was not representative of his work. His firm would have been expected to represent the Silverstein Trust, not fight against it, and until five years ago this would have been the case. The Board of Trustees had undergone a lot of changes and the new Chairman had used his influence to bring in a well-known law firm from the East Coast. Jack Goldman had refused to share the work (and lose the retainer fee) and parted ways with the Museum. So when Littlejohn approached him, Goldman felt it was a good opportunity to show the Silverstein Museum and its Board how wrong they had been.

Goldman adjusted his gold-rimmed glasses and asked for directions to the conservatory where Tarquin Littlejohn was waiting for him. The concierge pointed him in the right direction and he strode along the corridor, noticing that the carpet was thicker than the Bermuda grass of his lawn at home.

The two men shook hands. Littlejohn sat down again and beckoned over the waiter.

"What will you drink?" he asked his guest.

"What are you having?"

"Whisky, single malt."

The lawyer smiled but did not join Littlejohn and asked for a glass of California white wine.

Littlejohn emptied the rest of his glass, handed it to the waiter, then turned to Jack Goldman.

"You must be tired from your flight so let's cut to the chase. What do you need to review?"

The lawyer sat back against the thick upholstery of the armchair and flipped open his briefcase. He fished out a writing pad and a gold pen.

"As I explained to you over the phone, we may have to let the trial start before the Museum agrees to a settlement. So we are not caught unawares, we have to prepare ourselves as well as possible."

"What is there to prepare?"

"We need to be ready for the Museum's possible lines of attack."

"I am suing them, not the other way around! I am suing them for fraud, conspiracy and breach of contract!"

"You are indeed, and you are doing so by claiming the moral ground when you brought the Museum's attention to the fact that they had acquired forgeries. Your claim is based on your undisputed expertise, and your motivation is dictated by your scholarly ethics and duty to reveal the truth."

The former curator nodded approvingly.

"The Museum is therefore likely to attack you on both fronts and observe how you defend yourself."

"Go on," he said.

Both men remained silent while the waiter brought their drinks. At this point, Littlejohn knew that some unpleasant questions were in the offing and he braced himself for them.

"You had affairs with several employees of the Silverstein, did you not?"

"What does this have to do…?"

"True or not true? Think of me as the Museum's counsel."

Littlejohn hesitated.

"Yes, I did, but I don't see the relevance."

"It is if it goes to show that your sense of morality can be questioned. With morality come ethics of course," the lawyer continued, "So how many women employees of the Museum did you have a relationship with?"

"Several."

The lawyer frowned in disapproval.

"Believe me, you do not want the opposition to be the ones to reveal the details. So how many were married?"

"Can't I refuse to answer that?"

"You can, but you also lose the possibility of giving your version and give the impression you have something to hide."

Littlejohn drank some whisky, as much to steady himself as to divert the lawyer's attention, but to no effect.

"Fine, let's go back to Kathleen Corby. You at least admit to having had a sexual relationship with her, don't you?"

"Yes, of course."

"She was married, wasn't she?"

"She was in the middle of a divorce!"

"But still married at the time she went out with you?"

"Yes."

"What happened then?"

"I broke off the affair; she was furious that I did and she harassed me. When it didn't work, she sued for sexual harassment out of spite."

"Please avoid comments like that."

"Like what?"

"'Out of spite'. It's an unnecessary comment. In addition, the more you show the question rattles you, the longer they will dwell on it. Stick to the facts."

The former curator sighed in exasperation and drank more whisky.

"The Museum cleared me of sexual harassment."

"Good, this is the answer you need to give."

The lawyer studied his notes, scribbled a few words in the margin and turned the page to address the next argument.

"It was said that you had a high opinion of your expertise and a low opinion of that of other people."

"Who said that?" Littlejohn snapped angrily.

"Of no importance. One of your colleagues probably. Please remember not to react to this kind of provocation! So tell me why, you are so sure several drawings from the Silverstein collection are forgeries?"

"I was in charge of the V&A department of drawings and, during my career I must have catalogued several thousand drawings, including drawings from the personal collection of the English Crown."

"Good. However, it can be argued that an expert only delivers a personal judgment over the quality of a drawing, not a definite conclusion that can be demonstrated scientifically. Wouldn't you agree?"

"First of all, after over twenty years of studying, handling, and researching Old Masters' drawings you become familiar with artists' styles, their handwriting, with the fluidity of their lines. If you are presented with a drawing that is not genuine, you feel there is something wrong. So, it is your duty, it was my duty as curator, to study it in more detail to determine whether this feeling was correct or not."

"What made you suspicious to start with?"

"A Raphael sketch of a woman. The drawing was clumsy, the cross hatching careless and I doubted it was drawn from a live model."

"What about tests, scientific kits?"

"I submitted the Raphael, for instance, to a scientist who examined it with an x-ray fluorescent spectroscopy and discovered a substantial amount of titanium on the paper's surface; titanium oxides were not manufactured until the 1950s, that is, more than 400 years after Raphael had lived. This confirmed my judgment."

"Couldn't the titanium have come from something the drawing was in contact with years later, for instance? Like a passé-partout or a cardboard support?"

"Highly unlikely. If it was the case, we would have found other ingredients on the paper, like glue or fibres, but there was nothing."

"What about provenance?"

"The provenance of the six drawings identified as forgeries was incomplete. Each drawing appeared out of nowhere and none could be traced much further than thirty or forty years back."

The lawyer looked at Littlejohn attentively. He listened to his answers, watched his body language, in the way he knew the legal counsels of the Silverstein Museum would. What he saw was not entirely convincing. It was easy to see why Tarquin Littlejohn was disliked by his colleagues despite his obvious expertise. And the problem for Goldman came from Littlejohn's impatient and arrogant attitude. If the judges disliked him enough, they would discount his statements and make it difficult for him to win the damages he sought. However, when Littlejohn spoke about drawings, he managed to sound confident, passionate and knowledgeable. Somehow, Goldman thought, he would have to focus on Littlejohn's professional judgment and play down his personality.

"You claim that the six drawings you identified as forgeries were all drawn by the same person. What an extraordinary claim! How can you be so sure?"

Littlejohn had gone over his arguments a hundred times in his head.

"Several findings led me to this conclusion. Firstly, the ink used in all six drawings appeared faded, which is not consistent with their ageing. The iron-gall ink used during the 15th and 16th centuries tend to darken with age, not lighten. Then, the cross hatching in five out of six showed similarities. The parallel lines that indicate shadow – they were clumsy and clearly done by the same hand."

"Do you have any idea who could have made these drawings?"

"Eric Hargrave, the English forger who wrote his autobiography a few years ago!"

"Why him?"

"I saw an exhibition of his drawings and studied them carefully and there is no doubt in my mind. Besides, two of the drawings passed through the gallery Hargrave owned in Rome back in the early 70s."

"Did you confront Hargrave with these findings?"

For a moment Littlejohn froze, as if the question had caught him by surprise. When he regained his composure he replied, "I did not need to meet Hargrave to reach my conclusions!"

The lawyer did not miss a beat but noticed that the former curator had not answered the question. He wrote something down on his writing block and looked straight at Littlejohn.

"Did you meet him or not?"

After a second's hesitation, Littlejohn said he had met Hargrave briefly when he came to San Francisco to attend the opening night of his exhibition. The lawyer took a sip of his white wine and wiped his mouth carefully with the white napkin. He stabbed an olive with a toothpick and put it into his mouth. There was one more question he needed to ask.

"You maintain that the Silverstein is trying to avoid admitting they bought forgeries and therefore tried to suppress the publication of your catalogue and forced you out of the Museum. Why do you think the Museum took this position?"

"Obviously, because it would be an embarrassment for the Museum and the Trustees, not to mention the previous curator."

"Isn't it true that the Silverstein is the richest museum in the U.S. and has more than 200 million dollars a year to spend on acquisitions and that a loss of a couple of millions would therefore be insignificant in their budget?"

Littljohn shrugged and finished his whisky. He was still thirsty and summoned the waiter.

"Couldn't it be argued that you jumped to conclusions, both to discredit your predecessor and several Board members of the Silverstein who openly stated that you were not the right man for the position and that your predecessor should not have been allowed to go?"

The question felt like a personal blow to Littlejohn who recoiled inwardly. For an instant, he forgot who was asking him the question and he glared at Jack Goldman malevolently.

"That is a bloody lie! I take great pride in my work. My only motivation was to fulfil my duty as curator of the Silverstein Museum, nothing else. And if some of the Board Members did not like me, that's not my problem. No one forced them to hire me. But what can you expect from people who cannot tell the difference between Andy Warhol and Raphael?"

The lawyer cleared his throat before rebuking Littlejohn for his outburst, once again. The former curator seemed edgy, irritable and impatient. Goldman suddenly wondered whether it was such a good idea to let the trial start before discussing an out-of-court settlement. The trial was not scheduled for another month but Littlejohn would have to be prepared and made to rehearse extensively. The Englishman ordered another whisky without asking his lawyer if he wanted anything.

Chapter 36

The Porters lived in a three level town house not far from Angel tube station. The houses surrounding St. Mark's Church that stood in the middle of the square had seen better days but now showed various stages of dilapidation. Several houses, including that of the Porters, stood on subsiding land and displayed crooked doors and window sills that climbing vines did not quite conceal.

Although Giulia had only met the Porters a couple of times, she was always made to feel welcome. Clara was always ready with a cup of coffee and a home-made cake to share around the table in their homely kitchen overlooking the square.

"We had lots of lively discussions with Eric in this kitchen," Andrew remembered with a sad smile.

"That's because I was here; it was safer here than in the living room as those two needed a referee for their arguments," Clara added wistfully.

"Clara, we did not argue, we debated."

"You debated until the first bottle of wine was emptied, no, the second or third, then you argued," she corrected him.

Andrew raised his eyes to the ceiling and drank some coffee.

Giulia smiled at Clara. She liked her determination.

"You were both very close to Eric; you must miss him a lot."

Andrew looked away without answering but Clara did.

"He was part of the family. He was our eldest daughter's godfather in fact."

For a moment neither of them said anything, their thoughts on their friend. It was Clara who broke the silence.

"Eric had asked Andrew to write the foreword of his book. Did you know that? "

"Which book?" Giulia asked.

"*The History of Line*", Clara said.

"*The Language of Line,*" Andrew corrected her.

"I talked to him a few days before…before the accident, and he told me he would bring the manuscript to London. Seldom House was interested in publishing it," Clara said, offering Giulia another piece of apple pie.

"Yes, he told me Seldom House wanted to publish it," Andrew repeated. "What's going to happen to it now? Will it get published?"

Giulia said she hoped it would but explained that the illustrations and examples were missing.

"He talked about this book as his legacy, he wanted to share what he had learned about drawing, explain how to read a drawing the way a graphologist reads handwriting."

Giulia nodded and noticed that Clara's eyes were misty.

"His autobiography was not what he wanted to be remembered by. He enjoyed writing it and he acknowledged he had done it for money, but he saw it almost as a practical joke on the establishment. It would be a pity if the *The Language of Line* was not printed. And he wrote other things as well. He translated Garcia Lorca, Michelangelo's sonnets, the epic of Gilgamesh, Ovid's poems." Giulia hesitated before asking the next question.

"You know that I work on a freelance basis for Seldom House, don't you?"

Andrew nodded and Clara said Eric had told them.

"He was very fond of you," Clara added.

"I didn't know him as well as you did of course, but he was a dear friend and I would really like to see his book in print," Giulia continued, "but with the missing bits I am not sure Seldom House will go ahead. I was hoping that…perhaps Eric had said something to you about the illustrations?"

The Porters looked at each other and Andrew shook his head.

"We talked about his theories but he didn't show me the manuscript. I was expecting him to tell us all about it on his next visit," he said.

"We would, of course, like to help, but we're not sure what exactly we can do," Clara added.

"If you hear anything, please let me know. Maybe some of his friends in Rome helped him put the book together."

"Have you spoken to his brother about this?" Clara asked.

"Yes, I went over to see Bernard in Brighton but neither he nor his sister have any idea."

Clara walked towards the kitchen counter to make a fresh pot of coffee. Andrew pulled out a hand rolled cigarette, offered Giulia one, who declined, and then asked her if she minded if he smoked.

Giulia said she didn't, but Clara reached out to open the kitchen window. Between puffs, Andrew continued to speak of Eric, the good times they had spent together, and the visits to Anticoli Corrado, recalling how once, after a wine-fuelled night in town, they got lost in the woods walking back from the village to Eric's house, and ended up falling asleep among the oak trees.

"He was well liked in Anticoli and after the publication of his autobiography he worked more than ever before. He told me that art dealers from all over Italy continued to approach him to commission Old Master drawings."

"I thought he had stopped after his book. Or at least he had said so in an interview," Giulia said. She suddenly remembered what Willie had told her, that Eric was expecting to be paid a substantial sum of money in exchange for his work .

She was brought back into the conversation by Andrew laughing and coughing. "Eric was always up for a challenge. If he needed the money he would accept the work. But he did say that he no longer added collectors' seals or signatures. He said that he sometimes drew meaningless doodles in the margins to see if anyone complained."

"And did anyone complain?"

Andrew laughed again, and said no, no one complained.

"Besides, how could they? Eric loved practical jokes. He told me that one of the biggest auction houses in London once sold one of his drawings attributed to Pontormo with a drawing of a penis in the margin! We laughed about this, and he brought out the catalogue to show us."

Clara smiled at the recollection, then quickly frowned.

"He enjoyed a joke but he was also aware that not everyone appreciated his sense of humour. He said several times that if he was not careful someone might make him 'disappear' one day; yes, 'disappear', that's how he put it."

For a while nobody spoke.

Remembering that Andrew wrote poetry, Giulia asked him whether he had published anything lately. He straight away went to the next room and returned with a little yellow book, a new collection of his poems, that included one on Anticoli. He scribbled a few words in the front and told Giulia he would be happy if she would accept it as a present.

"Thank you," she half muttered, "thank you very much. I appreciate it."

Andrew left the kitchen and, alone with Clara, Giulia said. "Clara, I didn't want to insist or to give you the wrong impression when I asked whether you knew anything about Eric's last book. I do work for Seldom House, it's true, but I am not doing this because it's my job. I would like to see Eric's book published so that he can be acknowledged and remembered as a scholar, and not only as a forger of Old Masters. I think you can understand how I feel."

"I know, Giulia, and I promise you that if we come across anything useful, I will let you know immediately."

Giulia thanked her and gave her a quick hug.

When Andrew came back with a few magazines in his hand the conversation soon returned to the subject of Eric.

"Eric made a lot of people look bad, experts, dealers, curators, and it is possible that someone he had not named was afraid he would expose him one day. If you ask me, the police should look at the dealers Eric worked with over the years, especially those in Italy."

"The police are still actively investigating Eric's death but I'm not even sure they are really convinced it was suspicious," Giulia stated.

Andrew shook his head angrily.

"Scotland Yard should get involved. I think this could be a bit too complicated for the Italian police to handle on their own."

"I think a representative from the British Embassy in Rome has been assigned to look into the case. Of course, given Eric's reputation as a rogue and an anti-establishment figure who created trouble and was associated with Blunt, the spy, it is little wonder the police don't want to put men or resources into the investigation, although the Italian police are doing what they can," Giulia commented, thinking of Conti and his determination to get to the bottom of it all.

Andrew Porter paused, all the time clutching the magazines which regularly published his poetry and which he intended to show Giulia.

On her way home from the Porters, Giulia stopped at a 24-hour kiosk to buy a newspaper, and then hopped on a bus. She read the paper's headlines, but could not concentrate on the news as bits of conversation with the Porters kept coming back to her – a copy of Eric's manuscript mysteriously turning up, but the illustrations still missing; more possible suspects for his murder – Italian art dealers from Eric's past, and, according to Andrew, a number who still came to see him for commissions after the publication of his book.

Eric, in death as in life, was shrouded in as much mystery as his claim to have produced and sold more than a thousand paintings in the style of the Old Masters. He lived for his art, did he die because if it? Was her friend turning in his grave watching the development of events? No, thought Giulia, knowing Eric, he was having a good chuckle over this whole story.

Giulia got off at Piccadilly Circus and walked the rest of the way home. It was a pleasant evening and she felt like losing herself in a crowd of people and sauntered slowly down Oxford Street. She enjoyed the hours spent with the Porters and although they had welcomed her with open arms, she came away with a feeling of loneliness. Andrew and Clara had each other. And Giulia was alone. After Robert died, Eric would call her in the evenings to find out how she was. He wrote her little notes, that he never sent, and would end up reading them to her over the phone instead. He talked to her of art, she listened avidly to his stories, and she would scold him when he called to tell her he was not feeling too well after drinking too much. On one occasion, he lost a lot of blood after gashing his leg badly, and was adamant he wouldn't have a transfusion because it might give him Aids; Giulia realised then that life with Eric around was never going to be dull. When the opportunity to work for Seldom House in London came along, Giulia knew it was time to leave Rome and move on with her life. She believed that the job would give her a new sense of belonging and purpose. Eric encouraged her, and told her that he was only a phone call away; as he visited London often enough, and he was sure that Giulia would be flying into Rome as often, there would be plenty of occasions to meet up. So, they never said good-bye properly and kept in touch regularly.

Giulia passed the big brightly lit window of *Wagamama* and popped in to pick up an order of noodles. She was more determined than ever to find a way to get Eric's book printed. The illustrations had to be somewhere. And propelled by this conviction she started to walk more quickly.

Chapter 37

It was a miserable day. The rain had pelted down all morning and patches of dark clouds reflected on the streets and pavements of London. Pedestrians huddled against buildings and ran from one protective awning to the next. A gusty wind blew, pushing umbrellas inside out. It was certainly not anyone's idea of spring.

Behind the window of his art gallery, Christopher Donovan repressed a sneeze and cursed himself for having taken his motorbike to work instead of his car. The day was as bleak as the precarious state of his gallery. His main financial backer had run into some ill fortune and was calling back some of the funds he had invested in Donovan's business, insisting that Donovan was late on his repayments. He demanded that Donovan speed up the sale of the Picasso drawing, a reclining nude of Genevieve Laporte, one of Picasso's many mistresses, even at a small profit.

Donovan had a good eye and a sharp mind. He dealt with high-end pieces but also had regular gallery exhibitions for those with a more modest budget. He got along well with his ever growing client list: keen collectors from his auction house days, novices who had made money in the investment sector and were ready to spend substantial amounts to join the art crowd, and art enthusiasts who would attend his openings and find something that their pocketbooks could afford.

Like his main investor, who was an English commodity trader in Singapore, Donovan was also a risk taker. He was a generous man and not dishonest by nature, but gambled with what came to him. He used to say that in London, to make money, you had to make people believe you had money. And, true to his words, he was surrounded by a group of rich clients who became friends; some were ready to invest in what they saw not only as a successful but a culturally uplifting experiment. For Donovan to fit in with his new crowd he stretched himself to the limit and, sometimes, beyond.

The deal was simple and, if everyone respected his part of the bargain, straightforward. Christopher and his investor had agreed to acquire the Picasso sketch for one hundred and fifty thousand pounds on a fifty-fifty basis. Donovan was confident he could, within six months, resell the sketch at double their investment, earning them a healthy profit. The funds were channelled through an offshore company Donovan controlled, to avoid taxes.

However, Donovan did not have his share of the money to put into the painting and to make matters worse, had already helped himself to the newly arrived funds, transferring them to his personal account. But he did have a buyer waiting in the wings and to Donovan, the sale was as good as done. He had also cut a deal with the seller of the Picasso, who not only agreed to wait for payment until the drawing had been flipped over to the new buyer, but had brought his asking price down to a hundred thousand, a detail he conveniently forgot to tell his investor. Donovan had always said that trading in art was a business like any other, and business was about making deals. Everything looked sunny and bright until his "good as done deal" had collapsed, his prospective buyer defaulting on him and his investor calling for a quick sale of the Picasso to get his money plus profit back. The timing was particularly bad as his books were not looking good, and the outstanding balance on his personal credit cards was reaching its uppermost limits.

Donovan rubbed his forehead with his outstretched fingers as he stared blankly at the fax on his desk. He crumpled the fax demanding the return of the money ASAP and threw it into the wastebasket, aware this did not rid him of the problem, but, at least, he figured, it was not staring him in the face.

He had to keep up appearances with his wife as well. There was no doubt that they made a handsome couple, and she was under the impression she had married a financial genius and revelled in the fact that they got invited to events that featured in the glossy magazines which carelessly adorned her coffee table. She seldom ventured far from Sloane Square to do her shopping, and her biggest problem was deciding whether to soak up the winter sun at the Sandy Lane in Barbados or head for the white beaches and the promise of a sublime holiday at the much talked about Amanpulo.

Until now, banks had been willing to lend him money and each time he had fallen out with an investor, a new one had materialised. Why should it all unravel now? He refused to contemplate this possibility. A bump in the road, that was all. He would ride over it and land smoothly on the other side. Neither his wife nor his partner would be any the wiser.

He walked down to the front door of the gallery and bolted it from the inside. He was in no mood to let visitors drift through and waste his time. Besides, what he needed to do required his utmost concentration. He opened his computer, searched through his data base for the name he was looking for and started to dial.

Bernard Hargrave was understandably reluctant to speak to the art dealer but was curious to know why he called. The dealer had, until now, refused to give the heirs any information about his dealings with Eric Hargrave, claiming Eric owed him money, was in breach of contract, and that the heirs had no rights over any of the works still at St.George's gallery. The first exhibition of Eric Hargrave was not the sell-out Donovan expected and he faced a barrage of criticism from the press. Eric was unable to meet deadlines and Donovan suspected he still accepted commissions in Italy. Eric took the monthly payments from London for granted and literally forgot the terms of his agreement with Donovan. When the dealer reminded him of their arrangement and threatened to stop the monthly payments, Eric seemed offended and proposed they part company. They exchanged polite but cutting letters until a few days before Eric's death.

In spite of his misgivings, Donovan had commissioned a view of Venice in the style of Canaletto, bought a canvas from the eighteenth century for Eric to paint on, and travelled twice to Rome to check on Eric's progress.

When Giulia announced that the Canaletto had been found in Italy he had felt a wave of relief, but when she added that the painting was in police custody his heart had missed a beat. To complicate matters further, Bernard Hargrave, on behalf of the heirs, claimed ownership of the painting, and there was nothing Donovan could legally do to prevent the police from releasing it to Eric's brother.

"Mr. Hargrave, I believe it is in both our interests to clear up any misunderstanding and start all over again, so to speak."

"Really?" Bernard tried not to sound sarcastic.

"Eric's death was tragic of course, but it also left me in a delicate financial situation. I advanced Eric a sizeable amount of money and obviously, now, the gallery does not have the possibility to recoup this investment. That is why I may have answered you a little…abruptly when you asked for accounts. I would like to apologise for that."

"Ah, well, yes…I mean, thank you for this," Bernard Hargrave mumbled.

"I am ready to go through the accounts with you and will be glad to show you the drawings I have in the gallery."

"Well, very good…very good. Thank you for that."

"Can I suggest we meet at the gallery? Maybe sometime this week if you can make it?"

"I will try. Friday perhaps?"

"Friday will be fine, late morning or early afternoon," Donovan suggested.

"Friday afternoon then, Mr. Donovan."

"There is one more thing, Mr. Hargrave."

"Yes?"

"I had commissioned a painting of Venice from Eric that he was scheduled to deliver the week he died. Would you by any chance be in possession of this painting? It is quite a large canvas."

Bernard Hargrave finally understood why Donovan had called him, but with the prospect of having a first-hand look at his brother's accounts with the dealer, he found himself telling Donovan that the painting would be arriving in England any day soon, and that yes, they could discuss it.

Christopher Donovan was pleased with himself. The conversation had gone smoothly. Bernard Hargrave had all but agreed to let him have the Canaletto. Donovan did not doubt he would find a way to get his buyer to agree to wait another week.

Chapter 38

Inspector Conti decided he had time for a smoke before hailing a taxi from Milan central station to the Brera area. He felt inexplicably calm and pleased with himself, although his investigation into Eric Hargrave's death had not brought him any closer to the truth. He sensed that political pressures would soon place additional obstacles in his path. He found himself, once again, swimming against the tide, a position for which his ex-wife had criticized him countless times and, for as many times, stated that she had given up hope he would ever progress in his career.

He wondered briefly why he felt the need to argue with everyone and stick to his position in spite of everything. He took a long, deep puff from his cigar and blew away the thought. He was ready to face Enzo Zangara.

Enzo Zangara was a brilliant scholar and one of the most successful art dealers in Milan. His ability to inspire confidence, and his natural sense of timing, had made him arguably a prominent figure in the Milanese art establishment. He was referred to as an art critic, a collector and a dealer in Renaissance paintings, constantly associated with major exhibitions, auction sales or private collectors' acquisitions, and the cataloguing of major private collections. He also wrote a regular column in one of the main newspapers. His office occupied the first floor of a beautifully restored 17th century palazzo in the heart of Milan. Half a dozen chosen art pieces hung in a large room with half-closed shutters and well-placed spot lights with soft classical music playing in the background.

Conti was under no illusion that someone like Zangara would admit to knowing Hargrave personally or being in Rome at the time of his death. But he felt that, in the absence of a better plan, the further he cast his net, the more likely he was to provoke reactions.

Alberto Conti introduced himself and was immediately ushered into the expert's office.

"*Inspettore*, how can I help you?"

Zangara indicated one of two chairs in front of his desk to the policeman, before sitting down himself and adjusting his thin gold-framed spectacles with his middle finger.

"Professor Zangara, I need a few minutes of your time. I have a couple of questions to ask you."

"And you have come all the way from Rome to ask them? I am honoured."

Zangara smiled and joined his hands in front of him to form a steeple, his eyes focused and alert.

"I am investigating the death of Eric Hargrave," he stated flatly.

Zangara's face clouded briefly, but he said nothing.

"You knew Eric Hargrave, I presume?"

"If you mean, whether I knew of Eric Hargrave, the answer is obviously yes."

"What do you think of Eric Hargrave?"

The expert shrugged and raised his eyebrows in mock surprise.

"If you read my article you must know my position, *Inspettore*. Hargrave was a forger who copied Old Masters, passed them off as originals and sold them for years with impunity."

Conti waited for Zangara to continue but the dealer just stared at him impassively.

"Professor Zangara, have you ever conducted any business deal with Mr. Hargrave or his gallery in Rome over the years?"

The question was direct and if Zangara was bothered he certainly did not show it.

"No, I have not. Mr. Hargrave's forgeries were really not that good. The man was a bit delusional."

"A lot of experts say this now that he is dead and cannot challenge them," Conti commented.

This time the dealer reacted to the provocation.

"I would never have been fooled by Hargrave and never was. I cannot speak for other experts but I was not fooled. Anyway, the man brought only disrepute to the art world and the sooner he is forgotten, the better it will be for everyone."

Changing his approach, Conti asked Zangara whether he knew anyone who could have had dealings with Eric Hargrave. "I believe a small gallery in Trastevere showed some of his work," he added as if the thought had just struck him.

Conti was surprised that Zangara should know such a trivial detail as that about Eric.

Zangara was unfazed when Conti asked whether he was in Rome on the 8th of January and replied confidently that he was not. "I was in Milan attending a function," he said.

He adjusted his glasses again. "Is there anything else, *Inspettore?*"

"Just one last question," Conti paused.

Zangara waited.

"Let's say I have an Old Master's drawing, and would like to find out who it's by and where it comes from. How do I go about it?"

"Is that a purely hypothetical question or is it linked to your investigation?" Zangara asked.

Conti did not answer. Instead he described the photocopy he found in the portfolio of Eric's drawings in Monticello's apartment. Behind the image, Eric had inscribed, "ZGR".

"The drawing I'm interested in represents four figures in front of a tomb. Three men with sticks and a woman. There are trees in the background."

Zangara frowned and hesitated.

"From what you describe, it could be a memorial to someone who died…but without seeing the drawing itself I can't be more helpful."

"I understand. But how do I find out who drew it and what the subject is?" Conti insisted.

"You could show it to an expert or you could start looking at art books, catalogues, auction catalogues, for instance. But if you have no idea at all who drew it, it could take you a long time."

Conti could see Zangara's patience was fast running out. "Thank you for your help. I have no more questions."

"Well, then have a good trip back to Rome," Zangara said curtly, motioning Conti to the door.

As soon as he had gone, Zangara dialled a number in Venice he knew by heart.

"Enzo here, we need to talk, and the sooner the better."

Chapter 39

It was close to ten-thirty in the evening when Conti got into the Rome central station, so he hailed a taxi and gave the driver his address. The cab stopped in front of his building, and Conti paid and slowly got out. He looked up and saw many of the windows were lit, some of them open, and loud music streamed from the second floor apartment next to his. On the opposite side of the street, the bar was still open and the owner waved at him. Conti crossed the road and greeted Renato who was pouring a malt whisky for one of his customers.

"Good evening, *Inspettore*. You're working late tonight."

"Who says I was working? I was with a girlfriend."

"I don't think so, *Inspettore*."

Conti pretended to be annoyed. "How would you know? I am the policeman, not you."

"If you were with a girlfriend, you would still be with her. The night is young," Renato teased, after which he burst out into song.

The inspector shook his head and asked for a glass of whisky. "Is there anything left to eat, Renato?"

"*Tramezzini…*"

"Anything warm?" Conti asked, noticing the sandwich looked dry and curled up at the edges.

"No, but I have a cold rice salad and *prosciutto crudo*."

"All right, give me what you have."

A young police inspector ran down the stairs and almost collided with Conti, avoiding him only by side-stepping at the very last moment, and apologised. In the same breath, he warned Conti that the *Commissario* had been asking for him since the day before.

"He's in a foul mood, Conti, I warn you."

Conti shrugged and went inside.

Once at his desk, he took time to check his in-tray before

crossing the room and knocking at his superior's door.

"Conti! How nice to see you. Very kind of you to drop by."

The dripping sarcasm left the inspector cold. He noticed one man, a stranger, standing in front of the *Commissario's* desk. He had his coat on and was ready to leave. He shook the *Commissario*'s hand.

"Please make sure the matter is handled with discretion," the man said before greeting Conti with a nod.

"Who was he?" Conti asked.

"From the Ministry of Justice," the inspector's chief answered with a sigh.

"He asked me to drop the Hargrave case and focus on more important things."

Conti frowned.

"Look, even the newspaper has pushed its article to one of the back pages," the *Commissario* said.

He picked up the *Corriere* from his desk and opened it to find a short write-up.

"Let me read this to you, Conti, in case you have not seen it. Here*: Death of Forger; art dealer arrested in Rome.* That's the headline. Let us see what the journalist tells us about your investigation. Hmm, here it is…*Eric Hargrave, the famous forger of more than a thousand drawings which now hang in the most prominent museums in the world was found dying in the streets of Trastevere on the 8th of January. Many theories have been put forward to explain the mysterious circumstances of Hargrave's death. But so far the police have not come up with anything concrete.*"

"Do you agree with it so far?" the *Commissario* asked with exaggerated obsequiousness.

Conti tilted his head to the right without replying. It was obviously a rhetorical question, given that his chief was clearly not finished. "Now it gets more interesting. Here: *An art dealer from Rome, Giorgio Monticello, was arrested by the police and questioned in relation to the death of Eric Hargrave. Mr. Monticello appeared to have had a business arrangement with the Englishman and various artworks were found in his possession at the time of his arrest. Are we getting closer to finding out who killed Eric Hargrave or why he was killed? We have no official comments from the police but…etc. etc.*"

"Can I have your thoughts, *Inspettore*?" the *Commissario* prompted Conti.

"My thoughts about what, exactly?" Conti asked calmly.

"First of all, your thoughts on who passed the information to the journalist, Bruno Ferrara, of the *Corriere*?"

"I have no idea. Monticello's arrest did not take place in the middle of the night. His lawyer was there, he had neighbours…"

"So you are suggesting his lawyer leaked the news of his arrest to the press. Why?"

"I am not suggesting anything. Actually, you are," Conti countered, irritated by the innuendo he was somehow responsible for the leak, but also noticing that the *Commissario*'s voice betrayed a high level of stress that started to concern Conti.

"Would you care to enlighten me on the progress of your investigation, Conti? Isn't it correct that you still have no suspect?"

Conti chose his words carefully.

"Eric Hargrave's death is still being investigated as a possible homicide. Although it is true we are not in a position to indict anyone yet, the list of people with a motive for wanting Hargrave dead is long and difficult to investigate. I do not expect to solve this case quickly. As for Monticello, he was stopped while trying to leave the country, with a number of stolen artworks from Hargrave's studio in the trunk of his car. We are not done interrogating him."

The *Commissario* raised both hands and looked at the ceiling exasperated. He stared at Conti for several seconds before answering. As usual he could not decide whether he disliked the inspector's stubbornness and apparent impervious attitude to the realities of public service or envied it.

"Alberto, maybe one day you will understand that we have to operate in a world where the line between civil servants and politicians is often blurred. I have been instructed by the man who just left, to drop this case. Besides, what is the probability that you will find who killed Eric Hargrave if, and this is not even sure, he was actually murdered? I understand he made a lot of enemies when he wrote his autobiography, but this was almost five years ago. So why should someone wait for so long before doing something to him?"

Alberto Conti wondered why someone would have used his political influence with the Ministry of Justice to get the case closed.

"Chief, you asked why someone would have waited five years before doing something? I might be able to answer this question, although it still doesn't prove anything."

In spite of himself, the *Commissario* motioned for Conti to continue.

"Eric Hargrave was about to publish another book this year. In this book he intended to explain in detail how to recognise a genuine work from a forgery. Some people must have feared that he would say a lot more than he did in his autobiography."

"Are you sure?"

"Yes, the manuscript has only just been found but an important part is missing."

"I see. And where is the manuscript now?"

"In London."

"Which means we cannot examine it and…"

"I could try and get a copy," Conti interrupted.

The *Commissario* ignored Conti's comment and continued "and since whoever has his hands on the manuscript is in England, we cannot question him to find out how it came into his possession."

Conti acknowledged the international ramifications were a serious difficulty but suggested that Interpol could get involved.

"Conti, we cannot involve Interpol based on a mere suspicion. You assume that Hargrave's manuscript contains incriminating evidence that someone could be worried about, and I will grant you that it is possible. But the manuscript has disappeared and resurfaced in London. If there were revelations that could damage someone's reputation they have probably been taken out. So where do we go from here? Nowhere! I doubt Hargrave kept a record of all his transactions or left a list of the drawings he made over the years."

"It is very unlikely he left records, but I am confident we can identify some of the dealers he worked with during the last two or three years!"

"You really are stubborn!"

"It's in my nature. I'm never satisfied and cannot leave things half done!"

"Even when you know that you cannot finish what you've started?"

"I still don't know that. I may not find the right answers but I am determined to examine and exhaust all possible areas."

"Conti, you will never become *Commissario*."

"I do not wish to be."

The chief shook his head and looked hard at Conti.

"Drop this investigation. There are other cases that need to be solved."

Conti stared back. "I can't, unless you want to instruct me in writing, of course."

He knew this was unlikely to happen.

"If you find yourself transferred to Sicily, don't come and ask me why."

Chapter 40

Conti confronted Monticello once more, hoping that Monticello would come up with some new information that would help in solving the case. Monticello, visibly shaken by having his name linked as a suspect in the article in the *Corriere*, again vehemently denied his involvement with Hargrave's death.

"Tell me, Monticello, how did Hargrave justify the fact that he was doing forgeries?" Conti persisted.

"Hargrave argued that the questions of style and attribution were purely commercial concepts and that a drawing or a painting should be judged on whether it was well executed or not. He said that Degas reckoned he never had a style and claimed that Van Dyck spent his entire life trying to work in the manner of Rubens, as most Masters started by copying the works of their predecessors."

Monticello, noticing that he had Conti's full attention, carried on.

"Eric further argued that visual artists should be appreciated for their skill, and therefore, his work should be judged for what it was, not for what a so-called expert claimed it to be. If a painting in the style of Van Dyck ended up in the British Museum it was surely because of its high quality."

"And did you agree?" Conti asked Monticello.

"Yes, in theory, but I said to him that the claim it was by the hand of Van Dyck was still a deception to the public, not to mention the museum, who paid a lot more for an oil attributed to Van Dyck than for an oil painted by Hargrave."

"And how did Hargrave react to your reply?" Conti asked.

"I clearly remember his words. He had a mischievous smile when he said that 'On this point, his conscience was clear'."

Conti asked how Hargrave could claim a clear conscience when he contributed to the false claims.

Monticello, more relaxed at this point, said, "If I remember correctly, Eric had argued that, 'his drawings in the style of an Old Master were unsigned. He also claimed he never received more money for his drawings than what he would have taken had the work been signed with his name. He pointed out that he earned a good living selling drawings and lithographs through my gallery for example, as well as watercolours and paintings. He said it was the dealers who took his unsigned works and claimed they recognised a Brueghel or a Mantegna and sold them at an enormous profit."

At which point Conti interjected, "And were you planning to do the same with the Hargrave drawings we found in your possession?"

"No, no." Monticello blurted, his nervousness showing.

"I would have waited a while, and later sold them on as Hargraves', or as a follower or in the style of the artist who influenced Hargrave…"

Conti made no comment.

Monticello, relieved that Conti did not pursue the matter in more depth, and to deter further exchange on the particular subject, hurriedly continued, totally unaware that what he was about to say next brought the subject right back to dealers and their unscrupulous ways.

"I asked Eric whether he thought the Italian dealers were more dishonest than the English, to which Eric had laughed and said he did not think so. According to him, the Italians were proud of their craftsmanship, of their ability to recognise the work of an Old Master. If you fooled an Italian expert, his pride was hurt. The English, according to Eric, took the moral high ground and felt it was not right to sell someone a Rubens if it was not a Rubens. But in the end both the Italian and the English closed their eyes if they stood to earn a lot of money."

Conti smiled to himself. The conversation was going in the right direction, and Monticello needed little prompting from him, He asked Monticello whether Hargrave had discussed the impact of his autobiography on his life. Monticello said that Eric claimed that it was true that part of him wanted revenge on the art establishment. But he said that he also had more dealers than before coming to commission drawings or paintings in the style of Old Masters since its publication! In fact, one of the biggest galleries in Milan had been in contact with him.

Trying to sound and appear calm not to steer Monticello away from his readiness to talk, Conti asked, "Did Hargrave mention the name of the dealer?"

Unfazed, Monticello, just eager to continue with his story,

answered, "No, but Eric expressed his surprise that people did not think that he could reveal who they were!"

I asked him whether he was planning to tell more, to which Eric had teasingly answered, 'I just might, Giorgio."

"What did he mean by this?" Conti asked.

The dealer shrugged, "Just what he implied, tell more... that he might write another book."

"This is exactly what he did," Conti said to Monticello, whose look of astonishment appeared genuine. Conti thought that if Monticello was acting, he certainly acted well.

After his encounter with Monticello, Conti decided he was in no hurry to return to the Commissariato and risk facing his boss. He bought a newspaper, chose a table by the window of the bar and ordered an espresso and a Danish. He quickly scanned the headlines before putting the newspaper away and lit a cigar. His boss had a point. Although he had made some progress, he was far from confident he would be able to solve this murder, if it even was that.

Chapter 41

Giulia had agreed to meet Bernard Hargrave for lunch at the newly opened café at Sotheby's before meeting Christopher Donovan at his gallery. Bernard looked frail and apprehensive as he hauled himself out of the taxi. He had visibly not recovered from his illness, which was not surprising as he was almost seventy, and he grabbed the metal barrier at the pedestrian crossing to steady himself. Giulia kissed him and took his arm.

The doors of the auction house were opened by a doorman in uniform, and Giulia and Bernard walked the few steps to the Square Meal. Giulia had booked a table for two for one o'clock, and was glad she had as all the tables looked full. They were led to a table in the rear of the café and quickly ordered, both deciding to try the devilled quail with avocado salsa followed by a roast fillet of plaice. They shared a half-bottle of white wine and Bernard seemed more at ease.

"Giulia, I am so glad you agreed to help us. I'm not sure I would have had the courage to go and meet this man alone, you know," Bernard said quietly.

"Donovan? He's not so bad. He is smart and can be generous, as we know he was to your brother. But he may be a bit too obsessed with making money."

"All the same Giulia, I am glad for your company."

They ordered tea and coffee and shared the plate of petit fours that came with it. Seeing Bernard fully recovered, Giulia suggested they make their way to see Donovan.

St. George's Fine Art Gallery was just up the road. Bernard rang the doorbell several times but no one answered. The door remained closed and the intercom silent. Giulia asked Bernard if he was sure the appointment was for that day and he confirmed it emphatically. She tried her mobile phone but she got the gallery's answering service.

"You've come all the way from Brighton, and if Donovan has been delayed he might still show up. It would be a pity for you to have to make the trip again," she said. She left a note and slipped it between the frame and the front door of the gallery.

She led Bernard to one of the ubiquitous coffee houses around the block and assured him that Donovan had her mobile number and would call when he found her note.

Giulia told Bernard that she had been on the phone with the Italian police inspector who was investigating his brother's death.

"Monticello has been taken into police custody. They found a portfolio of Eric's drawings in his apartment and he confessed to taking them and other objects, including the oil painting that Donovan had commissioned. Conti doesn't believe he had anything to do with Eric's death."

Bernard nodded. He seemed relieved that Monticello, the distinguished Italian gentleman whom he had met in Rome and who had offered his help, was not a murderer.

"He also said, however, that a number of art dealers could have had a reason to want Eric silenced, especially if they knew he was about to publish another book."

"What does he say in his new book?"

"Well, the manuscript doesn't look complete. From what I have read there is nothing controversial in it, but since a lot of information is missing, one cannot be sure what Eric intended to reveal."

"What do you think, Giulia? You must have discussed it with him?"

"I don't know what to say. He gave me the general idea behind his new book but that was all. I remember when he first told us about his autobiography in Rome, he hinted that it would make a sensation, but I was as surprised as anyone else when I read the book. Goes to show how little we know about even our dearest friends!"

"Ah, yes, Eric liked secrets, he liked to surround himself in mystery and he was always embroidering to make a story more interesting."

Giulia smiled and agreed that Eric was indeed a very good story teller.

"By the way, I had a surprise visit from Willie, Eric's boyfriend," she said casually.

"Willie! Good grief, what did he want from you?"

"He was on his way to Manila from Canada and just wanted to

talk. He did mention something interesting, that Eric was constantly writing important ideas in a black leather-bound notebook. According to him, that book contained very important information."

Bernard listened attentively but showed little emotion.

"Would you mind looking through Eric's boxes again? If such a notebook actually exists it may contain notes related to the book."

"I will look again but I have no recollection of a black notebook with Eric's writing. I would have remembered that."

"I wonder what happened to Donovan? It's not like him to make an appointment and not show up! I hope nothing bad has happened."

"I don't like Donovan very much, but I hope he makes an appearance eventually," Bernard added. "Giulia, I meant to tell you, that unpleasant fellow, Littlejohn, called again. He was very insistent. What do you think I should tell him? Should I inform him that the Italian police confiscated some of Eric's works?"

Giulia offered to speak to Alberto Conti to ask for his advice.

"All right then. I will not mention this till I hear from you. You know, I'm thinking of buying an answering machine so that I'm not forced to speak with everyone who calls."

Giulia told him it was a good idea.

"I had not spoken with Eric for maybe ten years, you know, when he sent me an invitation to attend the launch of his autobiography in London. It was quite strange to meet with him again after all that time. He was the same Eric, yet he was so different. I asked him why he wrote what he wrote…about us… about our family, half-truths. And I also asked him why he had decided to become a forger. After all, he was a very talented boy; he won prizes and scholarships when he was young."

"And what did he say?"

He said he would instead tell me why he wrote the book.

"He said an important dealer had been to see him one day and told him he understood that Eric was sometimes able to find important drawings. He said that if Eric could find twenty drawings by Old Masters he would be prepared to pay him twenty million lire for them. At first Eric figured that he was offering less per drawing than what Eric sold his own works for, so he haggled, and the dealer agreed to pay one and a half million lire per drawing."

"And he knew that Eric would prepare the Old Masters himself?"

"I don't know," Bernard replied. "Anyway, Eric said he made the drawings, presented them to him and was paid. But a few months later, he happened to get his hands on the catalogue of an auction sale in Milan and recognised one of his drawings in the manner of Tiepolo. The dealer had sold it for 120 million lire. Almost ten times what he had paid Eric!"

It was getting late and Bernard did not want to miss his train home. Christopher Donovan had neither phoned nor returned to his gallery. The lights were still switched off and Giulia's note still where they had left it, slotted in between the main door and its frame.

Chapter 42

Two days after his meeting with his lawyer at the Dorchester Hotel, Tarquin Littlejohn ran into Kathleen Corby at the entrance to the National Portrait Gallery in Trafalgar Square. For a moment he thought of avoiding her, and the idea that their bumping into each other might not be accidental crossed his mind. But the American woman had not seen him and was busy rifling through the art books in the gift shop, hardly what she should be doing, he thought, if she was stalking him. Besides, how would she have known he would be visiting the NPG on this precise day? To make sure, he observed her for a while from the hall outside the shop and waited until she had paid for a book and exited. He then approached her in front of the museum.

"Hello, Kathleen. This is a surprise!" he said.

She turned around slowly, and froze. Regaining her composure, she smiled meekly and returned his greeting.

"I thought you had lost all interest in anything English," Littlejohn said, only half in jest.

"That's not fair, Tarquin. I never said that," she protested.

"Your lawyers said it all for you when they sued me for sexual harassment," he reminded her.

"I can explain…it is not…it is not so simple," she mumbled under her breath.

Littlejohn knew he ought to be careful and that there was still a possibility that this fortuitous meeting had been contrived. The first stage of his court case with the Silverstein was fast approaching and he would be flying to California in a couple of weeks. However, Kathleen was an attractive woman; the temptation to flirt was strong and he did enjoy the idea of playing with fire.

"Are you alone?" he asked casually.

Kathleen coyly said she was for the moment, entertaining what she perceived to be Littlejohn's subtle invitation, but that she would be joining the rest of the Silverstein delegation in the evening.

"Well, let's go and have a drink then. There is a pub I like not too far from here."

Littlejohn led her away from the museum to the White Horse pub. He smiled smugly to himself; it felt as if they were two adversaries saving their energy for a fight.

He ordered a malt whisky for himself and a gin and tonic for Kathleen. The waiter returned with their drinks and a bowl of crisps he placed between them. They sat by a window facing each other across a narrow table, their backs to wooden dividers that reached over their heads, affording them as much privacy as one could find in a noisy London pub in the middle of the afternoon.

"Cheers!" Littlejohn said, as he tilted his glass towards her.

"Cheers, Tarquin!"

He drank half his whisky in one go and put his glass down with exaggerated care on the coaster before looking Kathleen in the eye.

"So Kathleen, how has the Museum fared since I left, and did you miss me?"

"The atmosphere has changed, people seem to be more careful…more careful. I heard that your court case against the Museum caused a major row at the Board of Trustees."

"Tell me more, my dear."

"Oh, I don't know much more. I overheard my boss, Jeff, talking about it over the phone. Apparently the Board of Trustees was split right down the middle on whether to fight you or settle."

"And what did old Jeff have to say about it?"

"That he didn't know what to think. That it was better to stay out of it. You know Jeff."

"Yes, I know Jeff. As much backbone as a jellyfish."

"You're not being fair, Jeff actually defended you when…" she stopped herself.

"Jeff could barely find the energy to defend himself. When did he try to defend me?"

The woman played nervously with her hair, pulling it back repeatedly over her ears, unsure whether to answer or not.

"So?" Littlejohn insisted.

"When I had to sue you for sexual harassment."

Her voice trembled slightly but Littlejohn felt no pity. He remembered their affair that had lasted almost four months; the passionate love-making at the motel in Sunset Boulevard and the even more exciting encounters in his office where they could have been exposed while the blinds shifted automatically to adjust to the level of sunlight.

"And what did he say or do?"

"He told Human Resources that he would talk to you, and me, and that it was probably an overreaction on my side."

"Did he tell you that?"

"Of course not! Sheila, the Human Resources Vice-President did."

"Ah, that doesn't surprise me. She must have been happy with the idea of suing me."

Kathleen nodded and said she was quite aggressive.

"But why did you agree?" he asked accusingly.

"I was...I was very upset when we broke up and I thought... you know, I hoped we would get together again. So I waited and... tried to talk to you but you just laughed at me. I was in tears when Sheila entered my office and...and I told her what happened."

"But why the sexual harassment, for Christ's sake?"

"It was Sheila's idea," Kathleen said very quietly.

"What?"

"She asked if I was sure that you had not put pressure on me, you know, because of your position, to go out on a date. I said maybe, so she said she would take it up with the Board and let me know. She came back a couple of weeks later and said I should sue you for sexual harassment."

"And you went along?" Littlejohn exclaimed in disbelief.

"I told her I wasn't at all sure it was such a good idea, but she insisted that I couldn't back out, and that if I did, my credibility at the Museum would be ruined. She didn't say I would lose my job, but that's what I understood then."

Littlejohn sat back and mused over these revelations quietly. The timing of the harassment case coincided with the first memorandum he had written the Board about the forgeries acquired by his predecessor. Somehow, it was too much of a coincidence.

"Kathleen, would you be prepared to repeat what you just told me?"

"In court, you mean?"

"Yes."

"Please don't ask me that, Tarquin. I know it wasn't right but you won your case and I would certainly lose my job and who knows what else."

"Don't you see they used you? Sheila, the Board, maybe even Jeff?"

"Why? How?"

"My claim that the Museum had spent several million dollars to acquire forgeries was an embarrassment to the Museum. They used the court case to discredit me, to cast doubt on my character and therefore my claims. I was made to understand that if I withdrew my claims that the drawings were forgeries then they would make sure the sexual harassment case against me was dropped. Of course, I didn't agree!"

"Oh!"

"Kathleen, I didn't mean to hurt your feelings when we broke up, but you seemed to have taken it well and when you later said we should get together again I thought you meant...well you know...to get together one more time. And I didn't laugh at you, I laughed because it was quite unlike you. You were...I mean, you are serious. Intense and sexy but...well, serious."

Kathleen blushed and shook her head.

"I am sorry about the court case. Really, I mean that."

"How about making up for it this afternoon then?" Littlejohn suggested with a glint in his eyes.

Kathleen's eyes opened wide in amazement.

"You don't mean that, do you?"

"I certainly mean it. Let bygones be bygones."

He took her hand in his. At first she tried to pull it away but he did not let her go. Their eyes locked and Kathleen Corby knew that Tarquin Littlejohn was dead serious.

Littlejohn did not return to the Museum after leaving Kathleen Corby's hotel later in the afternoon, but he felt better than he had for months. Whether Kathleen wanted it or not, she was going to help him fight for his rights.

He decided to have an early dinner in London before going back home and hailed a taxi to take him to the Dorchester Hotel. The waiter recognised him and asked him if he wanted a malt whisky on ice. Littlejohn asked for a double whisky and a white notepad.

The sex with Kathleen had been good, but now Littlejohn had more important things on his mind. He started to scribble on his pad.

Point 1. Call Giulia.

This morning, before he had taken the train to London, he had made one of his regular calls to Bernard Hargrave with only one objective in mind, to inquire whether there was any news on the whereabouts of his drawing. Littlejohn thought that by insisting doggedly Hargrave would step up his efforts, but until this morning nothing had come out of it. So, Littlejohn was delighted to hear that Hargrave finally had news for him, but did not let it show. Bernard Hargrave asked Littlejohn to call Giulia, who was going to Rome in a few days, on behalf of the Hargraves, to look over the portfolio of drawings that had belonged to Eric Hargrave and recently resurfaced. There just might be a good chance that Littlejohn's was one of them, and if he briefed Giulia she could verify whether in fact Littlejohn's drawing was in Rome.

Littlejohn thanked Bernard Hargrave, grateful that his persistence had paid off.

Littlejohn ordered a second whisky and wrote down point 2. Call Goldman.

The afternoon had been more than pleasant; not only had he had his fun in bed with Kathleen, but he had also obtained information that would strengthen his case against the Silverstein. He would have to talk to Goldman about this and see how this development could be best used to their advantage.

Point 3, he wrote. Check bank balance.

Beside this he entered, "trip to Rome, trip to California, hotel stays, duration of stay, living expenses etc." His lawyers had warned him that even if a settlement was reached it could take as long as a month before the exact wording of the agreement could be finalised and, therefore, before any payout could occur. He would have to talk to the bank manager in the morning about extending his overdraft facility.

His bank balance was not looking healthy.

Littlejohn downed his whisky and asked for another. As the waiter poured him his third he said,

"Go on, my boy, don't be stingy. I'm staying here tonight."

With a great deal of reluctance Littlejohn scrawled the name Doctor Jones as point number 4. He glanced at his fingers and confirmed the whitish colour of his nail plates; his breath had been smelling funny and he was a bit more tired than normal. His urine had been darker than usual and he was bruising easily. He mildly suspected it had something to do with his intake of whisky, nothing new there, but he fought the idea of a troubled liver with the fact that he had no difficulty making love to Kathleen.

Anyway, Littlejohn thought, the way his luck had gone today, he should pass the doctor's examination without any problem.

Chapter 43

At the end of the seventies, Eric Hargrave's nefarious activities were exposed by a British journalist. She followed the trail of a Francesco del Cossa, sold to the Pierpoint Morgan Library in New York through one of the most prominent art galleries in London specialised in Old Masters.

A curator took a closer look at the drawing and noticed that some of the ink had been scraped away with a razor blade to give the artwork a more authentic fifteenth-century look. The Directors of the London gallery panicked, offered to take the drawing back and refund the museum. They placed an advertisement in a daily newspaper to announce they would take back drawings sold by their gallery, if buyers had any doubt.

Alison French visited Eric Hargrave in his house at the foot of Anticoli and found a soft-spoken Englishman of great erudition with a mischievous sense of humour. He was far too clever to admit to anything, and calmly answered the questions fired at him by the journalist, without compromising himself.

His long-haired Filipino boyfriend, Eduardo, graciously poured each of them a generous glass of red wine and passed around a blue and white bowl filled with pitted olives. The atmosphere was convivial and Eric felt the interview was going well.

He then pointed at the elegant marble head of a youth on a small desk.

"This head, for instance, is Roman, probably from the third or fourth century BC, but, it could equally be Greek. In ancient Rome it was quite usual for Italian sculptors to imitate Greek sculptors, and senators and generals did not mind whether they bought a copy, or an original. It is only much later, when art became a traded commodity, that the distinction between genuine and copy became relevant. The corruption of money!"

Eric excused himself to check whether the water for the pasta was boiling. Alison and Eduardo exchanged a few words and Eduardo must have said something funny as Eric heard laughter as he emptied the contents of a bag of penne into the pot before returning to his guest. He poured Alison and Eduardo some more wine, sat down and poured himself the rest of the bottle and picked up on his discourse.

"Many artists could not even distinguish between their own paintings and those of the forgers. Cezanne, Vlaminck and Utrillo, for example, were all fooled at some point, and admitted they could not see the difference. So, if an artist can be fooled, it should not surprise anyone that a museum or a so-called expert can make a mistake. Museum basements are full of artworks of dubious origin."

Eric chuckled and drank some red wine and told the journalist the story of the theft of the Mona Lisa from the Louvre Museum.

"In Paris at the turn of the century, a group of forgers had found a way to sell their works to unscrupulous buyers. They would copy an artwork from the museum, and use genuine Louvre stationery to produce allegedly confidential documents that said the original had been stolen and been replaced by a copy to avoid a scandal. In 1911, this group decided to sell the Mona Lisa to five American collectors at the same time. They painted the copies, smuggled them into the United States, and hid them there. A week later they walked out of the museum with the genuine Mona Lisa wrapped in a blanket. When the newspapers announced the theft, the forgers sold their works and became a lot richer.

Several years later, the head of the gang, who was Italian by the way, was arrested. The authorities recovered the original Mona Lisa. But did they really recover the original or was this another excellent copy? Who can tell?"

Alison French commented that it was an entertaining story, but added that modern technology would soon put an end to forgeries with the use of x-rays, ultra violet light and chemical analyses that made it possible to look under the surface of a painting or date the exact origin of a pigment used.

Eric replied, "But all these tests cost a lot of money; they can damage the painting and are not always entirely reliable. For instance, Van Gogh, who was quite poor, often painted over a canvas he had already used because he couldn't afford to buy a new one. So an x-ray can show you that there is a Van Gogh under your Van Gogh, but it cannot tell you with any degree of certainty whether it is a genuine one or not. A clever forger could then paint two Van Goghs, one on top of the other, and send the result to be tested, thereby providing an additional proof that Van Gogh was the author."

The journalist agreed that science was not able to offer a guarantee, but pointed out that new technology would continue to be developed.

"Scientific tests can prove that an artwork is not genuine, but they can never demonstrate that it is. And drawings, for instance, are much more difficult to test. To analyse a drawing means you must be prepared to damage it, because you will need to dissolve the ink or the wash to test it," he explained provocatively.

"Is this why you choose drawings?" the journalist asked, thinking he was about to make an admission.

"I do not choose drawings over paintings. I have sold both, in fact," he answered with a disarming smile.

"Do you deny that some of the drawings that passed through your hands were wrongly attributed to Old Masters?"

"It seems to be the case, but I did not claim, for instance, that the drawing that hangs in the Pierpoint was drawn by Francesco del Cossa."

"Because you knew who drew it!" Alison interjected.

Eric paused, a twinkle in his eye, as he explained with a smile.

"I liked the drawing and took it to an auction house in London to get a second opinion. They were interested in putting it in one of their sales, and did not even ask whether it was by Francesco del Cossa. It was subsequently acquired by the Museum on its artistic merit."

"But you knew it was a fake!" she insisted.

"There is no such thing as a fake drawing. A drawing is a drawing as a tree is a tree. There is a drawing in the British Museum by Rembrandt which is a copy of a drawing by Mantegna. Would you call the Rembrandt a fake?"

"Of course not, because it is attributed to the author of the drawing."

"You are correct, and it confirms my point. It is the attribution which is at the centre of the debate, not the drawing itself."

"I understand what you're saying," the journalist said guardedly.

"The artist produces a drawing and sells it to a dealer who shows it to an expert. The expert in question declares it was drawn by an Old Master. The dealer may or may not have his suspicions, but sells it at a huge profit. The guilty party is either the dealer or the expert."

"Unless the artist knows that his drawing is being sold with the wrong label."

"If the artist only receives a small amount of money for his work, he does not benefit from the false attribution, and, is therefore not guilty."

Alison French admitted that, in the situation he described, the dealer and the expert were the ones deceiving the buyer.

"Once a false attribution has been uncovered, the dealer and the expert are quick to blame the forger and to call him a criminal. In reality, it is the dealer and the expert who should be accused of deception."

"It is all about intention and knowledge then, if I follow you." she said.

"It is actually all about money. The dealers stand to make huge profits and do not want to rock the boat, so to speak. In fact, the whole art establishment would prefer that there be no debate on attribution. Experts can lose their reputation, museums might have to admit they wasted money and are not the authority they claim to be, and dealers…well, dealers should be the ones ending up in front of a judge!"

Lunch was served al fresco and the conversation flowed as freely as the wine for the rest of the afternoon. They talked about art, about life and about Italy. When Alison left her hosts, she realised it would be difficult for her to be entirely objective about Eric.

In her article published a week later, she was careful not to make any definite pronouncement about the role Eric Hargrave played in the sale or the production of the forged drawings. Was he an innocent middleman, buying and selling works he uncovered in Italy and passing them on to the experts to determine their origins? Or did Eric actually produce some of them himself?

Eric wrote to the English newspaper that published Alison's article, mocking the judgment of the so-called experts, and a few years later, when an Italian newspaper reprinted the article without disclaimers, he actually sued the paper and settled out of court. To his close friends he admitted, without shame, that he possessed the skills but lacked the imagination or the creativity to produce a masterpiece. But, Eric never lost his hunger for knowledge, trying his hand successfully at engraving, etching, sculpture, and writing.

When his autobiography was published, Eric Hargrave was vilified by the art establishment, who described him as a rogue and a crook. Experts came out of the woodwork to claim that no forgery by Eric Hargrave could really have fooled them.

Eric observed these reactions with detached amusement.

To a journalist who asked him what he thought of contemporary art and the likes of Damien Hirst he answered:

"Inasmuch as an artist questions the definition of art in an intelligent way – and many actually do – I believe their contribution is worthwhile. But placing a dead fish in an aquarium filled with formaldehyde? This is not art, at best it is a publicity stunt for the author!"

When Eric wrote the draft of the *The Language of Line*, he was not so much seeking fame as passing on the knowledge he had acquired to the next generations. He developed a theory that one could read a drawing, and recognise the hand that had produced the drawing, as one could recognise the literary style of a particular writer from a text.

In the presentation of his treatise he used as many illustrations by the Old Masters as works in his own hand. But he truly believed, as he had once told Giulia, "that a drawing should be appreciated for what it is, for its intrinsic quality, and not for what someone pretends to know it is."

Chapter 44

Most of the books that had filled Eric Hargrave's shelves in Rome and Anticoli had been moved from the guest room and were now piled up on the floor in his brother's garage. Some were still in the removal boxes together with copies of various art magazines and catalogues dating back thirty years.

The antiquarian bookseller who came to assess the value of Eric's collection was a small round man with a kind face and a seriously balding head. He wore a brightly coloured green jacket over a pair of chinos.

He grimaced when he saw the state of many of the volumes. Pages were missing, covers torn; humidity had stained many illustrations and a mouldy smell permeated the air in the windowless room.

He went through the piles methodically, picking up a couple of books from each one when he saw titles of particular interest. He lifted Gustave Dore's book, *Milton's Paradise*, that could have fetched several hundred pounds, only to find it had been rendered almost worthless by the heavily foxed illustrations. Still he patiently leafed through the pages and checked the publication date before putting it back on the floor with a frown.

In one of the cardboard boxes Bernard Hargrave had not had the energy to empty, the dealer found a notebook bound in black imitation leather filled with notes, sketches, and lists handwritten by Eric. He put it to the side, and once his examination of the books had been completed, handed it over to Bernard, and said he was prepared to buy the contents of Eric's library for nine hundred pounds.

"And this is only because we are friends and because it was your brother's library. There are some good reference books, but they're in such poor condition I'll make hardly any profit," he explained, standing with his arms crossed.

Bernard wanted to argue and thought of inviting another dealer for a second evaluation but his visitor pre-empted him.

"You are welcome to get someone in for another estimate, but I don't think you'll get more than seven hundred for the lot."

Bernard was tired and thanked the bookseller as he left. He said he would think about the offer and consult his sister before calling him back.

He skimmed through the black notebook and saw that it contained lists of artworks, some rough sketches, various notes and some telephone numbers, including Giulia's. Could this be the notebook that Giulia had asked him about? He was not sure as it did not seem to contain anything of particular importance. He phoned her and asked whether she would like to have a look at it; they agreed that Bernard would send it by express courier delivery.

Giulia received the package next day. The notebook itself was unremarkable, the type you could purchase in a stationery shop. The cover was scratched and a bit bent at the edges from constant handling, but it was otherwise in good condition.

The first pages contained several names with telephone numbers. Giulia recognised her own London number but also the names of Littlejohn with a number in California scribbled beside it, and that of Willie with several entries, one in Canada and one in the Philippines, she surmised. There were other names and numbers which were not familiar to her.

After several blank pages Eric had written a poem dedicated to Willie. Giulia read the first lines of the sonnet, hesitated, feeling she was intruding and turned onto the next page to find yet another poem. She leafed through about half a dozen of them and thought this is what Eric might have wanted Willie to have should anything happen to him. Willie had understood it to be a will. Giulia turned the pages and found what appeared to be a list of artworks, some described in detail with the size, the material they were drawn on and the medium used; others were only mentioned by their titles. Beside many of the descriptions Eric had added abbreviated notes and numbers. Giulia scrolled slowly though the list.

Claude, an Italian landscape, pen and wash over charcoal
Rembrandt, back of woman lying on her side, pen and sepia wash
Piranesi, carceri, pen and wash
Durer, Joachim, pen and charcoal
Raphael, combat of naked men, 25x40cm, pen & brown ink, 1975
Verrochio, head of angel looking up, 15x17cm, black chalk with white, 1978

The codes found most frequently were "BUR", "SO", "AP" and "CA". Beside each abbreviation were numbers Giulia guessed were dates. The Claude was associated with 0361, probably for March 1961. The Rembrandt was marked 0661, the Piranesi 1061 and so on. Towards the end of the list Eric had abandoned this system and simply listed the year.

She also noticed that several of the drawings were further highlighted with asterisks and wondered why. Eric had taken a lot of trouble in preparing this compilation.

The list with more artists' names was broken down in groups. Each group appeared to relate to one or two year periods. Several pages separated each group, themselves filled with notes, thoughts jotted down randomly and sketches with references. Two pages caught Giulia's attention, not because of the quality of the diagrams, but the remarks inscribed in the margin, "Line Fig. 1" and "Line Fig. 2" etc. She understood instantly that some of Eric's sketches and probably some of the drawings in the list were intended to illustrate *The Language of Line.*

Later in the afternoon Giulia tried to control the excitement in her voice as she called Bernard Hargrave to explain what she had discovered.

"Bernard, what you sent me brings us closer to identifying the illustrations for the book, *The Language of Line.*"

"You mean the notebook contained Eric's drawings?"

"Not really. There were a few rough sketches and a few diagrams but more importantly, lists of artworks he may have intended to illustrate the book. All we have to do now is to research the references and find the images," she said emphatically.

"And how will you do that, Giulia?" Bernard asked.

"I think the abbreviations beside each artwork may stand for a particular entry in a book or a catalogue. I haven't quite figured out what they are, but I'm working on it."

"So Eric's book will be published then?" Bernard asked hopefully.

"It's a little bit early to say for sure, but, we're making good progress. By the way, Bernard, have you sold Eric's books?" she asked.

Bernard explained that the book dealer had made him an offer he had not yet accepted. "Why do you ask?"

Giulia said that she believed that some of the drawings Eric had described in his notebook might be from books he owned.

"Also, were there old auction catalogues, exhibition catalogues, magazines?" Giulia added.

"Yes, they have been put to one side by the dealer. He wasn't interested in them. I remember seeing some Sotheby's auction catalogues and Burlington Reviews."

Giulia's heart skipped a beat. Eric's abbreviations "SO" and "BUR", could they possibly stand for Sotheby's and Burlington? "Bernard, this is very important. Please do not sell any of the catalogues or books until I've had a look at them."

He assured her that nothing would be shifted until her return.

Chapter 45

Conti had insisted on picking Giulia up at the airport and, after initially protesting, she agreed. The customs officials looked bored and tired and, just outside the arrivals door, a varied crowd pressed against the barriers to spot a familiar face among the arriving passengers.

The police inspector was standing aside from the crowd, close to the bar and the brightly lit bookshop when Giulia spotted him. He smiled and stepped forward to greet her.

On their way to the centre of Rome, Giulia told him about her conversation with Willie and her visit with the Porters, but did not speak about the black book.

"So, they confirmed that Eric had continued to make drawings in the style of the Old Masters even after his autobiography," he concluded matter-of-factly.

"That's what they said, yes. In fact, even Donovan had suspected it."

Not turning to Giulia, but keeping his eyes on the road, Conti said, "I have a few questions about Eric. Do you mind?"

"I'll answer what I can," Giulia replied.

"He appears to have been a man of certain means. A pied-a-terre in the city, a house in the country, books, paintings, travelling, dining out. How did he pay for all this?"

"Eric lived from his art and he liked to live well. He drank more than he should have, and never held back when he came across a book on art that would be useful in his studies. He had no concept of money beyond what he needed at the moment, but on the same score, he regarded debt as a matter of honour and his creditors were always eventually paid."

As the car crossed the Ponte di Testaccio, turning left on the Lungotevere where traffic was intense, Conti measured his words before asking Giulia "Did Eric frequent younger men in Rome?"

Giulia shrugged and said she doubted whether he made a habit of it, but believed the occasional encounter was possible. Eric was homosexual and had his needs, she reluctantly remembered him telling her once. Especially since Willie was always away in Canada.

Conti could hear her unwillingness to delve further into the subject.

"I'm sorry Giulia, I didn't mean to upset you, but during my interrogations I spoke to someone who said that Eric was often seen drinking with younger men. And I suppose he could have met the wrong kind and things might have ended up badly, and I was wondering whether this could have been the case."

"Oh?"

"And the man I interviewed said that Eric was with a male prostitute the night before his accident. But we have not been able to locate him for questioning," Conti continued.

"But didn't you tell me that Eric still had his wallet with cash and all on him when he was found in the street? So he was not robbed that night, and what motive could a one-night stand prostitute have to kill a client so openly in the street? Normally we hear of prostitutes as prey rather than perpetrators," Giulia countered.

Conti nodded in agreement.

Conti spotted a free parking space on the Lungotevere close to the Ponte Sisto and swerved his car into the opening. He leaned over to Giulia and asked, "Giulia, I was wondering whether you would join me for dinner tonight? I know it's a bit of a last minute thing…?"

"Of course I'll come and have dinner with you, gladly," she said smiling as they got out of the car.

Conti took Giulia's arm and steered her gently through the groups of people that crossed, lingered on, and performed on the Ponte Sisto. The scent of marijuana drifted through the air and one of the many dogs yawned and stretched out, nearly tripping a passer-by. Fake handbags, Prada, Vuitton, Chanel were displayed on yards of cloth. Conti ignored them; this was not his priority for the present.

They arrived in front of Piazza Trilussa and looked at each other in silence. They circled around the Piazza and headed towards the Via Benedetta and entered the restaurant *Checco er Carettiere*. They were both familiar with the menu and ordered a plate of antipasti to share and Conti ordered a dish of *spaghetti cacio e pepe* while Giulia remained faithful to her *scampi alla griglia*.

As they waited for their food, Giulia said, "Littlejohn will be here tomorrow."

"Bernard Hargrave told him that the drawing he was looking for might be in Rome and gave him my phone number. He insisted on coming over himself and we agreed to meet tomorrow, however, I didn't tell him the police had the portfolio of Eric's works so it might be quite a shock to him," she said with a half-smile.

"What do you know about Littlejohn?" Conti asked curiously.

Giulia told him what she had learned; his professional background, the forgery discoveries, the sexual harassment case. She also added the episodes that took place between Bernard Hargrave and Littlejohn during his visits to Brighton.

Enzo Zangara stepped on his brakes suddenly, avoiding collision with the oncoming white van by inches. The van's driver, a ponytailed, dark-skinned man in his late twenties, shouted obscenities as he swerved past his car. Zangara waved weakly in sign of apology and pretended he didn't hear the furious driver's shouts. He manoeuvred his way into one of the parking spots in the Piazzale Roma, hurriedly got out of his car, and headed for one of the water taxis moored by the pier.

He eased his way across the narrow gangway and into the boat, ignoring the driver's offer to help. He sat down wearily on a blue-upholstered bench, loosened his tie, and told the driver to take him to Santa Croce.

The water taxi pulled away from the quay and, once its bow faced the open water, picked up speed. Zangara mopped his brow and fiddled nervously with his glasses and the handle of his leather briefcase. Was he over-reacting, he wondered. Should he have waited before alerting Amato.

It was Angelo Amato's financial support and connections that had helped Zangara keep his gallery afloat and the story out of the press, when he was threatened with a very expensive lawsuit many years back. Amato had been a customer of Zangara's and his association with him gave him entry into the Northern Italian social elite and allowed him to gain respectability. Zangara, indebted to Amato, proposed that they form a silent partnership. Amato had money to invest, Zangara had artworks to sell. It came as a shock to

Zangara when he came to know that his partner represented one of the families of the '*Ndrangheta* of Calabria. He lived in a state of nervous tension for months, expecting the police to come knocking at his door, or even worse, his new partner to threaten him. But nothing bad happened. Instead, new customers were introduced, and offshore transactions made easy. He no longer considered his association a risk, and enjoyed Amato's company.

Amato owned the top two floors of a *palazzo* that fronted the Grand Canal.

They greeted each other and Amato led Zangara to his terrace overlooking the roofs of Venice.

"Angelo, why are the police still investigating Hargrave's death? I thought you said there would be no investigation."

"It's only a matter of days before the inspector who went to see you is ordered to close the case," Amato answered.

Zangara shrugged. "But in the meantime he's still investigating, and asked me about the Poussin drawing."

Amato frowned, "What did he ask exactly?"

He described the Nicolas Poussin we had commissioned from Hargrave. "How could he have made the connection and what else does he know?" Zangara asked nervously.

"I wouldn't worry. Hargrave is dead," Amato stated bluntly.

Chapter 46

The British Airways plane banked away from the shore and flew over the sea for a few minutes before making its final approach above the Leonardo da Vinci airport in Rome. The sky was cloudless and the sea sparkled under the glaring sun. Littlejohn looked through the window of the plane and saw the solitary silhouettes of umbrella pine trees and a few people on the beach despite the fact that summer had not officially started.

Littlejohn felt that nothing could go wrong. Kathleen Corby had provided him with a strong card in his legal battle with the museum, whether she testified or not. With a bit of luck, he might recover his drawing. Giulia Vasari had sounded helpful over the phone, confirmed that Bernard Hargrave had spoken to her about him, and yes, if the drawing that he was looking for was in Rome, she could check it out for him. When he suggested that he come to Rome himself Giulia had given him a number he could call so they could arrange the practical details for their meeting. He stood up, stretched his long frame in the narrow cabin and collected his hand luggage from the overhead compartment. He calculated that he would reach his hotel before six and would be able to call Giulia Vasari right away. The hotel was expensive and he did not intend to spend more than one night in the Italian capital.

The hotel doorman opened the back door of Littlejohn's taxi and gave him a bow.

"Welcome to the Hassler, Signore."

Littlejohn barely nodded and walked past him and the porter. Behind his back the doorman closed the door of the taxi and winked at the driver.

"Bet he didn't tip you?"

"*Inglese*," came the driver's reply.

"But he can afford the Hassler!"

"That's why he can afford the Hassler!" the driver replied sarcastically, switching on his engine and driving away.

From the third floor window of his room Littlejohn could see the whole stretch of the Spanish Steps from the church of the Triniti dei Monti down to the fountain on Piazza di Spagna, but he paid it scant attention. His visit had a clear purpose and nothing was going to distract him. He reached for the phone on the desk and quickly dialled Giulia's number. She responded after two rings and asked whether he had had a good trip. Littlejohn ignored her question.

"When can we meet so I can inspect this drawing?" he asked abruptly.

If Giulia was offended by his churlishness she did not show it and apologised for not being able to arrange a meeting that evening.

"I can pick you up at your hotel in the morning and we can go directly to see it. Would nine thirty be convenient for you?"

Littlejohn made no effort to mask his annoyance at the delay and insisted that he had little time and was flying back the next day. Giulia apologised again but did not suggest an alternative time. They would meet the next morning.

Littlejohn unpacked his bag and placed his toiletry set in the bathroom by the sink. It was too early for dinner, too crowded for a walk and he was not in the mood for a visit to a museum or to any of the many Roman churches. Absent-mindedly he picked up the Herald Tribune and started to read a review of the latest auction of Old Masters in London. For a moment the thought of calling Jack Goldman, his lawyer, to tell him about Kathleen Corby crossed his mind but he decided otherwise. He wanted to enjoy the surprise on Goldman's face when he announced his news.

Someone knocked at the door and he did not bother to answer. A key was put into the lock and a chambermaid stepped into the room before stopping abruptly.

"*Mi scusi signore*, I am here for the bed."

"The bed is already done and I don't need anything. Go away."

The woman hesitated, not sure she had understood the unfriendly Englishman. She noticed he had returned to his newspaper and so she stepped back as quietly as she could.

At exactly nine-thirty the next morning, Giulia presented herself at the reception of the Hassler and asked for Tarquin Littlejohn. The curator kept her waiting, taking his time to inspect her from the lobby where he was seated and when he finally walked to her he was at his most charming.

"Ms Vasari, a pleasure to meet you. Bernard did not tell me how beautiful you were!"

Giulia smiled politely and extended a hand he kissed in an exaggerated manner.

"Shall we go?" she said.

"After you."

Giulia led him across the lobby and into the street. She stopped in front of the car and indicated the back seat. Littlejohn was about to protest he wanted to sit in the front beside her when he noticed a man behind the wheel. So she has a driver, he mused, an interesting and intriguing woman.

She briefly introduced the driver as Alberto Conti but did not give any additional information.

He wondered how she was connected to the Hargraves. She was obviously not British; her accent was North American but there definitely was a hint of an Italian or Spanish accent. This would explain her dark hair and olive complexion, he thought.

The driver turned the car around and eased into the traffic away from the Villa Borghese towards Via delle Quattro Fontane then down Via Nazionale. The driver swerved in and out of the bus lanes despite the double yellow lines, adept in his profession, Littlejohn noted.

"Can I ask you how you came to know the Hargraves, Ms. Vasari?"

"I was a friend of Eric's," she answered.

"So you live in Rome then?"

"I used to live in Rome. At the moment, I live in London…but I am here quite often."

As Giulia said this she glanced towards Conti; he seemed uninterested in their conversation.

"Do you know who I am?"

"Bernard said you were the curator of an American museum in California. Is that right?"

"I was the curator of the Silverstein, yes. Have you ever been to California, Ms Vasari?"

"A couple of times. I have visited the Silverstein but only the villa where they keep the antiquities, not the main building in the hills."

"You should visit the main museum next time, it is well worth it."

"So why did you leave California?" Giulia asked quickly just as he was about to change the subject and ask where they were going.

"A long story. The museum and I had a difference of opinion on certain ethical matters."

"A question of attribution?" she asked.

Littlejohn was somewhat surprised that she had found out about his law suit against the Silverstein. He suddenly felt he had to be on his guard.

"A good way to describe it, but it is more complicated than that."

"I understand you are an eminent authority on Old Master drawings and that you worked at the V&A for a long period of time."

Littlejohn acknowledged the compliment. He watched Giulia's profile for a while, the line of her nose, her neck and caught a glimpse of her open blouse.

"Where is your driver taking us?" he asked suddenly.

"Alberto is not my driver…the drawings are in his safe keeping."

Littlejohn frowned, unsure he had understood. Conti continued to focus on the road and the curator wondered whether he actually understood English.

"We are almost there," Giulia said as they entered Viale Trastevere. No one spoke until Conti parked the car and stepped out. Littlejohn followed him out, looking in turn at Giulia and at Conti. The *Commissariato* was less than a block from where they stood.

"Coffee?" Conti asked.

"No, thank you. I had one at breakfast," Littlejohn replied.

"Well, I need one," Conti said and turned.

The Englishman looked puzzled and placed a hand on Giulia's arm to slow her down.

"Why does he have Hargrave's drawings? Who is he?" he asked.

"He's a friend, but I'll let him explain," she answered.

They entered a bar, walked past the cashier who was filling a form to play the *lotto* towards the green marble-topped counter. Conti and Giulia ordered coffee while Littlejohn stood waiting. Conti drank his espresso and turned him.

"Let's sit here for a minute," he suggested, motioning to a chair.

Littlejohn slowly sat down in front of Conti looking very concerned.

"I am Inspector Alberto Conti of the *Commissariato* of Trastevere," he said without preamble.

Littlejohn fixed his eyes on Conti incredulously. His discomfort did not escape Conti who asked whether he needed a glass of water.

"Can you explain to me what drawing it is you're looking for and why? I am very interested to know this," Conti said, not taking his eyes off him.

Littlejohn made an effort to straighten up in his chair and cleared his throat.

"Is this a police interrogation?" he asked.

"I am a policeman and I am asking you questions; so yes, we can call this a police interrogation. You do not have to answer me, but I believe I have something you are searching for and you might be able to answer a few questions for me, so we are in a position to trade."

Littlejohn was caught completely off guard. He realized he had two choices, stay and answer the questions, or leave and say good bye to the drawing. He decided to stay.

"When were you last in Rome?" Conti asked.

"I don't know exactly, seven, eight months ago, maybe more."

"And when did you meet Eric Hargrave for the first time?"

"In California, for the launch of his exhibition in downtown Los Angeles."

"Hadn't you met before? In England maybe?"

"No, or to be precise, I knew of him of course, but I had not met him until California."

"And what exactly do you mean by 'I knew of him'?"

"A woman journalist exposed him in the seventies; she came over here, to Italy, to interview him but he admitted to nothing. As a curator in London at the time I knew about it. Then in the early nineties his autobiography containing his confessions was published, and everyone in the art world got to know about him."

"So your relationship was…how do you say?…purely professional?"

Somehow the question unsettled Littlejohn and he began to stutter slightly.

"I…er…I wouldn't say we had a professional relationship…I mean, he was a crook and I was working for a museum so…" Littlejohn did not finish his sentence.

Conti asked for another espresso and said nothing else to Littlejohn. Something had clearly made him uncomfortable and Conti observed his discomfort with clinical detachment. After a few seconds Littlejohn felt the need to clarify what he meant, to explain that a man in his position, a man of his reputation, could not possibly be associated with Eric Hargrave. The inspector nodded inattentively as if what he said had no importance.

"So, you didn't meet Eric Hargrave in Rome during the last six months, and you say you can't afford to be associated with him, right?"

"Correct."

"So why should Mr. Hargrave have a drawing that you claim belongs to you?"

Littlejohn felt on safe ground again and explained that he suspected several drawings from the Silverstein museum attributed to Old Masters were, in fact, forgeries by Eric Hargrave and that he had asked Mr. Hargrave to confirm this was the case.

"Mr. Littlejohn, was it not a bit risky for someone in your position to be seen dealing with a known forger?"

"It was a risk, but…but I needed to have his confirmation. To have some of his work hanging at the Silverstein would be another feather in his cap, so to speak."

"And did he?"

"Did he what? Admit he had drawn them?"

Conti nodded.

Littlejohn looked away as he answered.

"Not directly, which is why I challenged him to do a new drawing in the style of Michelangelo."

"So, this is the drawing you're now looking for," Conti stated rather than asked.

Conti's eyes bored into his and Littlejohn found it unnerving. He volunteered, as Conti expected, more details about his dispute with the Silverstein and the fact that he saw himself as a man of principle, a man with ethical sense.

"Can you describe the drawing for me?"

"It's a study for the Virgin and Child. In fact, I've brought a copy of the original with me." He pulled a page folded in four from the right pocket of his blue blazer and placed it on the table.

Giulia glimpsed it and cast a quick glance at the inspector who nodded.

"Let's go and have a look at these drawings then," Conti proposed finally.

Giulia and Conti stood aside while Littlejohn took great care in examining each drawing carefully. He frowned at the photocopy inserted among the originals and put aside one of the drawings. "This is the drawing I'm looking for," he said, holding an exquisite pen and brown ink drawing showing a Madonna looking down and a Child looking up to her, his left hand stretching out to caress her face. The sheet contained additional sketches.

Conti said nothing.

"Well, can I take it with me then?"

The inspector said he would arrange to have the whole lot shipped to the heirs of Eric Hargrave within a week.

"You'll have to request it from them directly," Conti informed him.

Littlejohn stared at the drawing he wanted desperately to take home with him. He knew there was nothing he could do to change Conti's mind and his shoulders slumped.

"Ah, before you go, there is another thing I would like to ask you," Conti said casually.

He pulled the photocopy from the portfolio and placed it on the table in front of Littlejohn.

"It's a photocopy," Littlejohn said haughtily.

"I know that. What I would like to have is your professional opinion of the drawing. Is it good? Who drew it?"

Littlejohn was not really inclined to help Conti but his professional curiosity and his ego were not able to resist. He picked up the copy and glanced at it perfunctorily. Three shepherds and a woman stood by a tomb; one of the men kneeling in front of it pointed at carvings in the stone which read *"et in arcadia ego"*.

"It is probably by Nicholas Poussin, a French artist from the seventeenth century. It looks like a preparatory drawing for a painting that hangs in the Louvre. Easy enough to check, if you care to."

"Thank you, Mr. Littlejohn, that will be all," Conti said.

"But my drawing, when can I expect to see it in London?" Littlejohn asked wanting reassurance that it would be in his possession soon.

Conti repeated that the drawings would be released once arrangements had been made with the Hargraves on the practical details of the shipment.

Littlejohn was escorted to the front door of the *Commissariato* where he took his leave, and Conti and Giulia saw him hail a taxi to take him back to his hotel. He had only a few hours to spare before his return flight to London. Fridays were always busy days on the roads and Littlejohn was in great hurry to get back to London.

Giulia told Conti she would get on the phone to Bernard and make arrangements for the shipment of the drawings.

"And the Canaletto painting," Conti pointed out. He handed her a piece of paper with a full description and measurements and the contact details of the *Commissariato*. Giulia thanked him and made a mental note to call Donovan to let him know that the Venice painting would soon be on its way to the Hargraves.

Giulia asked him whether it would be possible to have the drawings and the painting professionally photographed before arranging for the packers to pick up the consignment.

Conti said he didn't see why not. Giulia glanced at her watch and noted that it was close to twelve. She was not sure Raimondo would be available at such short notice as he lived out in Tivoli, a good hour away from Rome. She told Conti she would try to make arrangements for the shoot on the following Monday if that was okay with him.

Conti said yes with a smile; it meant Giulia would be staying in Italy the whole weekend.

He walked her to the bar they had been to earlier and told her he had to get back to his desk to attend to some other urgent matters, but would be very happy if she would consider coming with him to Todi the following day.

"I try to get away from Rome as often as I can. I'll be going up to my house in Umbria and would like to invite you to lunch, show you the town of Todi and maybe meet up with a few friends for dinner. We could make a weekend of it. What do you say? Will you come?"

Giulia was pleasantly surprised by this impromptu out-of-town invitation. She wanted to get to know him better, and what better way than spending a whole day with him, away from his professional environment. But a whole weekend? Giulia threw caution to the wind, and gladly accepted his offer.

Chapter 47

A relaxed Alberto Conti stood waiting for Giulia at the entrance of the Locarno Hotel. He wore a striped blue and white shirt, beige Armani pants, and brown loafers. He had rolled up his sleeves and a pair of Raybans protected his eyes from the bright morning sun. Giulia felt butterflies in her stomach when she caught sight of him. She hadn't felt this in a long time and took it to be a good sign.

They walked over to his parked car and Conti put her case into the trunk and kissed her gently on both cheeks.

"I'm glad you're coming to Todi with me," was all he said.

"And I'm looking forward to this weekend," she replied.

They drove in comfortable silence, listening to a tape of Rachmaninoff's third piano concerto.

As they passed the exit to Orte, Giulia looked back and asked whether that wasn't the exit for Todi. Alberto said he normally would go that way but wanted to make a stop further north to pick up a few cases of white wine.

Giulia leaned back in the seat and closed her eyes. Half an hour later, Alberto gently nudged her to point out the bright red poppies that dotted the surrounding landscape. They stopped at Tordimonte, a medieval village between Baschi and Orvieto where Conti picked up his regular reserve of *La Carraia, Orvieto Classico* from a local wine producer.

The drive to Todi took them along the lake of Corbara, climbing up the sides of the mountain until they reached the top of the dam that formed the western part of the lake. The narrow road hugged the rock formation for a while before descending towards the shore of the lake as it approached the town of Pontecuti, a small cluster of houses that clung to the sides of the hill overlooking the Tiber valley. Conti pointed out the Chiesa della Consolazione, to the left, as they ascended the winding road that took them to the main piazza of the medieval city of Todi. He parked his car in front of the post office, close to the statue of Garibaldi, and walked Giulia to the Ristorante Umbria known for its local fare and stunning views.

"It's beautiful here, Alberto," Giulia said, admiring the panorama.

"And just under the woods, to the left of the red house that stands out in the fields, is where we are going after lunch," he pointed out to her.

They ordered their starters, the antipasti of the house followed by spaghetti with truffles. They skipped the main course, knowing a big meal was in store for them that evening, and ordered coffee and desserts instead.

Over lunch Conti told Giulia that the Eric Hargrave case was to be formally closed and the decision would be announced in the media the coming Monday.

"When did they decide this?" Giulia asked, wondering whether this was the important business Conti had to get back to after the meeting with Littlejohn.

"The *Commissario* was advised that it would be better for all concerned if the investigation ended. Influential people had a word with someone at the Ministry. Someone didn't like the way the inquiry was going, or the lack of answers so far."

"How do you feel about that, Alberto?" Giulia asked concerned that all her friend's energy and dedication had been to no avail.

"We did as thorough an investigation as we could, but we have nothing concrete. And the hospital medical report states that the injuries were caused by a fall."

"That serves their purpose, if they were afraid of being sued for having waited too long before attending to his injuries."

"Yes, you're right. But some things are just out of our hands, Giulia. We do the best we can but in this job, it is no guarantee that we come to a satisfactory conclusion."

Giulia then told Conti that she had made arrangements for a photographer to be at the *Commissariato* at nine Monday morning to take pictures of the drawings and the Canaletto. She also said she had spoken to Bernard Hargrave and that arrangements had been made with a company that specialised in the transportation of artworks to collect the drawings and the painting of Venice the same afternoon. Conti said that all seemed in order and he would be there to make sure things went smoothly.

They left the restaurant and returned to Conti's car. Giulia was relaxed in his company, but all the talk of work had slightly shifted the mood and only served to stress that theirs was, for the most part, a professional relationship. She glanced at him from the corner of her eye. His attention was fixed on the steep narrow road that took them down from the piazza, past a butcher, a jeweller, a few clothes shops, antique shops, more pizza places and bars. The afternoon sun was beating down strongly by now, and the route to Conti's house took them through olive groves interspersed with fields of grain and vineyards. They reached a dirt road that gently wound up the side of a mountain and turned into yet another scenic dirt road that passed a few farms along the way until they reached what appeared to be a dead end in the fields. They took a turn to the right and drove up a long driveway until Giulia noticed a terraced area with a pergola supporting grapevines. The house itself was a modest farmhouse that had been partly restored, with jasmine flowers in full bloom and wisteria hugging its front wall.

"Here we are, Giulia. Welcome to my humble country retreat," Conti said .

It was only when Giulia got out from the car and walked to the front of the house that she took in the beauty of the place. Lavender and rosemary and oleander bushes, apricot, plum, apple, pear and fig trees. Buds of pink peonies, roses of all colours, a magnolia tree in bloom. Little blue and white weeds carpeted the ground, cut off by a low stone wall that held the gravel away from the grass. The many colours, the many scents, that filled the senses. The gentle hills of Umbria with their patchwork of hues unrolled before her like the backdrop of a Renaissance painting. She spanned the view and realised that Conti's was undisturbed nature, 360 degrees. Giulia felt an overwhelming sense of peace. For a while she just enjoyed the silence, then turned to her host.

"Alberto, this is paradise on earth," she quietly said.

He smiled and took her hand, her case in his other hand, and led her towards the arched front door.

"Come on, we can enjoy the view later, when the sun is going down."

As they moved into the house Giulia noticed how thick the walls were and appreciated the sudden coolness they provided. Alberto led her up a few steps into a spacious living room where there was a sofa and a coffee table, around an old fireplace, with a small television in the corner of the room.

"Yes, even here I follow the news," he said deprecatingly. "Comes with the job."

The last remark stuck in Giulia's mind and was to nag her later.

A few scattered armchairs and pieces of antique furniture. An electric keyboard with a *Teach Yourself to Play* book by Olivieri propped up for the beginner.

"Filippo, is learning to play, and me with him," Conti said, "Or maybe the other way around."

His walls were full of paintings, big ones, small ones, watercolours, drawings and oils. In no particular order, they all hung together loosely. It reminded Giulia of the summer exhibitions at the Royal Academy in London.

Conti noticed her puzzled look, and quickly said,

"I tend to buy what I like, keep it in Rome for a couple of weeks then bring it out here to find a space on the wall. One day, I'll have to put them in better order. Maybe you could help me?"

"I'd love to, Alberto," Giulia answered, maybe a bit too quickly.

She remembered their trip to Monticello's gallery but could not locate his purchase on the walls. Must still be in Rome, she mused.

There was an eat-in kitchen to the left of the living room, with its own entrance from the outside as well, and an even larger fireplace.

Up a few steps, Conti showed her his studio which had a desk and papers and files piled high on every available space, and a door that led to a bathroom.

"The bedrooms are upstairs. You must be tired and might want a rest?" It sounded more like a suggestion than a question, but Giulia welcomed it.

There were three rooms upstairs, Alberto Conti's, his son's room for when he came over to visit on the odd weekend, and the guest bedroom that shared a bathroom with Filippo.

The rustic features of an old farmhouse had been carefully restored, the chestnut beams, the uneven red floor tiles, the doors and windows. Giulia knew she had the best view in the house. From her window she saw the same fields but even further. The room was simple and clean, and the bed had fresh crisp white sheets on it. On the dresser was a vase with red roses, a glass and a bottle of San Faustino water. In the corner there was a small writing desk. She opened her case and hung the one dress she had brought; it would do for the dinner they were going to this evening, she thought. She took a sip of water, went to wash her hands and fell into a deep sleep.

She was roused by a gentle knock on her door.

"Giulia, I thought you might like to catch the sunset," Alberto's voice came through the door.

"Yes, of course, thank you Alberto. I'll be down in a few minutes."

They sipped the chilled Orvieto wine as they watched the great golden ball of fire lose its way between the hills that had taken on another mood in the new light.

"And directly in front of you is Todi," Conti indicated.

Two falcons gracefully glided high up in the sky and Conti told Giulia how his parents had lived in a house in the centre of Todi, that his sister had later sold, and he had inherited the house in the countryside.

And as a dark blanket covered the hills and the sounds of night insects filled the air they lost track of time till they heard the piercing sound of the telephone ring with Virginia's voice on the line asking Alberto whether he could stop for some bread at Renzo's on their way to dinner.

Gianni and Virginia, Canadians, lived in a pink three-storey farm house with grey shutters facing the Monti Martani mountains. From their bedroom balcony, Virginia would pretend to sing arias to the gods as Gianni, from the veranda below, immortalised his wife in one of his many amusing caricatures.

"Hello, Alberto, and who is this lovely lady with you?" she asked, smiling warmly at Giulia.

"A friend from Rome. Well, no actually, she lives in London." Alberto turned to Giulia, "I think I'll leave it to you to explain, okay?"

Giulia was tempted to answer "I come with the job," a phrase he had earlier used that stuck in her mind, but thought better of it.

Around the terrace were flowering bushes of roses, and further down the garden Giulia could see the beginnings of a vegetable garden. She heard the low moo of a cow from the farm next door.

They were joined by other friends. Mario, a book restorer who worked on Vatican manuscripts with his Umbrian wife Mara, who much preferred the chaos of the city to the quiet of the countryside and never lost a chance to make this sentiment felt, to the great annoyance of her husband. Leonardo, a musicologist from Milan with his architect wife Cecilia, from Perugia and Valerio and Laura, a couple from down the road who owned the biggest furniture store in the area; Valerio's skilled hands had restored many a door and window to its former glory. The air was filled with the endless flow of conversation punctuated with laughter, and after the delicious dinner that Virginia had prepared was consumed, Leo played a Celtic tune on his guitar which reminded Giulia of Donovan, work and London. But as they all relaxed into their seats to listen to the Italian love song that followed, Alberto put his arm around Giulia's shoulders and drew her closer to him, bringing her back to the present, and she wished the moment would never end.

After a few more songs, Giulia and Laura helped Virginia clear the table, as the men said their good-byes. They all promised to meet again soon.

"Thank you for such a wonderful day, Alberto. You have a nice group of friends here in Umbria," Giulia said as they drove back to Alberto's house.

"They are now your friends as well. I'm happy to have you here; it has been a good day for me too." he replied.

They got to the house and lingered a few minutes outside, watching the flickering lights of the neighbouring towns and identifying star constellations when Alberto said,

"This is a great spot to watch the shooting stars on the night of San Lorenzo. If you're going to be in Italy, I would be happy if you would come and watch them with me."

She moved closer to him, and took his hand, and the perfume of her hair assailed his mind, awakening a desire he could not, and did not want to suppress.

He took her in his arms and kissed her lightly on the lips. She felt the tautness of his body; she held him tight, and gently opened her mouth. They kissed, a long and searching and tender kiss, under the open skies, oblivious to the hooting of the owl or the crickets that had started to play their music.

Giulia opened her eyes to a ray of light that had come through the slits of the closed window shutters. Beside her was Alberto, sleeping soundly. Smiling, she tiptoed to the guest room, donned her silk Japanese kimono, and went down to the kitchen to prepare coffee. Outside the window, Giulia could see a heavy mist had formed, enveloping the ground, and Todi appeared to float like a ship on an open sea. It was a magical sight and she closed her eyes as she remembered the passionate details of the night before.

Lost in her reverie Giulia did not hear Alberto steal up behind her and swoop her into his arms, carrying her back up to his bed.

"You're not getting away so easily. Coffee can wait," he said gently.

He kissed her cheeks, her nose, her eyes, her lips, her chin, then her neck, then her breasts. He tugged at one end of her belt and untied her kimono with his mouth revealing Giulia in all her sensual beauty. His one hand fondled her breast, his mouth consumed the other.

Giulia lifted Alberto's t-shirt over his head, and they pressed their nakedness against each other, firm breasts crushed against his ribs. He caressed her inner thighs to secure her excitement with his fingers, thrusting in and out. Alberto had not stopped kissing every inch of her body. He was like fire, travelling swiftly, searing her flesh.

She slipped away from under Alberto's embrace and turned him gently on his back. Alberto watched her face intently, as she straddled him and guided him into her. She let her body rise and fall in rhythmic pace, her hips moving in circular motion, and when she suddenly stopped, Alberto, wanting to keep up the movement started to stir.

"Not yet," whispered Giulia.

He felt her muscles gripping him, holding, releasing, holding, releasing and new waves of pleasure swept through him.

When he could no longer hold himself back, he moved in unison with her, performing the dance of love, till he poured into her, and she, receiving his passion, reached an orgasm like never before.

They lay in tight embrace, in blessed silence until Alberto whispered in Giulia's ear,

"I have waited for you for such a long time."

Chapter 48

The new premises of Seldom House in Clerkenwell were in stark contrast to their former office in the Bloomsbury area. They occupied the top two floors of a renovated old chocolate factory featuring the latest innovations in design. Gone were the sash windows, heavy curtains, high ceilings with friezes, carpeted floors and Victorian reproduction pieces of their former premises. All rooms were clad in a light oak flooring, big windows with Venetian blinds from floor to ceiling let in plenty of light, Philippe Stark was written all over the bathroom, and there was a top of the range kitchen; most of the furniture had been purchased from an interior design shop to complete the look. The piece de resistance was the rooftop garden, professionally landscaped, which overlooked the city of London, with the dome of St. Paul's a prominent highlight.

Giulia was greeted by Victor Edelman's secretary, who said a courier had just delivered two heavy boxes for her attention and that they were in one of the meeting rooms. Giulia thanked her and asked how she was. Edelman's secretary let her eyes roll before answering. "Conference in New York next week! Budgets to prepare. Pit Bull's in a frenzy! Can't wait for him to go."

Giulia smiled and wished her good luck before striding across towards the meeting room.

The boxes were those which had been used by the removal company to transport Eric's personal effects. She read the firm's name and label indicating Rome-Brighton. Rome, and Alberto came to mind. She briefly closed her eyes to shut out the world and treasure the fleeting moment.

Giulia tried to pull a box towards her; she could hardly move it. She realised she would need help to get all of them to her flat in Kensington. She opened the first box and saw it was filled with catalogues, art magazines, and a few badly damaged books that the antiquarian had cast aside. It would take her a couple of days to go through all this, she reckoned.

Edelman's powerful voice carried across through the open door of the meeting room. He was looking for his assistant, who was not at her desk, and instead spotted Giulia and looked surprised.

"Miss Vasari, I thought you were still in Rome enjoying yourself," he said.

Giulia was not sure whether he was being over-indulgent or sarcastic. She would find out soon enough, she thought.

"Since you are here, and no one else seems to be," he said, glancing at his assistant's empty desk irritably, "come in for a minute and let me know what you've been up to."

Giulia followed him into his office where chaos reigned. Stacks of books and newspapers in different languages were piled up on the small conference table and on the floor, files covered his desk and competed for space with notepads, a laptop, various colour mock-ups of book jackets, and computer print-outs.

"I'm off on Saturday. I need to have my presentation ready by Thursday!" he said to explain the mess around him.

Edelman's interest in Hargrave's book had waned rapidly when he understood that it would be neither controversial nor scandalous, appealing to only to a limited circle.

"Are you still working on the Hargrave book?" he asked.

"Yes, and I now believe Seldom House should publish it."

"But you yourself said that without illustrations it would be incomplete. I have no intention to publish a book I cannot sell. Besides, funds are tight and New York has asked us to reduce investments by ten percent."

Giulia, not wanting the project shelved at a time she was getting close to some answers, measured her words before replying.

"It may be a bit early to be sure, but I believe that we may be able to find the illustrations."

Edelman looked up sharply.

"Why didn't you say so?"

"Because I'm still working on it and need to do some more research. I meant to tell you later after all the checks had been done. And we may need an art historian to help us with the text and to match text to illustrations."

Edelman's tone became more conciliatory. Giulia must be closing in on something. She would not have mentioned help from an art historian if she didn't have those illustrations, he thought.

"Any chance you can find out before the end of the week?" he asked, assessing the potential extra sales of Eric's book.

"I need a couple of days."

"Okay, drop by the office, give me an update. Friday morning, can you do that?"

Giulia promised to return on Friday.

"By the way, is Greenwood going ahead with his film on Eric?"

"As far as I know, yes," Edelman answered.

"It will generate some publicity, I suppose."

"He's going to need to make some changes to his script first," Edelman replied.

The Vice-President of Seldom House pulled out a newspaper from the pile on the floor and pushed it towards Giulia.

"Page 4, top left," was all he said.

Giulia opened the paper and read the short article. According to the journalist, the Italian police had closed the case and declared Eric Hargrave's death an accident. The prosecutor "regretted the demise of Eric Hargrave" but stated that "the evidence did not point to homicide".

Giulia calmly placed the newspaper back on Edelman's desk and left.

The list of drawings in Eric Hargrave's notebook contained more than fifty items from artists as diverse as Rembrandt, Piranesi, Durer, Raphael, Tiepolo, van Dyck, Poussin and Michelangelo. Some modern masters such as Goya, Degas, Augustus John and William Blake had also been included.

Going through the contents of the two boxes Bernard had sent her took Giulia a few hours. They were humid, ink-stained, some showing signs of having been handled more than others. She separated the magazines from the catalogues by title and it was quickly obvious that the initials beside each drawing corresponded to a source.

BUR stood for Burlington Art Magazine, SO for Sotheby's, CA for Christie's, and AP for Apollo. The magazines and catalogues dated back to the thirties and Giulia placed them in chronological order to be able to match them with the dates Eric had included.

By evening, Giulia had been able to match some of the drawings in Eric's list with illustrations in the catalogues. She marked the relevant pages with post-its and set them aside.

The Burlington Magazine included articles on a wide variety of artists, collections put up for sale, works of art acquired by museums, a treatise on the painting or sculpture of certain periods. More than half the pages in these magazines were filled with notices from the main auction houses in London, New York and Paris, with numerous illustrations. Some of the pages had been earmarked, others had missing illustrations with only the outline of a scissors edge on what remained of the page, or a note or a sketch in the margin hastily done by Eric's hand.

She was ready to take a break when she happened to come across the inside cover of an open catalogue. It showed an etching, "first state of six" of Giovanni Battista Piranesi's *veduta di Campo Vaccino*, advertised by a London gallery specialising in Old Masters' prints. The illustration had been partly cut from the page but not removed completely. Giulia wondered whether Eric had used, or was planning to use, this particular engraving, as inspiration for a drawing in the style of Piranesi. The curator of the prints and drawings department in the State Gallery of Copenhagen had challenged Eric to produce another drawing in the style of Piranesi so Eric's style could be compared to the one hanging in the gallery Eric had claimed to be his. Giulia remembered Eric telling her about it and her asking him whether he was willing to take on the challenge. He had said he liked the Danish curator, and was going to start work on a Hargrave Piranesi.

Not all the material Bernard had sent her could be cross-referenced with Eric's list. Giulia noticed, in particular, a dozen copies of a magazine called "Old Master Drawings, a quarterly magazine for students and collectors" that were published in London in the 1930s and priced at five shillings. Did these magazines also contain examples Eric intended to use to illustrate his book?

Giulia was unrelenting in her research and worked into the early hours of the morning, fortified only with cups of coffee and a packet of prepared salad and fruit she had picked up at M&S. She had spoken briefly to Alberto on the phone, who told her that the drawings had been collected and were on their way to London. She told him she was busy working on the book and that she missed him.

"I'll see if I can manage to get a few days off work and come and visit you. Of course, if that's okay with you," he had said.

"I'd love that, Alberto," she had answered, pleasantly surprised by his suggestion.

Giulia found that two of the drawings in Eric's list had actually been used in his autobiography; a pen and wash drawing of the *Entombment* attributed to Peter Paul Reubens and the *Study of a Centaur* in the manner of Tiepolo. While it might not be proof that all drawings in the list were produced by Eric, it certainly suggested that some of them were.

On the dining table she placed the photographs of the drawings the Italian police had confiscated, and studied them carefully. The face of a woman looking down, the back of a youth with his arms behind his head, a view of what was probably the Roman forum, a child carrying a vase, the view of a square in Venice. She picked up Eric's black notebook. She carefully reread Eric's notes and comments in between the poems and the list of drawings.

On one of the pages were the following entries:

Cherub carrying a vase	Annibale Caracci
Study for the face of a Virgin	Bernardo Luini
Venetian square	Canaletto
Back of a youth	Michelangelo
Roman forum	unknown 17th century

These five drawings were among those being shipped to Bernard Hargrave and were in Eric's list, probably meant to illustrate *The Language of Line* as well.

Giulia checked her watch. It was three in the morning and there was still a lot to be done. She made a note to call Bernard. She would also call Professor Norman England of the Courtauld Institute for advice. Things were moving in the right direction but Giulia, tired, back sore, and eyes aching, reluctantly accepted that sleep would be the best elixir to prepare her for the workload that followed.

Chapter 49

"Stop right there! Are you saying that Hargrave has given us a list of drawings he has produced over the years that no one knows about?" Edelman could hardly contain his excitement. He still had a nose for a scoop, a carry-over from his journalistic days.

"Well, not exactly. He gives us a list, and some drawings are by him and others are by Old and New Masters. If the readers have paid attention to what he writes, he says they should be able to discover it for themselves."

"Tell a genuine from a fake! Great news, Giulia. Listen, don't tell anyone about this till I get back from the States. We'll then work out a time plan for the launch of this book. Actually, we should work around the dates of Sotheby's and Christie's Old Masters sales. That should shake them," he laughed.

"I thought the director of Christie's was a friend of yours?"

"Friends? Ah, just because he managed to twist my arm to publish his ridiculous book. So this, this is going to be my revenge, served on a cold platter."

Giulia tried to say that she first had to pick up the manuscript from Donovan, and the Hargraves had to be informed and rights discussed with them, but Edelman could not be sidetracked from the scenario in his head.

"I can just see the newspaper headlines, *Caveat emptor, let the buyer beware!*" Edelman continued.

"It will be a disaster for their sales and an enormous boost for the book," he continued, "and it may mean printing a new edition of his autobiography, with a new foreword highlighting the various tips and recipes Hargrave explained to create new Old Masters."

"This is really great news, Giulia," he went on, "and yes you take care of getting the Hargraves over to sign an agreement and I'll get Legal on the phone to forewarn them."

"Did you find what Donovan was looking for as well?"

"Yes, and he should be taking delivery of his painting as we talk!

And I'll be meeting him this afternoon to pick up the manuscript as agreed," she stated.

"And is it all right if I already make contact with Professor Norman England of the Courtauld Institute? He's a very discreet man and could recommend someone to help us understand where the illustrations fit in with the text. And we would definitely need some help with the editing too," Giulia asked, wanting to clear this with Edelman first.

"Yes, yes. Go ahead. But ask them to keep it under their hats until we are ready to go public. Understood?"

Edelman's ebullience was contagious. He congratulated her on her investigative work, making some allusion to Columbo, on the thoroughness of her research, wished her a good weekend, even gave her a big bear hug.

As Giulia stepped out of his office she thought, "Well, that was that," pleased with herself. She walked over to an empty office and dialled Norman England's number. He was pleased to hear her voice and could meet her on the following Monday.

Giulia had time on her hands. She had agreed to meet Donovan at his gallery at four in the afternoon, giving him ample time to drive down to Brighton, take care of business and drive back up. It was a beautiful sunny day and Giulia decided to walk. It would take her a leisurely hour to walk along the Embankment and give her time to grab a sandwich and catch the feeding of the pelicans at St. James' Park.

Bernard Hargrave's lawyer, David Walton, was a scrawny little man with black curly hair and full of nervous energy, who had been recommended by a common friend. He arrived early at Bernard's house, insisting on going through the document he had prepared and was pacing back and forth in the living room when Christopher Donovan rang the doorbell.

Donovan greeted Eric's brother, inquiring after his health and that of his sister's, and apologised profusely, without giving any good reason for not having turned up for their meeting in London. Bernard thanked him for coming all the way to Brighton and introduced him to Walton.

The gallery owner spoke of the next exhibition he was arranging and of a promising new artist he intended to represent. He reminisced about his past association with Eric.

Bernard sat on the sofa and waited for the right moment to bring up the reason for Donovan's visit while the lawyer fidgeted, constantly looking at his watch.

"Mr. Donovan…hmmm…there is the matter of my late brother's painting which…we ought to discuss, I believe." Bernard started.

He coughed slightly and waited for a reaction from Donovan.

"Yes, of course, we should talk about it," Donovan replied, waiting for Bernard to take the lead.

"Well, there is the painting, but…there are drawings in your possession as well as a few drawings we just found, and we should discuss those as well."

Donovan nodded gravely.

"As you already know, I paid Eric a retainer, that is a monthly salary, and in exchange I held the exclusive rights for all the work he produced during the term of the contract. As part of the agreement, Eric was obliged to generate a number of drawings that I was to sell through my gallery during the year. At the end of the year fifty percent of the proceeds were for me and the other fifty for Eric."

Donovan stopped to make sure both Bernard and Walton followed his explanation.

"The first year sales were however, disappointing, and if I look at what I earned compared to what I invested, I lost money."

At this point Walton asked him, whether he had any accounts with him to support his claim. Donovan ignored the question and continued.

"This being said, I am prepared to give you the last installment I owed Eric for the painting of Venice. But I would first like to see the painting to be sure we are talking about the same thing."

"Of course, if you will excuse me I will go and fetch it," Bernard said.

Donovan and Walton waited in silence, carefully eyeing each other, like predator and prey.

Bernard came back with the painting still covered in bubble wrap and carefully handed it to Donovan who meticulously peeled off the tape and the string that bound it together. The painting was splendid. Donovan examined it carefully before gently putting it down and turning to Bernard. "As I was saying, I am ready to pay you the last installment I owed Eric for the painting. I have a cheque for three thousand pounds with me," Donovan said, putting a cheque into Bernard's hand.

He waited for Bernard's reaction, but from his body language he knew he had made the right offer. He was eager to take the painting and head back to London as quickly as possible.

"That is very generous of you, Mr. Donovan. Thank you," Bernard said, handing the cheque over to his lawyer, who scrutinised it well to see if it was in order before handing it back to Donovan.

"However, before we can accept the cheque and allow you to bring the painting back, there is the question of accounts, and the drawings that you hold by my brother, and the drawings we have just found. Can we now come to some agreement about this?"

"Yes, yes," was all Donovan could muster.

"Kindly look over this document and if you are in agreement, all we need is your signature. Mr. Hargrave has already signed it," Walton said.

Donovan read the one-page sheet assiduously.

It said that both parties, Christopher Donovan, Director of St. George's Fine Art and Bernard Hargrave, representative of the Eric Hargrave estate, agreed that any works produced by Eric Hargrave and held at the gallery's premises belonged solely to the gallery; that the gallery did not have to present accounts to the Hargrave estate and therefore all accounts were considered closed from the date of the signing of the document; and that all drawings, paintings, manuscripts, et al, found in Eric Hargrave's property, executed before or during his contract with St. George's Fine Art, now belonged to the estate of Eric Hargrave.

Donovan was not prepared for this. But he had to have the Canaletto painting by hook or by crook. The agreement was short and straightforward, making no mention of the view of Venice and he was secretly grateful for that.

He looked up, poker-faced, at both men. He wanted to secure the painting before he signed any agreement. "And the painting?"

"That's between you and Mr. Hargrave," Walton said.

"Do we have a deal then, Bernard? I sign this document, I give you the cheque, and I take the painting?" He couldn't have put it more clearly, Donovan thought, trying to sound diplomatic.

"Yes, that sounds just fine, Mr. Donovan," Bernard replied.

Donovan signed the agreement, in triplicate. The lawyer dated and signed it, put his stamp on it, and handed both Donovan and Hargrave their copies.

Bernard Hargrave received the cheque from Donovan and watched as he carefully rewrapped the painting to transport it back to London.

"By the way, would it be possible to have a look at those drawings that you just mentioned?" Donovan politely inquired.

"Yes, of course. In case we decide to sell them, might you be interested?" Bernard ventured to ask.

Christopher Donovan examined drawing after drawing painstakingly. The superb quality of the painting, and now these drawings, reminded him why he had taken on representing Eric Hargrave in the first place.

"Interesting," he said as he picked up one of the drawings.

And on another drawing, "This one, I believe, has been commissioned by a certain Professor Tarquin Littlejohn, if I'm not mistaken," Donovan said casually.

"You know him?" Bernard asked sounding surprised.

"He came to my gallery asking if I had come across it and wanted it back. I told him I hadn't seen it but would let him know if it ever was found," Donovan answered.

"Well, maybe you could do us a favour, Christopher?" Bernard asked cautiously. "Would you mind delivering the drawing to Professor Littlejohn?"

"No problem."

"That would be most helpful. But let's give him a call first to make sure he agrees to this arrangement," Bernard suggested.

They phoned Littlejohn who agreed to meet Donovan the following day.

The three gentlemen said their farewells. Donovan left with his Canaletto painting and Littlejohn's Michelangelo drawing; Walton left with a copy of the agreement for his files discreetly indicating to Bernard the invoice he had left on the table in the foyer. Bernard felt for the cheque he had safely tucked into his jacket pocket. His first thoughts were to call Giulia and tell her the good news, but thought it could wait till later in the day. He needed to rest. There had been too much excitement for one morning.

Back in his gallery, Donovan let Giulia in. It had been a busy morning for both of them. Giulia asked how it went, and when Donovan said ,"Smoothly," she said she was glad and asked no more questions. She was certain Bernard would fill her in on the details later. He pulled out the top drawer of his desk and handed her the manuscript.

"Here you are, Giulia. It has been a long day and thank you. I owe you one," he smiled.

Giulia took the manuscript, returning his smile. "Thanks, Christopher. See you around."

Chapter 50

Tarquin Littlejohn paid the taxi driver and strode purposefully from the street towards the entrance of the Tate Modern. Without glancing at the monumental architecture of what used to be a power plant, he navigated through groups of visitors, huffing and mumbling under his breath. The ramp that led to the Turbine Hall was relatively clear of people and he made quick progress towards the escalator, past the reception desks. He found the height of the building, its visible steel skeleton and even the skylights overhead, oppressive, and was glad to be on the escalator, in a comparatively more confined space.

He left the first level and the towering spider sculpture by Louise Bourgeois and continued to rise towards the second level of the museum.

From the right, light came through massive bands of frosted glass; from the left side, narrow and tall windows sent beams of light into the gallery spaces. The former curator of the Silverstein was, however, in no mood to appreciate the subtleties of the Tate Modern architecture. His trip to California had been postponed twice and he had almost given up hope that the Silverstein was going to offer a settlement out of court. He was close to bankruptcy and forced to consider selling his house or at least remortgaging it.

At the top of the stairs he turned left and entered the restaurant. He was early and the crowd had not yet invaded this space, he noticed with relief, as he selected a table in a corner of the room and ordered coffee. Only then did he bother to look around in order to see whether the person he was due to meet had already arrived. He glanced at his watch, turned his chair slightly so that he was visible from the entrance and concentrated on his coffee.

A quarter of an hour later Christopher Donovan joined him at his table, easing himself onto the bench in front of him. He appeared to be in a good mood, in direct contrast to Littlejohn, who told him he was late.

"Traffic and all that, you understand. Anyway, I thought you would enjoy the place," Donovan replied cheerfully.

"Why on earth should I enjoy this post-industrial pile of bricks without imagination?"

"It is modern, spectacular and unique," came Donovan's reply.

"It was built after WWII and cannot claim anything unique about it. Even the French had already built something new in the middle of Paris, the Beaubourg, and God knows they are conservative when it comes to that."

Donovan shrugged and ordered two whiskies without asking Littlejohn whether he wanted one.

"So you didn't appreciate the Silverstein then?"

"The contemporary building was actually well designed and the exhibition space was efficient and practical. This building here, well, was designed to impress, not to display its contents in the best possible way. A typical case of form over contents."

The waitress brought them two glasses of whisky and a bowl of crisps and one of salted peanuts. Littlejohn grabbed his glass and drank half of its contents before slamming it on the table harder than he had meant to.

"Anyway, why could we not meet in your gallery?" he asked Donovan.

"I'm between appointments in the area. New artist on the rise, among other things. Thought you might want to have your drawing as soon as possible," Donovan answered rather flippantly. He had in fact just come from his gallery after having met Greg Watkins who took delivery of his "Canaletto". Donovan was relieved that Watkins was more than pleased with his painting and had lightly dismissed Donovan's apologies about the unforeseen delays. Donovan's bank balance would once again be beyond reproach even after his creditors had been taken care of. It had been more than just a good morning, and there was no way that Donovan wanted Littlejohn accidentally bumping into Watkins. Some people were better kept away from each other for the time being.

"I have your drawing here," Donovan said as he pointed to a thin cardboard portfolio lying on the seat beside him. "Good drawing, by the way. Michelangelo would have approved," he said with a mocking grin.

Littlejohn clenched his teeth and Donovan assumed it was the fact that his drawing had been seen by different people that upset him.

"I think we may be able to help each other," Donovan added in a more conciliatory tone.

"Help each other?"

"I consigned an oil painting in the style of Canaletto to a client of mine, an Englishman; more money and business sense than taste I would say. The "Canaletto" is by Eric, of course, but the buyer will actually have the eighteenth-century canvas restored! The restorers will, of course, confirm that, in their opinion, they have worked on a genuine Canaletto. Are you with me?"

"I follow you."

"In a few years, how many I don't know, my client may want to sell his "Canaletto" and will need an authentication."

He paused for a few seconds before continuing.

"If you were amenable to providing such a certificate, he would pay you a fair commission on the sale. Cash of course!"

"I am not an expert in this period."

"Yes, I'm aware of that, but you are the former curator of the Silverstein and a man whose sense of ethics cannot be questioned. It will be enough, believe me."

Littlejohn was non-committal and Donovan interpreted the simple fact that he had not turned down the suggestion outright, as an agreement.

The gallery owner handed the portfolio to Littlejohn who opened it cautiously and cast a glance at the drawing.

"Thank you," was all he said.

"A fair exchange. You helped me and I'm glad to have been able to do the same for you."

"Ah yes, the manuscript. What did you do with it?"

"It's now in the hands of the Hargraves. They decide what happens to it now."

"I'm rather curious. How did you lay your hands on it?" Donovan asked.

Littlejohn closed the portfolio carefully and looked outside. Through the windows he stared at the steel structure of the London Millennium Footbridge that appeared to end up right in the dome of St. Paul's Cathedral, rendered hazy by the late morning fog that had not yet lifted. He had no intention of helping Donovan or his client claim the Canaletto painted by Eric Hargrave was a genuine work by the Venetian painter but did not say so. Instead he reflected on the twist of fate that made him, the former curator of the

Silverstein, a man known for his expertise and integrity, depend on the work of a forger to defend his claim and therefore his reputation against the California museum.

Donovan read Littlejohn's silence as embarrassment and did not press him.

"He was a brilliant forger. He once drew the signature of a dozen Old Masters in front of me in a few minutes, and without consulting any documents. When I checked, each one was close enough to the authentic signature to pass for genuine," Donovan said.

The art dealer raised his glass.

"The man was a genius, of course. We should at least drink to that."

Littlejohn raised his glass but did not say anything. He remembered, to his own surprise, the day he received a copy of *The Language of Line* in the post with a note from Eric saying, "*Let me know what you think. I would appreciate your opinion. Yours sincerely, EH.*"

Eric Hargrave's life had crossed with that of crooks and honest men, dealers ready to forego ethics for profit and art historians who admitted their limitations, collectors looking for trophies and ordinary people who appreciated art for art's sake, for what it gave them and not for the price they had paid. Eric had changed the lives of a few, gained the respect and friendship of many.

On the other side of the Millennium Bridge, close to Embankment station, Giulia was making her way to the Courtauld Institute on the Strand.

Giulia had met Jane England at an art exhibition in the city the year she moved to London. Jane was an Australian sculptress with a warm heart and a contagious laugh whose work was influenced by aboriginal shapes. Her husband, Norman, was the Director of the Courtauld Institute. Giulia had struck an instant friendship with the couple and they saw each other regularly.

Norman England was a friendly and straight talking Scot whose particular area of expertise was medieval architecture. Of course he knew of Eric Hargrave, whose autobiography he had read, and did not hesitate to offer his help when Giulia called to explain she had a notebook with records and references in Eric's handwriting.

He received Giulia without ceremony in his wood panelled

office overlooking the Victoria Embankment. They sat at a mahogany table.

A library covered one of the walls, and two paintings hung between the windows. Giulia recognised a Gainsborough and guessed the second to be by a Flemish painter, perhaps a contemporary of van Dyck.

"How exactly can I help you, Giulia?"

She explained the thinking behind *The Language of Line*, the list of illustrations that accompanied it, and related what she knew of the police investigation into Hargrave's death.

"I'd be happy to look at the manuscript and the list," he volunteered.

Giulia thanked him and pulled out the notebook from her bag.

"I believe that some of the diagrams in this notebook are illustrations for the book," she said, pointing at several pages of simple lines of different thickness, cross hatchings, details of a hand, and representations of various geometrical figures. Then there is the list of works I found." She also handed to him.

Professor Norman England perused the treatise in front of him and the list of drawings as Giulia busied herself leafing through the latest copy of the Burlington Magazine.

After a few minutes, Norman England peered through the list and smiled. "Giulia, you have already accomplished a lot from what I can see. I would suggest that I call Professor Cortona, who is more qualified than I am in matters of Renaissance drawings. He will be glad to help, I am sure," Norman suggested helpfully.

"If he is willing and has the time that would be most useful," she countered.

"Professor Cortona is retired, which means he will not be hampered by his role at the Institute. You know that one of our goals is to determine the attribution of artworks of course. This work will be a little....controversial, let us say, and it will be easier for him to help you. Besides he was always a non-conformist, ready to challenge the order of things" he added with a grin.

Giulia smiled in return and said she was looking forward to meeting the Professor.

"You will most certainly like him; not only is he Italian, but after almost forty years he is still able to ignite fiery debates on matters of attribution."

Chapter 51

Six months later.

The publication of *The Language of Line* by Eric Hargrave, scheduled for the end of the year, was delayed. Giulia had completed her contribution to the decoding of Eric's entries in the black notebook against the drawings in the various catalogues. She had passed them on to Professor Cortona, who was to determine which illustration supported which explanation of Hargrave's theory. Professor Cortona had found a couple of serious discrepancies and needed more time to understand and rectify them. The fact that the book was being published posthumously made it even more difficult, as the author was not available for consultation. Professor Cortona was adamant in his position; he was not associating his name to a work that had not first gone through rigorous research and proper clarification.

Edelman was furious when he heard the news, but eventually calmed down when he was assured it was a matter of months. He wanted the publicity and sales but did not want Seldom House facing any unnecessary libel suits.

Giulia's work on the book was finished, but it had awakened a new interest in Old Masters Drawings, and she eagerly awaited the January sales scheduled by the two main auction houses.

The front cover of one of the auction catalogues caught Giulia's attention. It represented a beautiful drawing attributed to Nicolas Poussin in pen and ink and brown wash that was valued at three to four hundred thousand pounds. She opened the catalogue to read the description:

Nicolas Poussin
Les Andelys 1594-1665 Rome

Lot 35 *The Arcadian Shepherds*
Pen and brown ink and wash   36.4 x 44.3cm
with the artist's inscription in the back

Description

>This beautiful drawing, executed in a warm bistre and in a very fresh state of preservation, is a more pleasing example of the artist than many of his other elaborate designs, in which the pen line is often accompanied by wash.
>
>For Poussin, drawing has been more of a prerequisite rather than a sense of pleasure, however, not only has the artist shown more detail in this drawing, he has also been able to clearly evoke the atmosphere of bucolic tranquillity.
>
>This is a preparatory study for the famous second version of the pastoral painting Les bergers d'Arcadie (The Arcadian Shepherds) which also goes under the name "Et in Arcadia ego" (1638-1640) that hangs in the Louvre in Paris, and measures 121 x 185cm.
>
>The drawing represents four Arcadian shepherds, in a meditative and melancholy mood, arranged symmetrically on either side of the tomb, with an idyllic landscape in the background.
>
>One of the shepherds genuflects in front of the tomb, in a pose similar to Poussin's Adoration of the Shepherds (1637) and reads the inscription on the tomb, Et in Arcadia Ego, which can be translated as "Even in Arcadia I exist", the I being Death personified; it can also be interpreted to mean, "I, also used to live in Arcadia", where the I is the person buried in the tomb who once lived in Arcadia. Another shepherd, bent forward, points and looks at the inscription, as well. The third shepherd standing to the left looks up at the shepherdess who returns his gaze with graceful dignity. In the painting, the figures are represented in a more rigid and static pose.
>
>Arcadia was a harsh region in southern Greece inhabited by primitive herdsmen, rustic folk who led an unsophisticated yet happy life, their pastoral music later inspiring poets whose idealised shepherds sang about love and poetry in a world of bliss and beauty.
>
>The first appearance of a tomb in Arcadia is found in Virgil's (70-19BC) "Eclogues" and later in Jacopo Sannazaro's poem "Arcadia" in 1502.
>
>Poussin's painting takes its inspiration from the first pictorial representation of the familiar memento mori theme (Remember thou shalt die) popularised in 16th century Venice and made more powerful by the inscription "Et in Arcadia Ego" by the Bolognese artist Guercino (1591-1666) in his painting (ca.1618) that hangs in the Galleria Nazionale d'Arte Antica in Rome.

> The inscription, which also is the title of the painting, is given importance by the presence of a skull in the foreground, beneath which the words are carved.
> This painting has in fact been recognised as the precursor to Poussin's first version on the "Death in Arcadia" theme, now in Chatsworth House in England, showing two shepherds discovering the half-hidden tomb, that has replaced the skull in Guercino's painting, reading the inscription, "Et in Arcadia Ego" while a shepherdess poses in a sexually suggestive fashion in the manner of the Baroque style.

Sold by Order of the Trustees of the Martin Messmer Collection, Geneva.

It is interesting to note that this sheet was once part of the collection of the Orsini family of Rome who had about twenty drawings by Poussin, acquired during Poussin's first stay in Rome (1624-1640).

The cataloguing of the drawings in the Orsini collection was carried out in the 1980s under the responsibility of Professor Enzo Zangara.

Giulia purchased three copies of the catalogue and went straight home. She was sure that the drawing attributed to Nicolas Poussin bore a striking resemblance to one of Eric Hargrave's drawings in the portfolio confiscated from Giorgio Monticello by the Italian police. She still had the photographs taken at the Trastevere *Commissariato* and it was simply a matter of comparing the two. What did it mean? Could this drawing have been done by Eric? But how did it get to the auction house? A multitude of questions danced in Giulia's head and she could hardly contain her excitement when she finally got home and discovered that the Poussin drawing that featured on the cover of the catalogue and the image on the photocopy in Eric Hargrave's possession were one and same.

Giulia hurriedly called Conti to tell him what she had just come across.

"I'll send you a copy of the catalogue by express mail," she promised, "and I'll get in touch with Bernard Hargrave to see whether he has kept the 'original' of the photocopy, just to be absolutely sure. The photograph may have blurred a detail.

Bernard was pleased to hear from Giulia. They chatted for a while and he said he was coming up to London to meet with Donovan.

"Oh," Giulia said, sounding a bit surprised.

"Well, the man called and asked whether we were interested in selling any of Eric's drawings. He believed that with the publication of the book, there will be renewed interest in Eric's works. He's planning to put on a show."

"That sounds great, Bernard!" Giulia said encouragingly.

"Yes, but this time we'll have a straightforward agreement so there can be no misunderstandings. And the fact that all the drawings bear Eric's signature on the back, well, there can be no funny business, thank goodness."

Giulia was not too sure about Bernard's last statement. Eric had put down his signature in pencil, so easy to erase she thought, and even conveniently substitute with another.

"Do you remember the photocopy that came with the drawings? Would you still have that? she asked Bernard.

"Yes, in fact I thought of framing it for myself as it has no commercial value," he answered, "Why do you ask?"

"Well, if you don't mind, I'd like to have a closer look at it. Something I might have missed," she answered.

"Sure, I can bring it up tomorrow if that's convenient. I'm to meet Donovan after lunch at his gallery."

"What if we meet for lunch?" Giulia suggested.

"Only if you will allow me to treat you, and shall we say at the Café Richoux for old time's sake? Around twelve-thirty?"

"Why yes, thank you, Bernard. Until tomorrow then."

Conti received the catalogue the following day.

He recalled how Zangara had brushed aside the question about the drawing during the interview in Milan. He had also vehemently denied having had any dealings with Hargrave. Did Zangara commission the drawing from Eric? Zangara could also have sent a copy of the drawing to Eric for his opinion. But then, why deny he knew Eric? It was all circumstantial evidence. Conti could, at best, establish a connection between Eric Hargrave and Enzo Zangara, but he could not prove a forgery, even less, a murder.

On the same day that Conti received the catalogue, Giulia met with Bernard for lunch. He said he was glad to have a reason to come into London these days, and Giulia noticed that he appeared less stooped and moved and talked with more agility than when they had first met. She explained why she wanted to see the photocopy and showed him the cover of the catalogue. Bernard told her he had it with him and she was welcome to keep it for as long as necessary. They agreed that there would be no mention of it to anyone until more definite information could be gathered. He was happy for Giulia to deal with it. He had more pressing matters in hand, like getting his agreement with Donovan watertight, for the dozen or so drawings he had brought with him to sell. They enjoyed a pleasant lunch together and parted just before three, Bernard making his way by foot to Hanover Square, and Giulia catching a bus back to her apartment.

She put the catalogue on the dining table.

She put the A3 sized photocopy beside the catalogue.

She looked from one to the other, and, as with the photograph, they were identical; nothing new was revealed in the photocopy that the photograph may have blurred out or missed.

She then turned the photocopy over and saw the letters "ZGR" in what looked like Eric's handwriting. Could this have been the commission Willie was talking about that would make them rich if Eric behaved himself?

Giulia wondered whether the black notebook would hold additional clues. She meticulously studied the entries in Eric's book, first going through the telephone numbers. She noticed a telephone number with an 02 code. Milan, she thought, and jotted this down. The initials EZ preceded the number. She scrolled down through the various lists, inserted between the poems, between notes, between passages from the manuscript and came across an entry, *"follower of Guercino"* crossed out and followed by *"follower of Poussin"*

And the latin phrase *momento mori*. Remember you are mortal, remember you will die.

She hurriedly picked up the phone and dialled Alberto Conti's number. He asked her whether the photocopy of the Poussin drawing had the letters "ZGR" in pencil in the back. She said yes, and told him about the entries in the books she had just discovered.

In all probability, Enzo Zangara had commissioned a drawing from Eric Hargrave.

Whether he had commissioned more than one was another matter. Eric might have found out what Zangara intended to do with it. Realising that a good provenance would find its way into the history of the drawing, Eric knew that the three million lire he would have been paid by Zangara was a mere fraction of what he stood to gain from the onward sale. He must have tried to negotiate a larger sum for himself, sending a photocopy of the drawing to Zangara, instead of the original, through the middleman. He must have made another copy for himself for his records and prepared the original for delivery to Zangara once a new figure was agreed. This is what Eric must have meant when he told Willie more money would be coming in if he did not misbehave.

On the evening of Eric's fatal accident, nothing was taken from his person. His wallet was intact, his papers untouched. He was left alive at the foot of the steps of Piazza Trilussa. A call had been made to the emergency services to make sure he would be seen to. Police investigations showed that nothing was taken from his apartment, or so it appeared. Monticello confessed to taking some drawings and a painting, but was surprised by the photocopy in the portfolio of drawings. Could he have feigned surprise and taken the original drawing and unloaded it? Conti recalled Zangara mentioning that Eric exhibited in a gallery in Trastevere. However, it was highly unlikely. Monticello would not have kept the photocopy together with drawings he was going to offer for sale and had no record of previous dealings with Zangara.

No mention had ever been made about the keys to Eric's apartment. They were not on him when he was taken to hospital. Could the same person who pushed him have taken them and let himself into Eric's apartment and gone off only with the objects he was instructed to take? Would anyone have noticed the absence of a drawing? And what about the original of the manuscript, Hargrave's latest revelations? Was that taken too? Giulia only had the copy Donovan had given her; the copy Hargrave had sent to Littlejohn for his comments. Where was the original?

Together, Alberto and Giulia carefully went over the details, weaving a thread through events that would eventually lead to Eric's death. Their deduction led them to the following hypothesis:

The original drawing by a "follower of Poussin" and the draft of a manuscript by the "Prince of Forgers" were taken from Eric's apartment in the early hours of the morning of the 9th January, 1996. The drawing was by Eric Hargrave, and the manuscript was the draft of his upcoming book. Rumours had been circulating that it would not only present Hargrave's theories on drawing but include new confessions, indirectly implicating gallery owners and experts in the art world. A year on, the drawing makes an appearance on the cover page of one of the major auction houses in London. A genuine Hargrave, or a fake Poussin?

The Italian police, represented by Inspector Alberto Conti, explained their findings and their suspicion that the drawing on the cover of their catalogue was by Eric Hargrave and not Nicolas Poussin. They asked the auction house to reveal the consignee of the drawing in question and any papers in connection with the transaction. The authentication certificate and accompanying papers that came with the drawing pointed to a company with an offshore address as the owner of the artwork. Conti stated that it would take some time to get the information on the directors of the company, if this was even possible. The auction house, however, not wanting to take any risks, withdrew the drawing from the sale.

Enzo Zangara met with Amato and apologised for the failed sale of the Nicolas Poussin, but argued it was not his fault.

"You said there was no evidence Hargrave had made the drawing!" he stated nervously. "And the book! Have you seen the list of works he has included? Do you know how many were sold through my gallery? It is a disaster! A disaster! You told me you had destroyed the manuscript!"

Zangara was as agitated as Amato was composed.

"The manuscript was destroyed. Hargrave must have made a copy and sent it to someone. There was no way we could have known that," Amato replied coolly. "Anyway, you are not at risk. Deny everything and say Hargrave was a story teller, maybe even a good one. This will all die down in a few months."

Epilogue

Monticello was charged with attempting to smuggle Roman and Etruscan antiquities out of Italy. He pleaded guilty in exchange for the promise of a lenient sentence, and the judge had postponed his decision until the beginning of the following year.

As Eric's family declined to press charges for the theft of the drawings and of the painting in the style of Canaletto, the police closed the case before Monticello received his suspended jail sentence.

★ ★ ★

Littlejohn's lawyers and those of the Silverstein Museum reached an agreement to settle out of court a day before the first hearing was scheduled. The amount of the settlement was a multi-million dollar offer that vindicated Littlejohn, but the Museum refused to acknowledge publicly that their former curator was right, and persisted in their unwillingness to publish the catalogue of the museum's works prepared during his tenure.

Littlejohn accepted the settlement but negotiated hard on the wording in the confidentiality clause. He had suffered enough at the hands of the Silverstein he argued, stripped of his position, his important findings dismissed; there was no way that he would agree to their buying his complete silence as well. He had more research to carry out, papers to write, and the money he would receive would allow him the comfort, the time and the space to do this. It was not the last they would hear of Littlejohn, he said smugly to himself.

★ ★ ★

The Language of Line by Eric Hargrave was published by Seldom House and received wide press coverage. His theories were studied and debated by scholars, professors and students in the art world.

Once again, Hargrave had given the art establishment much to talk about.

Sebastian Greenwood's film on Hargrave was shown on television on the date of the publication of Hargrave's book. One of his short films had been selected for Cannes and another had been shortlisted for an Academy award.

★ ★ ★

Giulia informed Victor Edelman of her intention to leave London and move back to Rome. To her surprise he suggested that she continue to work freelance for Seldom House from Italy. Giulia thanked him and promised to think about his offer and let him know. She glanced at the ring that Alberto Conti had slipped onto her finger his last visit to London.

Hargrave's List of Drawings (A Selection)

Claude Lorrain, *An Italian landscape*
Pen and wash over charcoal (8x12 inches).
Landscape with mountains, a hill town and twisted tree trunks, a horse and goat in the foreground.
March 1961.

Rembrandt van Rijn, *Woman lying down*
Pen and sepia wash (3.6x6 inches)
Nude woman seen from the back.
June 1961

Giovanni Battista Piranesi, *Carceri*
Pen and wash.
Stairs, columns and arches. Theme used for known set of prints.
October 1961

Albrecht Durer, *Joachim*
Pen and charcoal (30x21 cm)
Joachim seated and looking up. A preparatory work for Joachim and the angel.
September 1962

Federico Barroccio, *Studies for San Sebastian*
Pen and pencil
Torso, legs and arms – studies used for the crucifixion in the Genoa Cathedral

Jan Brueghel, *Temple of Venus and Diana at Baia*
Sepia, pen and wash with blue watercolour (10x7.5 inches)
September 1964

Rogier van der Weyden, *Portrait of a Young Man*
Pen and charcoal
November 1967

Luca Cambiaso, *Madonna and Child*
Pen and brown ink, inscription in brown ink bottom right (18.7x12.47cm)

Jean-Honore Fragonard, *Danae and Jupiter*
Brush and brown wash (10.5x15 inches)

Peter Paul Rubens, *Man in Chinese dress*
Pen and charcoal

Francesco Guardi, *Venetian cloister*
Pen and wash

Anthony van Dyck, *Studies of women*
Pen and ink sketches
September 1969

Nicolas Poussin, *Study of a tree with hills in the background*
Brush and wash

Auguste Rodin, *Groups of Men in a Struggle*
Charcoal and ink wash (15x24cm)
April 1971

Edgar Degas, *Greek woman*
Pencil (25x19cm)
April 1971

William Blake, *Marriage of heaven and hell*
Pen and wash
April 1971

Theodore Gericault, *The kiss*
Sepia drawing (8x10.5 inches)
1971

Thomas Gainsborough, *Landscape with trees*
Blue chalk, wash and white chalk (9.5x13 inches)
1971

Annibale Carracci, *Peasant tilling land*
Pen and ink, brown wash (12x16.5cm)
1972

Georges Lallemant, *Study of seated Evangelist*
Black ink with brush. White, grey, and brown washes (26x18.5cm)
1972

Michelangelo, *Study of a Horse and a Horseman in Battle*
Pen and brown ink (38x24.5cm)
1972

Giambattista Tiepolo, *St John the Baptist*
Pen, brown ink and wash (20x31cm)
May 1972

Giovanni Francesco Barbieri called Il Guercino, *Judith with the head of Holofernes*
Pen and brown ink (20x19cm)
May 1972

Stefano della Bella, *A huntsman*
Pen and brown ink with grey wash, (16x30cm)
June 1972

Andrea del Sarto, *A Portrait of a Young Man*
Black chalk on paper (21x17cm)
July 1972

Sebastian del Piombo, *Virgin and Child*
black and white chalk on blue paper (25x19cm)
June 1974

Augustus John, *Portrait of a Woman*
Black chalk on blue paper (15.5x16 inches)
March 1975

Francesco Goya, *Quattro Figuras de Hombres*
Pen and ink
March 1975

Francois Boucher, *Woman seated in profile*
Red and brown chalk on blue grey paper (41x30cm)
May 1975

Raphael, *Study of Jonah*
Pen and brown wash heightened with white (26x20cm)
May 1975

Gian Lorenzo Bernini, *Portrait of young man*
Black and red chalk heightened with white chalk (12.5x9 inches)
January 1977

Eugene Delacroix, *Study of an Arab seen from the back*
Pencil (30x17cm)

Titian, *Study for Christ*
Blue chalk on blue green paper (23x20cm)
March 1977

Jacopo Pontormo, *Study of a nude boy*
Red chalk (38x23.5cm)
September 1977

Raphael, *Combat of naked men*
Pen and brown ink (25x40cm)
1975

Andrea del Verrocchio, *Head of an angel looking up*
Black chalk with white (17x15cm)
1978

George Romney, *Two women seated*
Pencil, pen and ink with sepia wash (11x9 inches)

Fra Bartolommeo, Head of a Child, an Angel and a Hand
Black and white chalk (9.5x6 inches)
1979

Francesco Maria Mazzola called Il Parmigianino, *Studies of the Madonna and Child (recto) $ sign right hand corner; Studies of the Madonna and Child and an architectural detail (verso)*
Pen and brown ink (4x3.5inches)

Taddeo Zuccari, *The Conversion of St. Paul*
Pen and brown ink, brown wash, black chalk heightened in white on blue paper
May 1979